Is This Love?

NEW YORK TIMES BESTSELLING AUTHOR

KAYLEE RYAN

The following story contains sexual situations and strong language. It is intended for adult readers.

Cover Design: Lori Jackson Designs
Cover Photography: RafaGCatala
Editing: Hot Tree Editing
Proofreading: Deaton Author Services, Jo Thompson, and Jess Hodge
Paperback Formatting: Integrity Formatting

KAYLEE RYAN

IS THIS LOVE?

LEGEND

PROLOGUE

THE WARM AUGUST SUN IS setting, casting a soft glow over Mr. and Mrs. Bailey's backyard. Roman has his new wife on his lap with his arms wrapped around her, one hand resting on her belly, and they're both wearing smiles that are bright enough to light up the darkening night sky.

The wedding ended hours ago, yet we're still here. We're a tight-knit group, so hanging out on a Saturday night is nothing new for us. What's new is the way Roman keeps referring to Emerson as his wife. His parents, as well as Monroe's, are here as well.

I'm smiling where I'm supposed to be, grinning and sipping on my bottle of beer, but my mind is still on the text message I received from my mom right after the ceremony. Her mother passed away. The grandmother I've never met. It's a long, dramatic story, but the CliffsNotes version is that my mom comes from money. Old money. The kind that takes generations to build. Her parents disapproved of my father. My mother didn't care. She married him anyway and walked away from the family she was born into for the one she was creating with my dad.

What I don't understand is why, after thirty-one years, they're reaching out, and to me? I've never met them. I've seen pictures and heard stories, but to me, they're strangers. Strangers who hated my father because of his bank balance. And trust me when I say this, my father is one of the greatest men you will ever meet.

He's patient and kind, and he loves my mother to the ends of the earth.

When I was younger, I used to get embarrassed by the way he always touched her or was constantly kissing her. Now that I'm older, I understand that the love they share is a bond that can't be broken. I've never known that kind of love. I love my parents and the guys—they're my brothers—but I've never felt that bone-deep intensity that alters my world.

Emerson's laugh pulls me from my thoughts, and I can't hide the smile that tilts my lips when I see the look on Roman's face. He's watching her as if she hung the moon. That's how my dad looks at my mom.

That's genuine romantic love.

I've never had it.

I've never felt it.

That doesn't mean I don't know that it exists. So, yeah, whatever it is, my grandmother felt she needed to say to me after all these years beyond her grave, I don't give a fuck. She made her choice. She pushed my mother away. I feel sorry for her. She missed out on so many laughs and good times over the last thirty-one years. It's her loss.

Tossing my warm bottle of beer, I shove my phone into my pocket. I'm having lunch at my parents' place tomorrow. We can figure it out then. For now, it's time to forget about the text and enjoy the here and now. The people in this backyard, they're my family. They chose me. And I'll damn well always choose them.

LEGEND 1

WHEN I PUSH OPEN THE front door of my parents' place, I hear Mom's laughter. I smile because I'm certain my dad is the reason for that laugh. "Parentals!" I call out. "I'm home."

It doesn't matter how old I am, I will forever refer to my parents' house as home. It's the house I grew up in, the house that holds countless memories. The house with the bedroom upstairs where the guys and I spent hours sneaking a look at the *Playboy* magazines that were given to us by upperclassmen.

Fun times.

This place will always feel like home to me. Sure, I have my own place. It's small, just a one-bedroom cottage-type house on the edge of town. I don't need much space, since it's just me. It's also mine. I own it free and clear, but this—the sounds of my mother's laughter, and my father's deep baritone voice.

This is home.

"In the kitchen, honey!" Mom calls back.

I round the corner and see my mom mixing something in a large bowl while my dad tries to dip his finger in for a taste. "What are you two up to?"

"I'm attempting to make cupcakes, but your dad keeps trying to eat all the batter." Mom playfully rolls her eyes.

"One small taste." Dad reaches out again, and Mom smacks his hand away.

"No." She scolds him like he's five, and I kid you not, the man juts out his bottom lip in a pout. In turn, Mom pulls open the silverware drawer, grabs a big spoon, and scoops him up a big bite.

"Damn, Dad. She never gave in to me that easily when I tried that growing up."

Dad wags his eyebrows and opens his mouth to speak, but I raise my hand to stop him.

"Nope. We're not going there. Not today, not tomorrow, not ever."

"Son, when two people love each other—" he starts, but Mom tosses a dishtowel at him, and all three of us are rolling with laughter.

"That ship has sailed, I'm afraid." I wink at him.

"Boys." Mom shakes her head, but there is a smile full of love and happiness tilting her lips. "I'm outnumbered by boys."

They wanted more kids, but it just wasn't in the cards for them. I never asked specifically why, and maybe one day I will. I know I was raised with so much love that I shared it with my best friends. Forrest was really the only one who had shit parents, but all four of the guys soaked up every ounce like a sponge.

Like I said, this is home.

"You love us and you know it." I round the counter and place a kiss on her cheek.

"Oh, I do, but you're going to need to find a nice woman to settle down with so I'm no longer outnumbered. Then I need a granddaughter, and yeah, the tables will turn." She gives me a bright smile, and all I can do is shake my head.

It's not that I don't want to settle down. I'm just not in a hurry to do it either. Although, I will admit that from watching Roman and Emerson, it's a little easier to see myself in that role. I always assumed I'd be a husband and a father. I had a perfect role model, at least in my eyes. I've yet to meet someone I can't live without.

"What are we having?"

"I made cheesy chicken and rice because Dad's been craving it and cupcakes for dessert. If I can keep this one"—she nods toward my dad—"out of the batter."

"Can't help it. You're cooking is addictive."

"He's not wrong," I say, grabbing my own spoon out of the drawer and dragging it through the batter in the bowl.

Mom shakes her head, the smile never leaving her face. "How was the wedding?"

"Good." I nod. "Rome's happier than I've ever seen him."

"Did you tell them we're sorry we couldn't make it? We had plans for dinner with Sara and John for months for their anniversary."

"I told them. They understood. It was a very small gathering." Reaching into my pocket, I grab my phone and pull up the few pictures I took of the happy couple.

"She looks beautiful, and Rome, that smile." Mom places her hand over her heart.

"Yeah." I chuckle. "He's smitten."

"As he should be." Dad stands and presses his lips to Mom's temple.

"And when is the baby due again?" Mom asks.

"Early spring, I think. March sometime." I try to think back, and I realize I don't know her exact due date. They mentioned it in the ER that night, but I was a little busy trying to make sure Forrest didn't strangle Roman.

"I'll be sure to get them a good gift."

"That's not necessary, but I'm sure they'll appreciate it. You know how Forrest and Emerson's parents are."

"Yeah." I can hear the sadness in my mom's voice. She wanted more kids, but it never worked out, and the Huntleys had two they neglected. This world is messed up and complicated, and sometimes, it's really hard for it to make sense.

"How's the shop?" Dad asks.

We fall into an easy conversation about work. I'm once again reminded of how incredible my parents are. When I told them that the guys and I wanted to open our own tattoo studio, they asked what they could do to help. I've never not had their unwavering support.

We catch up through lunch, and once the kitchen is cleaned up and we've all had one of Mom's mouth-watering cupcakes, I break the ice for the reason for today's visit.

"What did they send me?" I ask my parents as we settle in the living room.

"We didn't open it," Mom replies. "It's in your name."

"I told you that you could," I remind her.

"Not my place." She stands and moves toward the small desk in the corner of the living room, bringing back a white envelope. "Here."

"Thanks. Any idea what it might be?"

"No idea. She left a letter for me and your father as well."

"And?" I prompt her.

She shrugs. "She has regrets, just as I knew she would. She didn't come right out and apologize, but basically said, it's at the end of one's life that they understand their shortcomings, and pushing me away—" She glances over at my dad. "—pushing *us* away, and by association you, was one of hers."

Dad places his arm around Mom's shoulder and pulls her closer. "We suspect that whatever is in your envelope is much of the same."

I nod, tossing the envelope on the couch next to me. "I don't need to read it. She made her choice."

"Legend." There is a quiver in Mom's voice, and that's all it takes for me to reach for the envelope again.

"I'm sorry, but she can't make us feel guilty about her choices. I'm thirty-one years old and never met your parents. My grandparents. That was their choice. They made you choose, and that was wrong. You've done nothing but support me with every choice and life decision I've made. You've been my biggest cheerleaders. They were your parents. They should have been there for you. For all of us." I'm breathing heavily by the time I finish. One hand is clenched into a fist while the other grips the envelope like it's my mortal enemy that I'm fearful might slip away.

"She left this world with regret. That's on her shoulders, Legend," Mom says gently. "Whatever is in that envelope, it doesn't change who you are or who we are as a family. You're right, she made her choice." She looks up at my dad, and he leans in for a quick kiss, which makes her smile, before she turns her eyes back to mine. "We've built a life we're proud of. We have a son who has grown to be an incredible man. We're all happy and healthy, and there is nothing more that we could ask for. What's in there"—she points to the envelope—"has no relevancy in any of that. It's just a woman who carried around regret from the choice she and her husband made and wanted to make it known that she's aware of the mistake she made."

"What about your dad?" I ask her.

She shakes her head. "He passed away a few years ago. He had no regrets. My father was a hard man. He, too, chose to shut me out." She shrugs. "It's over. It's been years, and I'm happy, son. That's what's important here. Sometimes in life, you have to stand up for what's best for you. It's okay to walk away when it's not. That's what I did, and I have zero regrets. You and your father are the best things to ever happen to me." She smiles, and it's the one she used to give me when I was little and would scrape my knee. It's comforting and reassuring. It's her mom smile, and just as it always did when I was little, it settles me.

Loosening my grip on the envelope, I tear it open and pull out the small stack of papers, noticing a letter on top, and start to read it out loud.

Legend,

You don't know me, and that's on me, but I'm your grandmother. I'm sure by now you've heard all about me and your grandfather and how we pushed your mother out of our lives. I don't have many regrets in life, but that's my first and the biggest. The second is never getting to meet you, my grandson.

If you're reading this, then my time on this earth has passed. So many times I wanted to reach out to you, and to your parents, but I never did, and now, here I am, days left on this earth, and this is my last attempt to make things right.

Your grandfather and I talked extensively before he passed about what we would do with our family fortune. We've decided to donate most to the charities that were near and dear to our hearts, and the rest, my grandson, will go to you.

However, we have a few stipulations: you have one year from the date of this letter to marry the love of your life. You must remain married for one full year. On your one-year wedding anniversary, you will be required to meet with our family attorney, Edward Mullins. Regardless of what day this falls on, you and your wife must present together to receive your inheritance. You must arrive as a united front as proof you are indeed in a happy, healthy, and loving marriage. How you prove this is up to you. On your one-year anniversary, you and your wife will receive a lump sum of five million dollars.

You and your spouse must live in the same household. This will be verified by surprise home visits by Mr. Mullins. I have provided him with your home address, if this changes at any time you will need to make sure you provide him with your new information. Yes, this is controlling, but we must insert this rule to ensure that you are truly living as husband and wife. We want you to have that choice, to choose who you love and spend your life with. And, of course, Mr. Mullins will attend your wedding and handle the filing of the marriage certificate to ensure it's legal and binding.

I know this seems unorthodox, but, Legend, this is what we should have done for your mother. She should have been allowed to love whomever she wanted without being disowned by her family. It's at the end of one's life that you can see your mistakes clearly. This is how we right that wrong.

Should you fail to be married one year from the date of this letter or to show up on the date of your one-year wedding anniversary, you will lose all access to the funds, and Mr. Mullins will be instructed to disperse the remaining funds to our charities as well.

This may seem harsh, but I feel it's imperative that these stipulations remain in place. I assure you that the documentation that Mr. Mullins has prepared is ironclad, and this is the only way for you to gain access to your inheritance.

If you are currently married, you must submit your marriage license to Mr. Mullins, and the same rules apply. You must live with your spouse in the same house and present one year from the date you submit the license to Mr. Mullins to gain your inheritance.

Go live, love, and be happy, my grandson. Live up to your name, and be the legend of the family, and follow your heart.

Your grandmother,

Elaine Hammond

My hands holding the letter fall to my lap as I stare wide-eyed at my parents. "Is this a joke?"

My mother shakes her head, a sad look on her face. "No. That's who she is, who they both were. They had to maintain control at all costs."

"They can't control me," I seethe, tossing the letter to the couch as I stand and pace across the living room floor. "How dare she think she can just send some letter after she's dead and gone and dictate my life. For money. I don't need her damn money." I'm pissed. She abandoned my mom, which includes my father and me. She had years to reach out to us, and she refused, and now this? She thinks this is making things right? She's fucking delusional.

"Son," Dad warns.

"Did you not hear the words that I just read to you? To hell with her."

"You don't have to do anything you don't want to do," Mom assures me.

"Legend, son, that's a lot of money." This is from my dad.

I whip my head around, mouth falling open in shock, to look at him. "Do you hear yourself right now? That's not what we're about. We don't let money buy our love. We're Raines. Isn't that what you preached to me growing up? That money can't buy happiness, and you should be true to yourself. How can you even suggest that I entertain this idea?"

Dad holds up the hand that's not wrapped around Mom. "Son, that's not what I'm saying."

"What are you saying, Dad?" I stop pacing to place my hands on my hips and glare at my father.

"I think you should consider all of your options. If you fall in love within the next year and find a woman who you know without a doubt that you can't live without, then consider this and what it could do for you and your family."

"I do fine on my own. My home is paid for; I have a nice nest egg in the bank. My business is thriving. What more could I ask for?" I challenge.

"Legend, please sit." Mom's voice is calm and soothing, and I hate being short with her or denying her anything, so I do as she asks and park my ass back on the couch. "What your father is trying to say badly is that you don't know what the next year of life is going to toss your way. If you fall in love and get married, then why not show up on your one-year anniversary and collect the money?"

"Because they abandoned you. Us. That's why." I try to keep the anger out of my voice.

"That's in the past, Legend," Mom says gently. "We don't let our past hold us back. Instead, we live for today and all our tomorrows. If the timeline fits, then I say you do what you have to do to take the money. Technically, that money should have been mine, and I would love nothing more to know that you and your future family would be set for life because of it."

"Are you really saying I should go through with this?"

Mom shrugs. "Only if you want to."

"I'm not engaged. Hell, I'm not even dating anyone," I remind her.

"That could change. Just keep an open mind. You have one year from—" She leans over and grabs the envelope that's made its way to the coffee table. "—last Thursday. A lot can happen in a year."

"In thirty-one years, I've yet to find someone I feel I can't live without. The chance of that happening in the next twelve months is slim."

Mom nods. "You could be right, but you could also be wrong. We don't know our futures, Legend. The day I met your father, I was at the mall, waiting for food at the food court. I wasn't supposed to be there, but I defied my mother and went anyway. Your dad and a few of his friends were behind me in line. I dropped my wallet, and he picked it up for me. Our eyes met, and the rest is history."

"Come on now," I say, fighting the smile that wants to break through. I've heard this story a million times. "It wasn't that fast." Even as I say the words, I know they're not true. The story hasn't changed, not once over the years.

"I knew he was going to be important in my life."

"And I knew she was the most beautiful woman I'd ever seen," Dad chimes in with the same line I've heard countless times.

"It doesn't work like that for everyone. Look at Roman and Emerson. They fought hard to be together, fought against it, and then for it. It's not always that easy."

"Oh, it wasn't easy by any stretch of the imagination. My parents didn't approve and did everything in their power to keep us apart. Our hearts had other plans."

"You sound like a Hallmark movie."

"Oh, we should call them up, see if we can sell them our story," Dad jokes. "How much do you think we can make off that? Maybe we can remodel the kitchen and buy that new bass boat," he rambles on.

"Har har." I shake my head but smile despite the anger I harbor against my grandmother. I'd never met the woman, yet she still managed to insert herself into my life and strike up an anger deep in my gut all the way from her grave.

"Just keep an open mind. Life has a way of surprising you."

"Yeah, okay," I agree because I don't want to argue with her.

I spend a little more time with them before leaving. The plan was to head home, but I see a text from Roman telling me that everyone is invited to their place for leftovers. They had a small wedding but enough food to feed an army. Time with the guys—and well, now girls, if you count Emerson and her best friend, Monroe—is exactly what I need.

MONROE 2

SLEEPOVERS JUST AREN'T THE SAME. Spending the night at my best friend's house doesn't quite look like it used to. Emerson insisted I stay over last night, but it was their wedding night, so we compromised that I would stay in what we declared to be my room at Forrest's place.

Forrest has always been a big brother to me. A hot-as-hell big brother, but there is nothing romantic there. Sure, I like to flirt and tease him because I love to see him get all riled up. I don't see him that way. His friends, on the other hand, that's a completely different story. All five guys turn heads and drop panties wherever they go. Forrest is my brother. Not by blood, but in my heart. Roman, well, he's always been Emerson's. Those two, I saw the longing between them way before they gave into temptation. I couldn't be happier for them.

That leaves Lachlan, Maddox, and Legend. All are fine as hell, all great guys. I flirt with them without mercy every chance I get. Not because I think I have a chance with any of them, but because it's fun. The banter and flirting with them is safe, and for me, that's important. They know I'm teasing, and in turn, I don't have to worry about them getting handsy or trying to take advantage of me. Not that I would mind any of the three getting handsy, but you know what I mean. They don't take our banter as a green flag to take what they want. I've heard some horror stories, and after my last breakup with douchebag Henry, let's just say, safe is important.

Henry was one of those guys who liked to present one way but was someone altogether different behind closed doors. He was a fraud, and a fake, and had a mean streak a mile long. Thankfully, I ended things before they escalated too far. He wanted things he didn't earn, things I wasn't ready to give him. He still corners me if he sees me out somewhere, but thankfully, my best friend is having a baby, and we've been hanging out at her place, or Forrest's, since we've been back home. Not that we went out a lot before. We pretty much always ended up hanging out with Forrest and the guys because Emerson was smitten with Roman.

Everything worked out like it was supposed to. In my heart, I know those two are meant to be together, and I have no doubt they will go the distance. They fought hard to be where they are, and I'm thrilled to watch them flourish and start their family.

The sun peeking through the blinds tells me it's way past time for me to get up and get moving. Tossing off the covers, I grab some clothes that I've left here over the years and head to the shower. Twenty minutes later, I'm walking into the kitchen. There is no sign of Forrest, but his door remains shut, so I'm sure he's still asleep. I busy myself making coffee and decide to scramble us some eggs.

Just as I'm plating up the eggs, Forrest walks into the kitchen. His hair is rumpled, and there's a line across his right cheek from where he was sleeping. "Morning, Mo," he mumbles.

"Morning, sunshine. How did you sleep?" I've always been a morning person. It helps that I only had a couple of drinks last night and stopped earlier in the night so I could drive home and I still ended up staying over.

"Good. Too much celebrating," he replies.

"Ah, the dreaded hangover. Nothing some breakfast and a little caffeine won't fix." I slide a plate across the island to him and quickly pour him a cup of coffee—black, just like he likes it.

"You're an angel. How long have you been up?" he asks, taking his first sip of coffee.

"Not long. Thanks for letting me crash here last night. Emerson was insistent I stay and not drive home even though I was perfectly capable. I didn't want her to worry, and I didn't want to crash with the newlyweds."

Forrest shudders. "Let's not talk about *that*." He emphasizes the word, and I toss my head back in laughter.

"Come on, they're married and having a baby. You do know how babies are made, right?" I tease.

"We are not talking about this," he grumbles into his cup of coffee.

Silence falls between us, and I can't help but fill it. "They're happy, Forrest." I know he's accepted them, but the best friend in me feels compelled to cheer them on, just in case.

He sighs. It's a deep, resounding sound that tells me what he's going to say before he opens his mouth. "I know. I'm happy that they're happy, but it still doesn't mean I want to think about them and... that." His face scrunches up, and it's adorable. I keep that thought to myself. I'd hate to hurt his manly ego and all that.

"Just wait until your niece or nephew gets here. You're going to want them to do more of *that* to give you another one." I flash him a wide grin.

He shakes his head, but a small smile tugs at his lips. "Yeah," he agrees grudgingly. "You're probably right. This damn house is too quiet now that she's gone."

"She's next door," I remind him.

"Not the same, Mo. It's just not the same." He's pouting, and my heart swells in my chest for my best friend. She didn't have it easy growing up, but the man before me, her big brother, he stepped up for her in a big way, and I love that he's in her life.

"Eat your eggs before they get cold." I point to his plate with my fork, and he does as he's told.

"Thank you," he says a few minutes later, standing with his empty plate in his hand.

"Did you even chew?" I ask, looking down at my still half-full plate. He laughs and ruffles my still wet hair on top of my head.

"I'm going to shower. Are you sticking around?"

"I need to text Emerson and see if it's safe to go over. I told her I'd come back today and help clean up."

"Wait for me, and we can go over together. I'll be quick." He dashes up the stairs while I sit and enjoy the taste of my eggs instead of swallowing them whole.

Twenty minutes later, Forrest and I are knocking on the newlyweds' front door. Roman pulls it open, wearing the same grin he's had on his handsome face since he found out that Emerson was pregnant.

"Come on in." He steps back, allowing us to enter. "Em's on the couch."

"Because he won't let me get up!" my best friend calls from the living room.

"Spoiling her again, I see?" I chuckle, making my way to the living room to Emerson.

"Is there any other way?" Roman calls back.

I'm shaking my head, but my smile is genuine when I see her with a blanket and a bowl of fresh fruit in her lap. "Being held hostage again?" I tease.

"He's ridiculous. He won't let me do anything."

"He loves you."

"I love him, too, but come on. I can put some fruit in a bowl for breakfast."

I tilt my head to the side to study her. "He wants to take care of you, Emerson. You and your baby."

"I know, but I want to be his partner in life. Not an obligation or responsibility."

"You're not," a deep voice says from behind us. We both know without looking that it's Forrest. He steps into the room and bends over the back of the couch to kiss his sister on top of her head. "What makes you think that?"

"I don't know." Emerson stares down at her bowl of fruit.

"Spill it, Em." Forrest rounds the couch and takes a seat on the coffee table facing her.

"I just.... It's hard to wrap my head around the fact that this is my life, you know? It's all I ever wanted, and now here I am, living my dream. It all happened so fast. We found out about the baby, and then I moved into my dream house next to you, you found out about us, the wedding. I just.... I don't want to give him any reason to change his mind."

We both startle when Forrest tosses his head back in laughter. Not just ha-ha laughter. No, this is "shoulders shaking, gasping for air, can't stop it" kind of laughter. Emerson scowls at her brother, and I bite down on my cheek to keep from snickering. Not because what she said was in any way funny. Well, okay, it was kind of funny. She's not an obligation to Roman. She's his queen, and now that they don't have to hide, he's living his best life. I know she knows that. These pregnancy hormones must be getting to her.

"Are you done?" Emerson asks, folding her arms over her chest.

"Emerson Bailey." Forrest shakes his head. "You're his wife. He doesn't feel obligated to take care of you. That's who he is. We didn't see that growing up. We didn't have a good view of what a marriage should be, but you lean on one another. You can't tell me if Rome was sick, you wouldn't be fussing over him."

"I'm not sick, Forty. I'm pregnant."

"And doing all the work." Roman joins the conversation. He hands Forrest and me a bottle of water each before kneeling in front of where Emerson sits on the couch. "You're doing it all, baby girl." He moves the bowl of fruit from her lap and places it on the end table, then settles his hand over her still-flat belly. "You're growing and protecting our son or daughter. I want to do everything I can to make life easier for you. I don't feel obligated to do it. I want to do it. We're a team, Em. You and me for the rest of forever." He leans in and kisses her softly.

"Told you," Forrest says.

I kid you not, the man-child sticks his tongue out at his little sister, which makes her laugh, just as I'm sure he intended.

"Go off and do manly things. We need girl time." I wave my hand in the air at them.

"She's been my wife less than twenty-four hours and you want me to leave her?" Roman asks incredulously.

"Just to the kitchen or the backyard, big guy. Your wife needs to tell me all about her wedding night." I wag my eyebrows, and Roman gives me a saucy grin.

"Nope. No. Just no." Forrest stands, grabs his bottle of water, and stalks off toward the kitchen. He's mumbling about his ears bleeding, which makes us all laugh.

"You good, baby girl?" Roman asks.

"I'm good. I'm... overly emotional. I'm sorry."

"No apologies for feeling how you feel. Just remember to be open and honest with me so I can put your fears at ease." He stands, leans over, and captures her lips in a kiss before trailing toward the kitchen after Forrest.

"You good?" I ask her.

"Yeah." She smiles and waves me off. "These hormone swings are no joke, and I'm living this life, the one I've always dreamed of, with the man who I dreamed of having beside me, and this morning, when you and Forrest got here, it kind of hit me. I don't think yesterday quite set in for me until that moment. I got my happily ever after, Monroe."

Her smile lights up her face, and in turn, so does my own. Reaching over, I pull her into a hug and hold her tightly. "You deserve all the happiness in the world, Emerson. You fought for what you wanted, you never gave up, and here you are. Starting your own family with your husband."

"My husband." She stares down at her engagement ring that's now accompanied by a diamond wedding band. "It's all felt like a dream until the moment you and my brother stepped through the door. I don't know why, but it all hit me at once."

"How was the wedding night? And no, I don't want specifics because that's special between the two of you, but really, how was the wedding night?" I ask again, making us both laugh.

"Magical. Roman is... my husband. Gah, will I ever tire of saying that?"

"I hope not," Roman says, walking back into the room, reaching over the back of the couch, and rubbing her shoulders. "How do you feel about inviting the rest of the guys over to help us take care of some of this food? Maybe later for dinner?"

"That's a perfect idea." Emerson tilts her head back to look at her husband.

"Love you, baby girl," he says, kissing her nose before removing his hands from her shoulders and heading back toward the kitchen.

"I have to show you what we picked out for the nursery. With all the wedding planning, I keep forgetting to show you."

"Do you know which room you're going to use for the nursery?" I ask.

"We decided to use the one right across the hall from ours."

"And when can we go shopping?" I ask. "Aunt Monroe has some gifts to buy."

"We're waiting until the ultrasound to pick a paint color, but we're pretty sure we're going to go with white furniture, boy or girl."

"Well, you should hold off on buying too much, anyway. You know we're going to throw you a shower."

"I don't have anyone outside of you and Forrest and the guys. We're prepared to do the bulk on our own."

"You have Roman and his parents. You have Drake, Lisa, and Lyra, and I'm sure your work will throw you a shower," I remind her.

"Yeah, I just don't expect it, you know? I'm happy with our life, and I know the people who are in it want to be here. I'm okay with that number being small."

"It's not that small." I shake my head at her.

"You know what I mean. I don't have aunts and cousins to invite, and that doesn't bother me. I have a small circle, but it's bursting with love. I couldn't think of a single thing I could want more."

"You know, with four uncles, and Roman as thier daddy, and then there's me, the best aunt ever, this little one is going to be spoiled rotten."

"Good. I never want my child to know what it's like to not feel loved and cared for."

"That man you married, he's going to make damn sure that never happens."

"Come on, let's go upstairs and I can show you what we have planned."

I follow her up the steps and into the empty room. Emerson proceeds to tell me the vision that she and Roman have for their baby's room, and it's perfect.

"You should have Rome paint a mural on the wall. I'm sure the guys would help him."

"Yes! Why didn't we think of that?" she asks. She twirls in a slow circle. "That wall is where the bookshelf, toy box, and rocking chair are going to go. That's such a great idea."

"And I've already bought a couple of books," I confess. "Mom and I went shopping the other day, and I couldn't resist."

"Aunt Mo for the win," she cheers. "Just wait. When it's your turn, I'll be repaying the favor."

"If I ever get there. At this rate, I'll be an old spinster cat lady and have to live vicariously through you."

"Come on, that's not true."

I shrug. "Not all of us can be as lucky as you and have the man of our dreams sweep us off our feet."

"Henry messed with your head. Everything about you is beautiful. You're a great catch, and the right man is going to come along, and you'll forget he ever existed."

"A girl can dream," I say, sighing dramatically, making us both laugh.

We talk a little while longer. It's not until we hear deep voices that we know we've been up here most of the day, just talking, and planning, and catching up. "I'm surprised your husband left us alone this long."

"Stop." She playfully rolls her eyes. "Come on, I'm starving, and we need to make sure the guys don't eat everything before we have a chance to make our plates."

"Did you forget how much food you have left over? You'd have thought you were feeding a wedding of one hundred, not less than twenty."

"I know. My mother-in-law and I might have gone a little overboard."

"Might have?" I tease.

"Fine, way overboard, but it was the perfect day, and now we have those who are closest to us here to help us eat what's left."

"You did it on purpose." I call her out, but I already know the answer.

"I'll never tell," she sings, but the wink she gives me tells me I'm right.

My best friend, she has no idea that we'd all be here, food or not, if they invited us. That's what you do for your friends. You show up, you offer support, and you be their shoulder when they need it. Emerson will always have that from me, no matter where life takes us.

LEGEND 3

WHEN I PULL INTO THE driveway, I see that I'm the last to arrive. I should have been here earlier, but when I left my parents' place, I drove around for a little while, just trying to wrap my head around today. Talk about a mind-fuck.

I never could have imagined what would be in that letter. I hate that I never got to meet my grandparents, and on some level, I understand my grandmother's need to make things right. However, forcing me into marriage, even if I get to choose my bride, is not the way to do it. Besides, it's too late. They're both gone, and the chance to get to know them has long since passed.

Grabbing my keys and my phone, I climb out of the truck and make my way up the sidewalk. I knock once, and a chorus of voices that are more than just Roman's and Emerson's voices say "Come in."

I smile.

For the first time since reading that damn letter, the same one that's shoved in my back pocket, I smile. These are my people, and tonight, spending time with them is exactly what I need.

Stepping into the room, I see that the gang's all here. Roman is sitting in the recliner with Emerson on his lap. Forrest and Lachlan are on the couch, and Maddox is in the other recliner. Monroe is sitting on the love seat and laughing at who knows what with this crowd. It's always a good time when we get together.

"What did I miss?" I ask, stopping next to the love seat.

Monroe wipes at her eyes. "Nothing, really, but these two"—she points to Forrest and Lachlan—"made the mistake of looking up a labor and delivery video."

"Don't do it, man." Lachlan shudders. "You'll never see pussy the same way again."

"La-la-la-la," Forrest says, placing his hands over his ears. "I'm not talking about this shit. She's my sister," he grumbles.

"And she's my wife, and trust me, the pu—" Rome starts, but Emerson manages to slap her hand over his mouth before he can finish what we all know he was going to say.

I laugh, because how can you not? That shit's funny. Forrest is Emerson's big brother, but with the age difference of ten years between them, he helped raise her, and well, he did more for her than their deadbeat parents ever did. So, in a way, he's her father figure. I don't have kids, but yeah, if I had a daughter—hell, if I had a sister—I'm certain I'd feel the same way as Forrest does right now.

It's still funny as hell.

Monroe taps the cushion next to her on the love seat, and I plop down next to her. "What got this started?" I ask her.

"So, Maddox asked Rome if he was nervous about the delivery. Then I spoke up and said that Emerson would be doing all the work. One thing led to another, and they ended up on their phones, and it all went downhill from there." She wipes another tear caused by her laughter from her cheek.

"Well?" I look over at Rome. "Are you nervous?"

"Yes." He nods, his face sober. "It's going to be hell on my wife, but I'll be there every step of the way, for every single one."

Emerson's eyes widen in surprise as she turns to look at him over her shoulder. "How many?"

Roman presses his lips to her nose. “At least two, but I’m down for a houseful. We can add on if we have to. Or, we can just do lots of practicing until we decide.” He winks at her and her cheeks turn pink.

“Let’s get this one here and see how we do as parents, and then we can talk,” Emerson replies.

“You’re going to be great. Both of you,” Monroe tells them.

“What she said.” I point at Monroe. “And you have a room full of babysitters.” I wave my hand around the room.

“You going to do diapers?” Monroe asks me.

“Sure.” I shrug. “We all have to shit.”

She cracks up at my reply, making her big blue eyes sparkle. Monroe is a knockout. She’s fucking gorgeous with those electric-blue eyes and all that dark curly hair. It’s long and thick, hanging down her back. It’s the kind of hair a man can’t help but think about wrapping around his fist. That includes me. I’ve thought about it—more times than I care to admit.

Monroe is a flirt, and she lays it on thick with the guys and me. Well, that’s not true. She never flirted much with Roman, if at all. It makes more sense now that the truth about Roman and Emerson is out. She wasn’t going to flirt with her best friend’s man, and yeah, he’s always been hers. It just took them a while to get there.

None of us has ever made a move on Monroe. Lachlan, Maddox, and me. We flirt back relentlessly. Forrest doesn’t, but he’s more of a brother to her. Monroe has just always been around. She was always with Emerson, who was always with Forrest. I’ve watched both of them grow into the women they are today.

Monroe leans her shoulder into mine as she laughs, and her warm vanilla scent invades my space. She’s gorgeous and smells good enough to eat. This one, she’s dangerous.

“I finally heard from the realtor on that plot of land on the edge of town,” Maddox speaks up.

“And?” Roman asks.

Maddox whistles and shakes his head. “It’s pricey. The land and the cost of a new facility would strap each of us financially.”

My gut twists. We've all wanted this for so long. "What about other locations? Buildings that we can renovate to suit our needs?" I ask.

"No luck." Lachlan shakes his head. "We all agreed that we want to stay in Ashby, and there just isn't anything on the market that's better or bigger than our current space."

"Damn," Forrest mutters. "What are you guys thinking?"

Maddox looks at Roman, and I can see the resolve in his eyes. He knows our friend just got married and has a baby on the way. No way do we want him to not be able to provide for his family. I can see Maddox's reply in his eyes before he answers.

"I say we hold off. At that price, I doubt the land will go anywhere. It's too small for farmers, and it's been for sale for months."

"Yeah," Roman agrees. "It's just—not the right time." I can hear it in his voice. It kills him to say it, but there will never be a time he won't put his family first. We would never expect him to.

My mind drifts to the letter in my pocket. I have access, or could have access, to the money we need to fund our new facility. The money could take Everlasting Ink to the next level, but it's wrong. Right? To marry for money? Besides, I don't trust anyone outside of this room other than my parents, and the parents of the guys, Forrest and Emerson's excluded. I love my brothers, but I'm sure as hell not marrying one of them.

"Where you been, man? I texted you a while ago," Roman asks, pulling me out of my thoughts.

I pull my attention from the damn letter to Roman. "I was at my parents' having lunch when I got your message." I don't tell him I drove around for close to an hour when I left their place. That would only lead to more questions I don't want to answer. How can I when I'm still trying to comprehend it all?

I haven't decided whether I'm going to tell them at all. I mean, Roman knows I got a text and that my grandma, whom I've never met, passed away, but we can leave the details alone. Guilt hits me because I don't keep things from the guys, but this feels... like even from the grave, she's dictating my life just as she tried to do with my mother.

It feels wrong.

It would be selfish to get married to gain access to the trust fund I don't really need. Don't get me wrong. I'm nowhere near a millionaire. However, the guys and I have built a very successful business that I'm damn proud of, and I make a damn good living. My house is small, but it's paid for, free and clear.

"How's your mom?" he asks.

"Wait, is she not well?" Emerson asks, sitting up straighter on his lap.

"She's fine," I assure Emerson. "Her mom passed away. They hadn't talked in over thirty years," I explain. I know the guys already know, but I wasn't sure if Monroe or Emerson did. By the way Emerson nods and Monroe places her hand on my arm, giving it a soft squeeze, I know they don't need further explanation.

"I'm sorry," Monroe says softly.

I give her a smile that I hope says I'm unaffected. "Thank you. I didn't know her. She and my grandfather made my mother choose between loving my father or being a part of their family. Mom chose Dad, and well, here I am." I wave and huff out a laugh.

"What did she send you?" Roman asks.

"A letter."

There's a long pause, and I'm not sure anyone in the room is breathing. It's obvious that I'm upset, and they know I wasn't close to her. My friends are smart, and they know something about that letter is what's causing my sour mood.

"And?" Forrest prompts.

"Just a letter." I shrug as if the letter was insignificant. It *is* insignificant. She has no control over my life. However, the reminder of those words on the page still lingers in my mind.

"Ladies, shit's starting to get deep in here. You might want to roll up your pants legs," Maddox says, crossing his arms over his chest.

I chuckle, because they're my friends and my family, and they know me better than anyone. I should have known I wouldn't be able to fool them. "Har har." I barely contain the urge to roll my eyes. I'm irritated that I can't keep this contained, but at the same time, I need to talk about this. To someone other than my parents. They're too close to this. Too close to me to think about this objectively.

Not that there is anything to think about. It's a bogus apology and an attempt to control my life.

"Listen, man," Lachlan speaks up. "You don't have to tell us, but we're your family. Something is bothering you, so you might as well get it off your chest."

I hang my head and expel a heavy sigh. The letter burns a hole in my back pocket. "My grandparents left me some money." I scoff. "But there are terms I have to meet in order to get it."

"What? Like reach a certain age?" Emerson asks.

"No. Like get married."

"Seriously? What the fuck?" Lachlan blurts. "Can they do that?"

"The letter was accompanied by legal documents from their attorney, so yeah, she can do that." Leaning my head back on the couch, I close my eyes. How is this my life?

"How much money are we talking about, Legend?" Forrest asks.

"Enough that we can buy the plot a few times over and still have money to build a state-of-the-art facility." I pause, letting that sink in. "Five million dollars." My voice is gruff, and it feels like gravel coats my throat as I tell them the amount.

A chorus of colorful words and disbelief fill the room.

Reaching into my back pocket, I pull out the crumpled letter, holding it up. "It says it all right here in black and white. If I marry and remain married for twelve months, I'm to meet with their attorney on the date of my one-year wedding anniversary, and I will receive a cool five mil."

"Damn," Lachlan mutters. "That's some heavy shit."

"What are you thinking?" Maddox asks.

"Five million?" Forrest repeats.

"You're not even dating anyone," Roman adds.

"I'm thinking this is her final fuck you from the grave. They made my mother choose between my dad and her family. Not once in my life did they try to reach out to my parents or to me. They obviously knew about me. They're trying to control me, just as they did her."

"What does the letter say?" Emerson asks.

I hold it up, and she stands from Roman's lap and walks toward me. When she's close enough to grab the letter, she does, but she also keeps walking until she's close enough to pull me into a tight hug. On instinct, my arms wrap around her and return her embrace.

When she stands and makes her way back to Roman, he welcomes her, wrapping his arms around her, his hand resting over her belly where their child is growing. My best friend is one lucky bastard.

"Read it," I tell Emerson. It was inevitable that I tell them the details. They might as well hear it word for word. I hang my head, my elbows resting on my knees, and keep my eyes on the floor as Emerson reads the letter out loud.

I feel a hand on my back, and I know it's Monroe trying to offer me comfort. I don't know why I can't get past this. I didn't know them. Now, from the grave, they're trying to control me just as they did my mother. I think that's the crux of all of this. They hurt my mother, disowned her, and made her choose the love of her life, her soul mate, over her family. She should have been able to love whoever she chose and have the support of her family behind her.

She didn't.

Now, from the grave, my grandmother wants to make it up to her by putting stipulations on me for marriage to gain access to my inheritance. It's all fucked up, and I hate them for putting me in this position and for what they did to my parents.

There is so much I could do with that money. My parents could retire. I could secure the land and the facility for the new Everlasting Ink location here in Ashby. Hell, the list goes on and on, but damn, I can't just marry someone for money. I don't even like anyone enough to let them in on this and to stay married to them for a full 365 days.

I'm fucked.

Just like my mother was all those years ago. That's where my anger is coming from.

"What are you going to do?" Forrest asks once Emerson has finished reading the letter.

"What can I do? I'm not dating anyone. I won't marry a complete stranger just to gain access to the money, no matter how many people's lives I can make better with it."

"Legend, bro, that's five million dollars. That's a lot of thousands and more than any of us will make in our lifetimes," Maddox says.

"I know, but fuck. I can't just walk up to some woman and say hey, let's get married for a year, and I'll give you a million dollars for your trouble. That has complicated and disaster written all over it."

"There has to be someone," Lachlan adds. "Did you go through your phone?"

"No." I grind out the word. "I didn't go through my phone. Do you hear yourselves? It's wrong. Right? Tell me I'm not alone in this." I scan the room, making eye contact with everyone. My eyes land on Monroe, who has been quiet, other than her hand that still sits softly on my back. My eyes land on Forrest. "Right?"

He shrugs. "It's a lot of money, Legend. I know the shop does well, and we're all financially stable, but this—it's fuck-you money."

"What?" I huff out a laugh.

"Fuck-you money. You know, you don't give a fuck what it costs because you have money to throw away."

"Money changes people."

Lachlan shakes his head. "Not you. You're solid. Good head on your shoulders and all that jazz."

I huff out a laugh. "It would have to be someone I trust, and that's the people in this room and my parents."

My words have all eyes going to Monroe. I turn to look at her as well. She's been silent through all of this. Her electric-blue eyes meet mine, and there's something there, something swirling that I can't name.

"What am I, chopped liver?" she asks. Her smile lights up her face.

"I included you in the list of those I trust," I remind her.

"Yeah, but you didn't consider me for the position."

"What position?"

"Your wife."

Those two words falling from her plump lips stir something inside me. Something other than anger and resentment. "My wife?" I repeat.

She shrugs. "Sure, why not? It's only a year, right? I'm not dating anyone, and you know you can trust me. You get your millions, and we get divorced."

"Just like that?"

This time, she nods. "It doesn't have to be complicated, Legend. I know you don't want this. You're against marrying for money, and I get that, but it's a lot of money. You said it yourself: it could change lives. Besides, if I were in your shoes, you'd do it for me." She pauses as her eyes bounce around the room. "All of you would."

"Not me," Roman speaks up, and we all laugh.

"We know, bud." Forrest laughs. "You're married. We get it."

"It deserves repeating." Roman grins as he snuggles Emerson closer.

Monroe rolls those big blue eyes of hers, then focuses on me. "It's not a big deal. If you want to do this to satisfy the terms of that archaic letter, I'm your girl."

My girl.

Why is my heart racing at the thought of Monroe being mine?

MONROE 4

LEGEND'S STARING AT ME LIKE I've lost my damn mind. I fight the urge to fidget under his gaze. Not because I regret my offer, but the look he's giving me is so intense and, let's face it, sexy as hell. His face is all stonelike and brooding, and those full kissable lips of his are being tortured by his white teeth as he clamps down on his lip.

"No pressure." I raise my hands in defense. "I won't be offended if you don't think it's a good idea, but you can trust me. Once you meet the requirements, we'll get a divorce, and all will be right in the world."

"That's a year of your life, Monroe. Longer, because we'd have to date, plan the wedding. It has to look real." His eyes never leave mine. He's likely looking for regret, but he won't find it. Legend is a good guy and a friend. This is what you do for your friends. At least in our circle, you do.

I nod. "Understood. Look, the offer stands, but the ball is in your court. I'm just trying to help out a friend."

"You sure about this, Mo?" Emerson asks.

I pull my gaze from the sexy, brooding man sitting next to me and look across the room at my best friend. "It's two years maximum. I'm single and unattached, as is Legend. We've known each other for years, and he knows I'd never try to gain access to his money at the end of this. I'm twenty-one. I'll be twenty-three at the oldest when this is over. Plenty of time to meet Mr. Right and start my happily ever after. This old man, though." Reaching over, I pat Legend on the back. "He'll be ready for retirement by the time our marriage is over," I tease.

"I'm thirty-one," Legend grouses. "I'd be thirty-three. That's far from retirement." His eyes bore into mine, and it's obvious he's failed to find the humor in my words.

"You're right. Semiretired." I lean my shoulder into his and offer him a bright smile. Surprisingly, the corner of his mouth twitches. Mr. Sexy and Brooding isn't immune to my humor after all. I hate seeing him this way. Legend is usually happy and upbeat.

I lean my head on his shoulder and keep my next words low, just for him. "I don't expect or want anything, Legend. I'm just offering to help. I'm available to do so, and that's what friends do."

I can feel him nod, but he doesn't reply for the longest time.

"One million dollars," Legend says. His voice is low and rumbly, and it's hot as hell.

I lift my head from his shoulder and meet his gaze. "What?" I'm too lost in the sound of his voice and the deliciousness of the man next to me to comprehend what he's trying to say. "I thought it was five million?"

"I'll give you one million dollars." He penetrates me with his gaze.

My mouth falls open. "No. Absolutely not. If we do this, Legend Raines, it's because I'm helping out a friend. I don't want your money." It's the absolute truth. He's in a jam, and I understand where he's coming from. He doesn't want to marry a stranger, and who can blame him?

"You'll be my *wife*."

Something in the way he says wife sends a ripple of desire through me. I don't understand why I'm having this reaction to him. Sure, he's hot as hell. They all are, but I've never felt this way around any of the guys before. I flirt with them, shamelessly, because I know they won't think of me as a tease and try to take more than I'm willing to give. They're safe, fun, lovable, sexy men. I enjoy the banter with each of them, but this... this is new.

"And you'll be my husband." My words are soft, meant just for him, and from the flare in his eyes, my words have an effect on him just as his did on me.

"This is huge, Monroe," Emerson speaks up. "That's a long time to put your life on hold."

Blinking hard, I force myself to tear my gaze from Legend and address my best friend. She has valid concerns, but I don't see it that way. "My life won't be on hold. I just started my job as a dental hygienist. I'm in the early stages of my career. I still live at home with my parents now that we're home from college, and I'll still get to hang out with my people."

"As his wife." Roman nods toward Legend.

"We wouldn't be able to tell anyone outside of this room the truth." Legend turns so that he's facing me. "We'd have to appear like a real married couple for this to work. Not even my parents can know."

I shrug. "How hard can it be?" To prove my point, I stand and turn before sitting on his lap. I glance at him over my shoulder at the same time his large, muscular hands grip my hips. "See? We've got this."

"She flirts with all of us all the time. She's never hidden that. You could spin it that she always had a thing for you," Maddox suggests.

"That would have to stop," Legend's deep voice says, his lips next to my ear. "My wife can't flirt with my friends. No, fuck that. My wife can't flirt with anyone but me." There's a growl in his voice that's not usually there, and I can admit to myself that it's doing it for me. I feel that sound between my thighs.

I laugh nervously, but I hope it sounds carefree. "Good thing I'm a pro at flirting. You sure you can handle all of my attention?" I tease. At least I hope it sounds teasing. I'm trying to mask the desire I feel from his thumb tracing over the waistline of my shorts. We're always laughing and teasing, but this feels different.

I know it's because of what's at stake. If this gets out, it would have all been for nothing, and we can't have that. I want to do this for him. I don't want his money. I just want to help him. The guys have been a huge part of my life. Where Emerson went, I went, and well, they were just always there. I have no doubt in my mind that if it were me, one of them, hell, all of them, except for Roman, who only has eyes for his wife, would step up to help me.

"As long as it's on me," Legend replies huskily.

"Done."

"Just like that?" Forrest asks.

"Why is it so hard to believe that I'd want to help him? I'd do it for any of you. This is huge. Five million dollars is life-changing. I understand why he's not willing to marry a stranger. We've known each other for a long time. We all spend a lot of time together. It's believable that something has been brewing between us. I'm the best candidate. Besides, Legend can trust me. I'm not out to take over his life or his bank account." I turn sideways in his lap to face him. "The offer is on the table. You're not going to hurt my feelings if you say you don't want to go through with it. However, I think you should consider it. It's too much money to pass up. I know you, Legend Raines. I know you'd give back to those who matter to you. The shop, your parents, your future wife and kids, the real one." I wink.

"We need to talk about this." He stands with me in his arms. "We're using a guest room," he announces as he turns and heads up the stairs.

"That comes after the wedding, buddy!" Lachlan calls out.

I laugh and loop my arms around Legend's neck. "I can walk, you know."

He grunts but doesn't put me down as he ascends the stairs.

With heavy steps, he pushes into the first guest room and kicks the door closed. The room is empty. Emerson and Roman have only lived here a short time. He's not even breathing heavily when he places me on my feet. I watch him as he rakes his hands through his hair and paces across the room.

"Legend." I whisper his name into the quiet room.

He stops pacing and his ice-blue eyes lock on me. "Why?"

"Why what?"

"Why are you doing this? Why offer up potentially two years of your life for me?"

"You're a good guy. I hate what your grandparents did to your mother, and I hate what they're doing to you. They're trying to control you. I want what's best for you, and with that money, you'd be set for life, Legend."

"I do well for myself now. Money changes you." He crosses his arms over his chest. It's a protective stance, but he doesn't need protecting. Not from me. I know what this is, or what it will be, rather. An understanding. An agreement between two friends.

Nothing more. Nothing less.

"I agree with you. It does change some people, but I can't see it changing you. You're such a down-to-earth person, and you'd do anything for your friends and family. I know how you helped Roman and then again when you talked to Forrest once he found out about them. You care about those who are close to you. You would never let something like the balance in your bank account change that."

"Will it change you?"

"Considering I'm not making millions on my dental hygienist salary, I'm going with a no. Even if I were making millions, the answer would still be no."

"I won't let you do this for free."

"Then no deal."

"Monroe." He sighs. "If we do this, you're giving up so much for me. I have to pay you for your time."

"Let me ask you something. If I were to call you in the middle of the night and tell you I was stranded in another state—let's say Kentucky—on my way home from school. What would you do?"

"I'd get to you as fast as I could."

"Would you charge me?"

"No. Of course not," he scoffs.

I give him a pointed look.

"It's not the same. This is giving up your life for over a year. Probably a year and a half because we'll have to date, get married, and then be married for a year."

"I'm aware of the timeline. We won't have to do much dating. Just be seen together, holding hands or whatnot, and announce the engagement. It's plausible that we've been dating secretly, given how much time we are together. My only stipulation is that my parents be there."

"You can't tell them the truth. You'd be lying to them."

I shrug. "It's a little white lie. I'm going to be marrying a good man. A man who will make sure I'm taken care of and protected long after we're divorced. I want them there because life is messy, and sometimes things don't work out. I might never find my one true love, and I'd like for my parents to witness me getting married. This might be my one and only wedding, and I'd hate for them to miss it."

"So, no guilt?"

"We're going to be married, Legend. I care about you. We're friends. There have been marriages based on less. We're both going into this with our eyes wide open. It's not going to be miserable. We're not tied together by obligation. I'm offering to do this of my own free will. We get along well. It could be fun. We can look at it as an adventure."

"You'd have to move in with me."

"Most married folks live together," I tease.

"I live in a tiny one-bedroom house. Well, there are two bedrooms, but as you already know the second was the size of a closet, so I tore out the walls and made a larger living area. It was just me, and works for me."

"What size bed?"

"What?" He tilts his head to the side.

"What size bed do you have?"

"California King."

"Perfect. That's big enough for both of us. You can stay on your side, and I'll stay on mine. What else you got for me?" I raise my eyebrows in question.

"You want to sleep next to me every night?"

"Do you have cooties?" I chuckle. "Legend, come on. We're adults. We can do this. Does it suck hairy donkey balls? Yes. Absolutely. I hate that they've put you in this position, but that's okay, because we have a solution. We'll announce that we've been dating, then our engagement, and then the wedding."

"What kind of wedding?"

"Honestly, Em and Rome's was perfect. Small and intimate. Huge weddings are more for the guests than for the couple. Our friends, our parents, and we live happily married for the next year. We get your inheritance, and we get divorced. Easy."

"I'm going to have to hold your hand, hold you, kiss you, touch you. We're going to have to sell this." He takes small steps until he's standing before me. His large palm rests against my cheek. "Can you handle that?"

I smile up at him. "I can. Can you?"

"Of course."

"Our friends know. When we're with them, here or at Forrest's, which are our two usual hangout spots, we don't have to pretend. We can be us. It's when we're outside in the world we have to put on a show. It will be minimal at best. We both work full time. We can do this, Legend. You deserve the money. Your mom deserves the chunk that I know you're going to give her. What bigger fuck you to your controlling grandparents? Scam their fucked-up rules, and let's do this."

"If we do this, Monroe, we do it right. I'm going to buy you a ring. I'm going to ask your father's permission, and I'll treat you like a man should treat his wife."

I swallow hard. "That's not necessary. I know you'll be good to me."

"Damn right. Anyone who knows me knows that if I'm with someone and asking her to marry me, I'm all in. It will be to sell it to everyone and because you deserve nothing less."

"Fine." I roll my eyes dramatically, as if the notion annoys me. When in reality there are a swarm of butterflies taking flight inside me. "There is one small thing." I hold up my thumb and index finger about a half an inch apart.

"What's that?"

"Other women."

He rears back as if I've slapped him. "Mo, if I'm with you, if you're my wife, and you take my last name, there will be no other women. I don't cheat."

"But this won't be real."

"It will be in all the ways that matter. We might not be sleeping together, but we're going to stand before our family and friends and take a vow. I take that seriously." He pauses, those ice-blue irises holding my gaze. "Is that the kind of man you think I am?" There's hurt in his tone.

"No." I'm quick to assure him. "I just know that a year, well, more like a year and a half, is a long time to go without sex."

This time it's both of his hands that cradle my face as he angles my head to look up at him. "My wife." The words are a deep, rumbly growl from his lips. "Mine, Mo. There will be no one else. I'm not an animal. I can abstain for however long it takes."

Desire courses through my veins like hot lava rolling down a mountainside. Heat pools between my thighs. It wasn't my intention to anger him, but damn, he's hot when he's fired up. "I didn't mean to offend you, Legend. I just thought it was important that we discuss it before we announced to the world that we are an us."

"What about you?" he asks. "Can you go without?"

"Trust me. You have nothing to worry about."

He nods and drops his hands but doesn't step back. "So, we're doing this? We're going to tell everyone we've been dating for a while? Get engaged, get married, and be married for a year?"

"Give or take." I shrug. "We'll stay married as long as we need to."

"The letter outlined a year."

"We can't very well run and get divorced that afternoon or the next day. Once the money is yours and in your account, we'll end things."

"Monroe." He bends his head, resting his forehead against mine. His arms wrap around me. "This is huge. What you're doing for me, and for my family. I promise you, I'll be the best fake husband you could ever dream up. I'll also take care of you when this is over. I know you said you don't want money, but I'll find a way to repay you."

My heart melts at his words. I don't want any of that. I don't want a cut of his inheritance.. I just want to help him. I'm happy that I'm able to do this for him. "Just be happy. Don't let their negativity steal your light. You walked into this house today with the weight of the world on your shoulders. I hate seeing you that way."

"You're one of a kind, Monroe Morrison."

"Right back at ya, boyfriend."

He pulls back, kisses my forehead, and takes my hand, lacing our fingers. "We might as well get used to this."

"Yeah," I agree, feeling the warmth of his hold spread up my arm. He gives me a smile, a genuine Legend smile, and leads me out of the room and back downstairs.

As soon as we enter the living room, conversation stops and all eyes are on us. "Have you met my girlfriend?" Legend asks.

He leads me into the room, and back to the love seat, pulling me onto his lap. We tell them what we've decided and swear them all to secrecy. I know in my heart this is the right thing. It's eighteen months, tops. I'll focus on my job, save money, and at the end of this, I'll find my own place and start my life.

I glance at my best friend, who is snuggled up on her husband's lap. I might never find that kind of love, so this... this will give me a small taste of what that kind of love and devotion would feel like. If I know anything about Legend, it's that he's a good man and a man of his word. He'll be good to me. I just have to remind myself that this isn't real.

Let the adventure begin.

LEGEND 5

IT'S MONDAY MORNING, AND I'm dragging ass. I slept like shit last night. I'm not sure what I expected, considering my life just got flipped upside down.

I'm getting married.

To Monroe.

I'm still trying to wrap my head around all of this. She volunteered without hesitation, and no matter what I tossed at her, she wasn't backing down. That girl has a heart the size of Texas. Is this a good idea? Probably not. Are we doing it anyway? Yes, we are.

Starting today.

Everlasting Ink is usually closed on Sundays and Mondays. However, we shut down on Saturday for the wedding, so we moved the clients that were able to today. Monroe is not in today. She works four ten-hour days. Her day off fluctuates, but today she's free. She's bringing me lunch, and we're starting small. Letting the Everlasting Ink staff know about us. Forrest referred to it as a soft opening. It sounds crazy, but when you think about it, it makes sense. Small doses to get the word out there and for us to get used to being... close to one another. Closer than our flirting and banter made us before.

It's a ruse. All of it. However, I still find myself watching the clock, waiting for the moment my new girlfriend gets here with lunch. It's not because I'm hungry. That alone tells me this is a terrible fucking idea, but even knowing that, I'm not stopping it. There's something about the idea of her being mine. She's not really mine, but she will be for a while, and that's fucking with my head. I've never thought much about getting married. I assumed one day I'd find the one I couldn't live without, and it would happen. Now that it's here, it feels wrong, yet there's a small part of me that knows it also feels right.

The money can do a lot of good for the people I love. I wouldn't be doing this if it were anyone other than Monroe. She's a fucking knockout, and she's going to be my wife. There's a reason why I've always shamelessly flirted back with her all of these years. It wasn't just for fun. I can admit that.

Since the moment she spoke up last night, she's all I can think about. Not the money. Not deceiving our families. Her.

Just Monroe.

I'm fucked. This is going to be the hardest and probably the best eighteen or so months of my life.

"You're all set," I tell my client. He's a regular who just had a baby and wanted to add his name to his tattoo with his other kids' names. "You know the drill," I tell him.

"Thanks, man." He slides his shirt over his head and stands at the same time Monroe walks into my room.

"Hey, babe." She smiles. "You ready for lunch?" She holds up a bag from the deli down the street.

"Babe?" Martin asks. He looks from me to Monroe. "You didn't tell me you had a steady girl."

I hold my arm out for Monroe, and she steps into my side, wrapping her arms around me. "Can you blame me for wanting to keep her all to myself?" I ask, placing a kiss on her temple. Her body relaxes into mine as if she was always meant to be there.

Martin chuckles. "You got to show them off, Legend. Let her know you're proud to be her man." He winks at Monroe, and she laughs.

"We hid it for so long because all of our friends are friends. We just wanted to see where this was going before adding more complications," Monroe explains.

Martin nods. "Makes sense. Not hiding now?"

I look down at Monroe as she peers up at me. "Nah, not hiding." I brush Monroe's hair out of her eyes.

Martin huffs out his approval. "Enjoy your lunch." He waves and makes his way out to the desk, where Lyra is working today.

"How did I do?" Monroe asks. Her arms are still wrapped around my waist, and my hand is still sitting firmly at the small of her back. Before I can reply, we're interrupted.

"Hey, Legend." Lyra walks into the room and freezes when she sees us. "Oh—I—I'll just — " She points over her shoulder.

"It's fine, Lyra. What's up?" I pretend like having Monroe wrapped up in my arms is a normal everyday occurrence. Maybe on a day when we're teasing and flirting, but every moment since the words "your wife" fell from her lips last night has felt different.

"O-kay. What did I miss?" She waves her index finger in a circle, pointing at the two of us.

"You've met my girlfriend, right?" I ask Lyra. I ignore the way my chest wants to expand, claiming Monroe as mine.

"Girlfriend? How did I miss that?" Lyra places her hands on her hips and tilts her head to the side as she studies us.

"We were keeping things quiet until we knew what this was." Monroe smiles up at me. "Until we knew we were going to last."

A huge grin breaks out across Lyra's face. "So, this means you're going to last? Are you playing a trick on me? Is there a camera in here?" She twirls around, looking at all four corners of the room, searching for cameras.

I can't help but laugh at her. "Stop being so dramatic. We're not playing a trick on you. We actually told everyone last night at Rome and Em's place. We're going to last." My voice is strong, and if I didn't know better, I'd believe me. Maybe this won't be as hard as I thought.

"That's awesome!" Lyra rushes toward us and pulls us into a hug. "Two down, and three to go." She grins.

"What?" Monroe asks.

"The men of Everlasting Ink are dropping like flies. Roman's married. You two are going to last." She winks at us. "That just leaves Forrest, Lachlan, and Maddox."

"What about you?" Monroe asks her. "You're still single."

Lyra waves her hand in the air. "Meh, I've had my fair share of dramatic relationships. I'm good with sitting out a few innings. Besides, these guys don't really date, so for them to acknowledge a relationship is a big deal."

She's not wrong, but I'm not going to tell her that. We've all dated casually, but never enough to claim an actual relationship. "You don't know us that well," I tell her.

She rolls her eyes. "I watch. I listen. I learn." She cackles at herself. "But for real, congrats, you two. This is the best news I've heard all day."

"Did you need something, Lyra?" I ask.

"Oh, yeah. Martin's all taken care of. He said he'll call you when his wife is ready to schedule her tattoo."

I nod. "Thanks."

She flashes us a wide grin. "I seriously love this. So much." She turns on her heel and rushes out of the room.

"That wasn't so hard to convince her," Monroe says.

I smile down at her. "Yeah, I think we make a pretty good team."

"Damn right we do."

I can't resist bending my head and placing a kiss on her forehead. "Thank you for this, Monroe. Are you sure? There's still time to back out."

"I'm not backing out, Legend."

I wrap both of my arms around her and pull her fully into my arms, hugging her tightly. "Thank you, Mo."

"Aw, the lovebirds," Lachlan coos.

Monroe's body shakes with laughter as she pulls away. She doesn't go far. I keep one arm around her waist and hold her close to me.

"Hey, Lachlan." She smiles at him.

"I was coming to see if you wanted to grab some lunch."

"I actually grabbed lunch for everyone." She points to the deli bag that's sitting on the desk.

"You better lock this one down, Legend. I might have to call dibs."

"She's going to be my wife." The words slip off my tongue as if it's the most natural thing in the world to refer to Monroe as mine.

"So I hear." Lachlan rummages through the bag, pulls out the sub with his name on it, and grabs a bag of chips. "Thanks for lunch, Mo." He reaches into his pocket, pulls out his wallet, and drops some cash on the desk. "Do you think you two lovebirds can keep it PG in here while I send in the others to grab their food?"

"I don't know." Monroe runs her hand over my chest. "You better have them hurry."

Lachlan's eyes go wide before a grin tugs at his lips. "I see how this is going to go." He wags his eyebrows.

"Get out of here. Send in the others."

"I don't know. I think I'll take my time."

"Then you can answer to them when they're pissed my door is locked and they can't get to their food."

"Hey, now. This is a respectable place of business. None of that newlywed stuff going on here."

"Make sure you remind Rome of that," I fire back.

"You two just need to learn how to control yourselves around your wives."

Reaching behind me, I pick up the first thing I can grab, which is a box of gloves, and toss them at him. He ducks and rushes out the door, his laughter following him all the way down the hall.

"Come on, boyfriend. Let's take this to the break room."

"We're getting married. I think that makes me your fiancé," I remind her.

"Hmm." She taps her index finger against her chin. "Did I miss you getting down on one knee and asking?"

"Is that what you want?" My hand slides up to cradle her cheek.

She shrugs. "I mean, this might be my one and only. It might be for appearances, but I'd still like the full experience."

I nod, knowing that there isn't a single thing she could ask from me that I wouldn't give her. She's giving up so much to help me. If it's the full experience she wants, the full experience she'll get.

"Come on." I lace her fingers through mine, enjoying the feel of her soft skin, grab the bag, and lead her to the break room.

It's been two days since I've seen Monroe. We've texted back and forth a little, but I've not laid eyes on her in over forty-eight hours. Something I know a man in love would never do. "You should go see her. Drop lunch or flowers off at her work," Roman tells me.

"Why are you not home with your wife?" I ask him.

"Trust me, I wish I were. She made me come in today. I was ready to cancel all my appointments."

"She's going to be there when you get home," I remind him, and a goofy, joyful look crosses his face.

"I know, man. Best fucking feeling ever to come home to her."

I nod like I actually understand, when I have no clue what it's like to have someone waiting at home for you at the end of a long day.

"Take her some flowers. When is your next client?" he asks.

"Not until two. I had one cancel."

"You've got plenty of time. Grab her a coffee and some flowers, and make a show of dropping them off to her in front of all of her coworkers."

"I don't know her favorite coffee."

"You do know I'm married to her best friend, right?" He grabs his phone from his desk and dials Emerson, hitting the speakerphone button so I can hear their conversation.

"Hey, how's your day?" she greets him. "You caught me on my break."

"Better now that I'm talking to you. Baby girl, I've got you on speaker. Legend is with me. He wants to take Monroe her favorite coffee and some flowers. What's her drink of choice?"

"Aw, Legend, she'll love that. Look at you being all husbandly already."

"It was my idea," Roman tells her.

Emerson laughs. "Why am I not surprised?"

"He hasn't seen her in two days, baby girl. The man needs to step up his game."

"They're easing everyone into this, Rome. Have patience. Legend?"

"I'm here."

"She's an iced-vanilla-latte girl. As far as flowers, we're women, and anything is always appreciated, especially when it means the man in our life is thinking about us. You can't go wrong with whatever you choose."

"Thanks, Emerson."

"Love you, baby girl. I'll be home around six."

"I'm working until six."

"I'll have dinner ready."

"I'll see you at home. Gotta go. Love you." The call ends before Roman can reply.

He shoves his phone back into his pocket and levels me with his stare. "You sure about all this, man?"

"It's a lot," I admit. "But the more I think about it, the more I know it wouldn't work with anyone but her. She's right about that. It's easy enough to get everyone to believe it."

He nods. "Who knows, maybe it will work out between the two of you."

"Don't go getting ideas there, Rome. I know you're in newlywed heaven, and in the daddy-to-be blissfulness of life, but that's not for all of us."

"Just know that when it gets to where you need to talk to someone, you can come to me. You were there for me with all that stuff with Emerson. I appreciate you always having my back."

"We all do."

"Forrest came around. Thanks to you."

"He would have anyway. There isn't a single person on this earth who can see the two of you together and not understand the love you have is soul deep."

"Yeah," he agrees. "Go. You've got an iced vanilla latte and flowers to deliver."

"Need anything while I'm out?"

"Nope, I'm all set."

"I'll be back." I rush down the hall to my room and grab my keys. I stop at the front desk and let Lyra, who's working again today, know I'm stepping out but will be back before my next client arrives and head out.

Twenty minutes later, I'm pulling my truck into the parking lot of the dentist's office on the edge of town where Monroe works. With her iced latte and flowers in hand, I head inside. All eyes turn toward me, but I ignore them as I approach the front desk.

"Hi, can I help you?" a young woman asks. She smiles and eyes the latte and flowers I'm holding.

"I'm here to see Monroe Morrison."

"Oh, sure. Let me see if she can come out to see you. I think she's just finishing up with a patient."

"Thanks." I turn, find an empty seat, and settle in to wait. I've got over an hour before I have to be back at the shop, and now that I'm here, I really want to see her. There's a TV on, but the sound is off. It's some kind of home renovation show. I watch, getting lost in the demolition they're doing, when I feel a hand on my shoulder. I turn and smile when I see her.

"Legend? What are you doing here?" Monroe's smile is welcoming, and her eyes soften when she sees what I'm holding.

"I missed you." The words tumble out without thought. They're the absolute truth. I have to get a handle on this, but for now, I push it all down and stand to greet her. Leaning in, I place a soft kiss on her cheek. "I thought you might need an afternoon pick-me-up, and well, these made me think of you." It's not a line either. I stopped at the local florist and the blue color of the flower reminded me of her eyes. "Your eyes," I clarify.

She takes the offered flowers and brings them in to smell them. "Thank you, Legend. That was sweet of you."

"You're welcome."

"I hate to rush, but I need to get back to work. I have a full schedule today."

"Right. Of course. You're off at seven, right?"

She nods in the middle of taking a sip of her drink. "Yes," she finally replies.

"How about you come over to my place, and I'll have dinner ready? You should see what you're getting yourself into."

"I'm in this, Legend."

"Me, too, Mo." My voice is soft and doesn't sound like my own.

"I'd like that."

"Any requests?"

"No seafood." She wrinkles up her nose, and it's fucking adorable.

"Got it. My girl hates seafood." I tap my temple with my index finger, and she smiles. "Enjoy the rest of your day."

"Thank you." She rises on her tiptoes and presses her lips to my cheek. "See you later."

"See you." I wave awkwardly. I stand still, watching, waiting for her to walk back behind the door and disappear out of sight. When I can no longer see her, I make my way back out to my truck.

I ignore the way my heart races just a little faster, knowing that I'll get to see her again tonight. That's not supposed to happen. She's a friend, the one who's doing me a huge solid. My family, both blood and my Everlasting Ink family, are going to benefit greatly from this arrangement. I know that, but I can't stop thinking about how, for a while, no matter how short that time will be, Monroe is going to be mine.

MONROE 6

I'VE BEEN HERE A FEW times before. It's always been with Emerson. However, it still feels like the first time as I pull into his driveway and put my car into Park. Taking a deep breath, I grab my phone and purse and push open the door. I'm barely at the front door when it's pulled open and a smiling Legend greets me.

He's wearing a black T-shirt that's molded to his muscular frame, a pair of well-worn jeans, and he's barefoot. Why is that so sexy? His full, kissable lips are tilted into a smile, all aimed at me. "There she is."

"Hey." I return his smile.

"I hope you're hungry." His ice-blue eyes rake over my body. I'm wearing my scrubs, having come straight from work, but the heat of his gaze makes me feel as though I'm in the skimpiest of outfits.

"Starving, actually. What are we having?"

"Nothing fancy. I grilled some chicken breasts and tossed a couple of baked potatoes on the grill as well."

"Perfect."

"Come on in. Make yourself at home." He holds the door open for me, and I step past him, my shoulder brushing his chest. A spark ignites as we touch, but I pretend to ignore it and keep walking.

"It smells amazing. What can I do to help?"

"Nothing. I just need to grab everything off the grill. You're right on time. Help yourself to whatever you can find to drink in the fridge. I'll be right back." He walks past me, pausing to give my arm a gentle squeeze as he does.

I follow him into the kitchen, grab us each a bottle of water from the fridge, and take a seat at the small dining room table. I allow my eyes to roam around the space. It's small but surprisingly roomy.

"I marinated the chicken," Legend says, stepping in from the patio doors. "Do you want any other sauces?"

"No, I should be good."

He sets a serving platter with grilled chicken and potatoes in the center of the table. "Let me grab the butter, cheese, and bacon bits." He rushes off to the fridge, and I decide to serve us both while he does.

"Thanks," he says, placing everything on the table before grabbing his water and taking a long pull. He sets the half-empty bottle on the table and gives me a shy smile that does nothing to ease the tension in the air.

"How was your day, dear?" I smirk, and the nervousness that surrounds us fizzles as we both chuckle at my question.

"I had a client cancel, so I surprised my girl with her favorite drink and some flowers. How about you?"

"That's so weird. My guy showed up with my favorite drink and flowers. It was a welcome surprise and a first for me."

"A first?"

"No one has ever given me flowers before."

"Never?"

"Nope."

Something happens. His eyes sharpen, and his chest rises and falls a little faster with each breath. "I'm glad I got to be your first."

It takes all of my focus and effort not to squirm in my seat. Why are his words so... hot? "They were beautiful. Thank you, Legend."

He nods. "You're welcome."

We make small talk throughout the meal. I've never had an issue talking with Legend, or any of the guys, for that matter, and tonight is no different. We talk about his client, who came in for a memorial tattoo for his little sister, and I tell him about the adorable little girl who got her first dental cleaning from me today. She was a challenge, but she left smiling and telling her mom she was excited to come back to see her new friend, Mo.

"That was delicious. Thank you." I stand to start clearing the table.

Legend leans over and places his hand on my arm. "I can get that later."

"Nope. We both worked today, and you cooked. The least I can do is help clean up." I grab his plate as his hand falls away. He stands as well, and together we work in silence as we clean up from dinner.

"So, how about a tour?"

"Sure."

He holds his hand out for me, and I take it, allowing him to entwine our fingers and lead me through the house. We're not in public, and there's no need to put on a show when it's just the two of us. The intimacy of holding his hand comes naturally. "Not much to see, really. You already know I tore out the wall between the two bedrooms to make the master bigger and to fit a walk-in shower."

"I remember," I tell him as he leads me down the hallway.

"So, this is the guest bathroom. Not much. A tub shower, a sink, and a toilet. Nothing fancy."

"It does what it's intended to do, I guess," I say with a short laugh.

Legend flashes me a wide grin. "You saw the kitchen and dining room area, as well as the living room, since it's an open concept. All that's left is the master suite and the laundry room, which is also a mudroom that leads out to the attached garage."

"Well, show me this masterpiece, Raines." I nod toward what I know is his bedroom door. "I need to see how the other half lives."

He huffs out a laugh. "I might have gone over the top, and I'm aware that resale value on the house now that it's a one-bedroom is going to suck, but I'm hoping the master suite makes up for it."

"You planning on selling?"

"Nah, it's just me. Well, soon to be us. Do you think we need more room?"

"It's only a year, Legend. I think we can manage."

"What happens when I drive you crazy and you need to get away from me? There aren't exactly a lot of options."

"One of us will sleep on the couch, or I'll crash in my room at Forrest's place, or with Emerson and Roman. Hell, I can even go back to my parents'."

"No." His voice is stern, and he's shaking his head as if the idea is mortifying to him. "If anyone sleeps on the couch, it's going to be me. I'll make every effort not to piss you off so that doesn't happen."

"I'm sure we're going to ruffle each other's feathers here and there, but it's all going to be just fine."

"Monroe, this is huge. You're giving up so much."

"Not really. Sure, I'm out of the dating game for a while, but I'd already planned on that. You're getting me out of my parents' place. Essentially giving me more freedom. But I'm not struggling to pay all the bills on my own."

"You won't pay a single bill while you're here."

"That's not fair, Legend. I want to help. Pull my own weight."

"It's nonnegotiable. You're giving up so much that's the least that I can do. Save your money. Blow it. I don't care what you do with it. It's no good here."

"We'll see." I can feel a smile tugging at my lips, knowing that this is going to be something that's going to ruffle his feathers for sure. No way can I just live here and not help out. That's not who I am.

He holds my stare for a beat longer. "This is where we'll sleep." He pushes open his bedroom door, and we step inside. The room is massive, with dark gray walls and a gray-and-white bedding set. The furniture is all black wood. It's very masculine and very Legend.

"That bed is massive!" I say, stepping next to it and pushing down on the mattress, testing its softness.

"Should be plenty of room for both of us, or I can move a bed to the living room for me, and you can stay in here."

I wave him off. "I think you, me, Emerson, and Roman could all sleep in this bed and never touch," I joke.

"Yeah, just us in our bed, Mo." His deep voice, along with the determined look in his eye, sends tingles down my spine.

"I agree. Em is a bed hog. Trust me, I speak from experience."

"The closets are in the bathroom. There is a his and hers. So you should have plenty of room for all of your things." He nods toward the bathroom.

I make my way to the door, pushing it open, and gasp. "Holy shit! Legend, that tub is massive, and its inside the shower. This is like something you'd see on that *Cribs* TV show. This is... wow." I turn to look at him. "Did you design this?"

"Yeah," he says, raising his hands and locking them behind his head. "The contractor was able to see my vision."

"Damn. Yeah, I don't think you have to worry about reselling once someone sees this bathroom. Is that a rain showerhead?"

"Yep. And jets all down the wall. There's another detachable showerhead. You know, in case two people want to shower at the same time."

I nod, pushing the thought of showering with Legend out of my mind. "Was it your idea to have the tub in the shower area too?"

"Yeah. That way, if the water sloshes over, and when you step out, you don't have to worry about dripping all over the floor."

"You put some thought into this."

"A little." He grins.

"No door. That's genius."

"Yeah, I didn't want to have to clean all that glass, and I hate shower curtains. They just get nasty, and I didn't want to deal with either."

"This is amazing, Legend. I'm already seeing myself soaking in that tub with a book and a glass of wine."

"Just tell me your favorite, and I'll make sure we keep it stocked."

"You don't have to do that."

He points at his chest. "You're doing me the favor, remember? Besides, as your husband, that'll be my job. It might not be a marriage in all the traditional ways, but I will take care of you, Monroe. Before, during, and after this is over. Always."

There is so much conviction in his tone, I don't bother to argue with him. I know he's feeling like I get nothing out of this. He doesn't understand that I want to help. It's still new, and I'm sure once it all settles, he'll stop worrying so much about me, and we'll just focus on getting through the year as man and wife.

"I have to admit, it might be hard to get me to move out once I'm here. This is like a resort." I laugh.

I hear his deep chuckle behind me. "I'm glad you like it." I can feel him as he draws closer, and his hand rests on the small of my back. "Can you see yourself living here? With me?"

Glancing at him over my shoulder, I find that he's closer than I thought. His lips are a breath from mine. I swallow hard and offer him what I hope is a charming, carefree smile. "You're stuck with me, roomie."

This close, I can smell his cologne and see every fleck in his ice-blue eyes. This man, this gorgeous, funny, talented, sexy man, is going to be my husband. I'm going to be sleeping next to him in this very room for a long while. I know what I signed up for. However, standing here in this room, the thought of what will be ours for the foreseeable future hits me.

I'm marrying Legend Raines.

He tosses his head back in laughter, and I feel the tight coil in my stomach unravel. "Come on, roomie." He snakes his arm around my shoulders. "Let's go watch a movie. I'll make you some of the best popcorn you've ever had."

"Oh, yeah? How long do you put it in the microwave for?"

"Two and a half minutes. The trick is to buy the movie theater butter flavor and not let the bag stop popping before you pull it out of the microwave."

"Then you have a bunch of unpopped kernels."

"A few, but you also don't have a bag full of burnt popcorn."

"You sound like you've tested this theory from experience?"

"A time or fifty." He chuckles. "You want to stay, Mo?"

"Yeah, but I get to pick the movie."

"What my wife wants, my wife gets."

He's teasing, but damn if hearing him say wife doesn't get my lady bits fired up for him. I need to get myself under control. This is all for show. This is to help Legend get his inheritance. It will help all the guys of Everlasting Ink, my best friend, her brother, who is so much like my brother as well, our friends, Legend's parents. This is the right thing to do. He shouldn't have to jump through hoops to get an inheritance. Either they wanted him to have the money or they didn't. It should be that simple.

"We can talk about what comes next."

"Not a bad idea. We need to decide when to tell our parents," I agree as he leads us back to the living room.

"Sit tight." He motions to the couch and rushes off to the kitchen.

I take a seat, grab the remote, and manage to pull up the streaming app and start scrolling through the movie options.

"Water okay to drink? I have beer as well, but I know you're driving home. Unless... you wanted to stay?"

"I have to work tomorrow, so I'll need clean scrubs. Water is perfect." I take the offered bottle and place it next to me on the end table. "So, this is the absolute best popcorn, huh?" I ask, as he places a large bowl between us on the couch.

"You know it." He nods, and I grab a handful, tossing a few pieces into my mouth.

"Not bad."

"Why, thank you." He reaches over and pats himself on the back, and we both laugh at his antics.

"All right, so the parents. What are you thinking?"

"Well, the sooner we tell them, the better. How long do you think we need to date before announcing the wedding?"

"I think there is no timeline for love. We've known each other for years. We hang out a lot, so it's believable. There shouldn't be any red flags from your grandparents' attorney."

"I was thinking the same thing. I don't think this would have worked with anyone but you. Thank you for doing this, Monroe." He pauses, then releases a heavy sigh. "It still feels wrong in a way. Getting married to get the money."

"You can't think about it that way. Think about what you can do for your family with that money. For the business. Besides, it was a shitty way to make amends. I get what they were trying to say. Marry who you want. But to put the stipulation that you have to be married within a year and for a year to get your inheritance...." I shake my head. "They should have given you that money, or hell, given it to your mom with no strings attached."

"Yeah. That's why I agreed to all of this. And to help you too. You'll be set for life after this. We both will be."

"I don't want any of it, Legend." Reaching over, I place my hand on his shoulder. "We're friends, and that's what friends are for. Time is going to pass us by in the blink of an eye, and the days where you once referred to me as your wife will be a distant memory." A look I can't name crosses his face. "Now, we need a game plan."

We spend the next hour hashing out our plan and eating the entire bowl of popcorn. The movie we planned to watch is long since forgotten.

"Okay, so I'll call my parents and tell them I want to bring someone for them to meet. I know you've met them multiple times, but this way we get to play it up." I grin.

"And I'll tell mine the same. I'll set something up for Sunday at my parents', and you said you're going to try for Saturday?"

"Yep. My parents are going on a cruise next week, so we'll catch them before they leave."

"Then we date?"

"Yep. Dinners, hanging out with the group. We'll let it ride for a few weeks, and then we can announce our engagement."

"I have to ask you."

"You don't technically have to. I mean, I did volunteer for the position."

"You said that was important to you. I'm going to ask you. Are you okay with me taking care of all of those details?"

"Yep." I ignore the flutter in my belly. "That's all you, Mr. Raines."

"Monroe Raines," he says softly. "I like it."

"Yeah, I like it too." I stand and pick up the now empty bowl. "I should get going. I have to be up early tomorrow."

"Text me when you get home?"

It's on the tip of my tongue to tell him I'll be fine, but this is my life for the foreseeable future. I need to get used to us pretending we're a couple. That's something a couple in love would do. Hell, Emerson and Roman know each other's every step. I'm sure it won't be like that, but I do understand checking in. Safety is important.

"Of course. Thank you for dinner and for the popcorn."

"Anytime, wife," he whispers.

I don't know if I was meant to hear him, but I did, and that sexy deep voice of his is hard to resist. He walks me to my car and waits until I'm buckled in before closing the door. I watch him stand in the driveway as I get further away from his place.

We have a plan for moving forward.

Now, I guess I need to start thinking about the wedding.

[illegible]

"No, no kidding," he says. [illegible]

[illegible] I stand and [illegible] my bowl. [illegible]

[illegible]

[illegible] important.

"Of course. Thank you for dinner and for the [illegible]."

"Anytime, with [illegible]."

I don't know if I was meant to hear this, but I did, and that [illegible] is hard to [illegible]. He walks me to [illegible] and waits until I'm buckled in before closing the door. I watch him stand in the driveway as I [illegible] away from the place.

We have enough for moving forward.

Now, I guess I need to start thinking about the wedding.

Legend 7

"We're early," Monroe says from where she sits in the passenger seat of my truck.

"I know, but I needed to make a good impression on your parents."

"You've met them. Besides, if you're who I chose to be with, and they know I'm happy, they'll be happy."

Her words help ease some of my worry about tonight's meeting. "They said seven, right?" I ask.

"Yes. They went shopping for a few last-minute items for their cruise and are heading home now. It works out great because who wants to cook and clean and finish packing the night before you leave for vacation?"

"I couldn't tell you. It's been too damn long since I've been on vacation."

"We should go."

I turn to face her. It's still light out, but the sun is setting, casting a warm glow across her cheeks. "Yeah? Where do you want to go?"

"I don't know. Maybe we can say we're going on our honeymoon, but really, it's just a vacation? Mom and Dad tried to get me to go on the cruise with them, but I'd just started my job and didn't want to take the time off. Not to mention, who wants to be the third wheel on a romantic cruise with their parents?" She makes a grossed-out facial expression, which makes me laugh.

"I see your point. So, what about a little time off for a honeymoon?"

"Yeah, I think I can make that work."

"Where do you want to go?"

"Nothing fancy. Maybe we just rent a cabin in the Smokies for a few days? Or, we could do a destination wedding there. Have the gang all go with us. Can your parents travel?"

"Yeah, they can. Is that what you want? How do you see our wedding day?"

"You know, I never really thought too much about the day. It was always the man who would be waiting for me at the altar."

"And what about the man?" It's not really any of my business, but over the last few days, we've been talking on the phone a lot at night after ending our days and texting throughout the day, and I've discovered that I'm desperate for any morsel of intel I can get on the dark-haired beauty.

I know her, but in a way, I don't know her.

Before Sunday night, I knew her on the surface. I knew she and Emerson were thick as thieves, and I knew she was someone we all trusted. What I didn't know is that she always wanted a sibling, that she wants a big family of her own, and that her favorite color is light pink. That's just the short list of things I now know about my future bride, and I'm eager for that list to keep growing.

"It was never his looks, you know?" She glances over at me, and her cheeks turn the sexiest shade of pink. "You don't want to hear this."

I glance at the clock on the dash. We still have twenty minutes, and I'd be content to sit here for all twenty of them and listen to her talk. "I do." Reaching over, I lace our fingers together. Her hand is a perfect fit within mine. Something I try not to think about. "I want to know." We need to get used to these kinds of touches. Not that it's new for us. We flirted like crazy, but it feels different knowing she's going to be my wife.

She nods and closes her eyes as she rests her head back against the seat of my truck. "He's someone who cares, who listens and appreciates what I have to say. Someone who will put his love for me and our family before anything else. I never wanted anything lavish, just a true, honest connection. Like Emerson and Roman. Their wedding was perfect. You could see the love they share, and everyone who was important to them was there as well. Small and intimate." She turns to face me, and her eyes slowly blink open. "What about you?"

Unable to resist, I reach over and tuck her hair behind her ear so I can have a clear view of those electric-blue eyes. "Something real." My words are soft. "My parents, they fought to be together, and they knew they were it for one another. I want to feel that. To know that no matter what, I have one person in my life who shares my last name, who is there for me through it all. It's not something I'll ever settle on." I shrug. "I guess that's why I'm still single."

"Not anymore you're not, mister." She points at me with a teasing smile. "Something real," she says, sobering her tone. "Can we do that?"

"I promise you, Mo, it will be as real as we can make it. This will be a real marriage. There will be no one else for me while you're my wife."

"Just us."

I nod. "Just us."

"So, yeah, a small, intimate wedding. I think here, in town somewhere, and then you and I can take a trip. We can have some fun and learn to be the new us, you know, married and all that, while we're gone. That will alleviate the pressure. We can learn how to be us without the eyes of everyone who knows watching us."

"Our friends know the truth."

"Yeah, but they're no help. They'll tease us, and I'm sure warn us to keep our emotions out of it. I can already hear Emerson now."

"Can you do that? Keep your emotions out of it?"

"Sure." She shrugs. "I mean, we're already close and connected. We're friends, so it won't be completely emotionless, but I'm not expecting for you to fall in love with me or anything."

Something tells me that wouldn't be hard to do. "So, a cabin in the mountains for a short honeymoon and a wedding close to home. Your parents' place? Mine?"

"Let's do mine, since they're paying for it."

"No. They're not. I can't let them do that. Not when we know this has an expiration date." The thought of putting that burden on her family has my stomach twisting in knots. She's doing this because her heart is pure gold. I'm paying for the wedding.

"My dad is going to struggle with that."

"Well, I, too, am an only child. So I can tell them my parents want to pay as well."

"It's not going to work, Legend. My father will insist."

"I don't like it. You keep track of every dime. I'm paying him back when this is over."

"We're never telling them the truth, so how are you going to do that?"

"I don't know, but we have to figure it out." I can't, just can't let them take this on knowing the real reasons behind the wedding.

"Okay, how about this? How about we tell them that we're both financially independent, and that we want to do this on our own? We're keeping it low-key anyway, so it should be easier to convince them. Maybe our moms can take care of the food, and then you and I will take care of the rest."

"Yes. That's perfect. My wife is a genius." I wink at her, and she laughs. The sound fills the truck, and I realize I'm the lucky bastard who gets to call this woman his. Even if just for a small amount of time.

"They're here," she says, holding up her phone. "Mom just texted me and said they're pulling in now."

"Stay put. Let me get your door for you."

"I can open my own door, Legend." She furrows her brow as if she can't understand why I'd want to do such a thing when she's capable of doing it on her own.

Leaning in close, I press the palm of my hand against her cheek. "You can also let your boyfriend, future fiancé, and husband open it for you. I'm in this, Monroe, which means you're mine, and I'll treat you as such." Unable to resist, I press my lips to her forehead. "Let me get your door, gorgeous." It takes effort for me to pull away from her. We're barely into this thing, and I'm already craving the connection between us.

Grabbing my phone and keys, I climb out of the truck, shoving them both in my pocket as I rush to open her door. I offer her my hand, helping her step down, and as soon as her feet are on the ground, I pull her into my arms, leading her into the restaurant.

When we reach the door, I freeze. "Shit."

"What?" Monroe stops walking when I do and peers up at me under long lashes.

"How are they going to take our age difference?"

"It's ten years?"

"That's a big gap."

"They didn't mention it when Emerson married Roman."

"Emerson isn't their daughter."

"She might as well be. Come on, old man." She winks. "You're worried for nothing." She laces her fingers through mine and gives our joined hands a gentle tug as she leads us into the restaurant.

"Mom. Dad." Monroe stops before her parents. Never letting go of my hand, she offers them both a one-armed hug. "You know Legend," she says, stepping to my side and smiling up at me.

"Mr. and Mrs. Morrison. Good to see you again," I reply politely, hoping they can't hear the nerves in my voice. It's at this moment I realize I've never met *the* parents, and it's important to me that they approve. Not because of the money, but because in their eyes, I'm the man their daughter has chosen to give her time to.

That's important.

"Of course. It's nice to see you again, Legend," her mom replies.

"Legend." Her dad offers me his hand. I accept his handshake immediately, maintain eye contact, and give him a nice firm shake.

"So, this is new?" her mom asks with a smile.

Monroe slides her arm around my waist and rests her hand on my chest, peering up at me. "Not really. It's complicated. At least we were afraid it would be. We wanted to be sure this could be something, *would* be something, before we brought everyone else into it. We're all friends, and that could cause some friction."

"And when it didn't work out, you thought that wouldn't happen?" Her dad laughs.

Monroe shrugs. "Doesn't matter now." The look that she gives me has me believing her.

"Well, I'm starving. Let's eat." Her mom links her arm with her dad's and turns to give the hostess their name for our table.

I bend my head, my lips next to Monroe's ear. "Just like that?" I ask.

She smiles. "Just like that. They trust me. They know you're a good man, Legend."

"They don't know me."

"They know Emerson, and they know Forrest. They lump you in with my association. I've talked about all of you over the years, and I can admit my crush has been noted." Her cheeks pinken. "This is going to work out. I'm the best candidate because of our extended history. Now, stop stressing so much, boyfriend, and feed your girl." Her grin is infectious.

Placing my hand on the small of her back, we follow her parents to the booth. I slide in next to her, and she snuggles up close to me.

"What sounds good, babe?" she asks.

"Not sure yet," I reply, still wrapping my head around her parents' easy acceptance of us.

"I kind of want the chicken strips and fries. They're hand-breaded and are so good, but I also kind of want the steak and shrimp."

"You get one, I'll get the other. You can have both."

"You sure?"

I press my lips to her temple. "Yeah, I'm sure."

"Aw," her mom coos.

I stiffen. It's easy to forget there's anyone else in the room when I have Monroe's full attention. I scoot over just a tad. Well, I try to. My new girlfriend isn't having any of it. She loops her arm through mine to hold me still.

We make small talk with her parents about what they're going to order, and to my surprise, they do the same thing as us, ordering two meals with the intention of sharing.

"She gets it honest." Her dad chuckles. "This one can never decide. We always end up sharing."

"Dear, I think he knows her pretty well. He agreed easily enough. I'm sure this isn't the first time for them," her mom says.

"Nope," Monroe chirps.

She thinks I made the offer to impress her parents. And while that might be true, it's also who I am. She's mine. We may be pretending, but in the eyes of the world and the law, she's going to be my wife, and I'll treat her accordingly. Just because I've never found a woman to become my world doesn't mean I don't know how to treat her and make her feel as though she is.

Our food is delivered, and the four of us eat and continue with the easy conversation. We talk about the shop, Monroe's job, her parents' cruise, and all the while, Monroe and I eat off each other's plates. It's not something I've done before, but then again, I don't date. I don't mind sharing anything of mine with her. Monroe is one of those people who are easy as hell to be around and talk to. She's gorgeous, smart, loyal, and well, she's the total package. We're pretending, but I'm one lucky son of a bitch to have her be mine. Any man would be, but I'm starting to see that there might not be a man who's actually good enough for her. The more time we talk and spend together, my fondness for her grows. We're a week into this thing, and I'm already struggling.

Not that I'll ever tell her that. We made a deal, and I won't go back on that.

I'm going to enjoy this time with her.

"You kids have fun. Be safe," Monroe tells her parents as we're standing outside on the sidewalk.

"Legend, thank you for dinner. You didn't have to do that." Her dad offers me his hand.

"It was my pleasure."

"Are you coming home tonight?" Monroe's mom asks.

"I'll probably stay at Legend's. We're going to have lunch with his parents tomorrow," she tells them. She steps out of my arms and hugs them both. "I love you."

"You, too, sweetheart," they say at the same time.

"Big weekend for the two of you as well." Her mom smiles at us.

"Yeah, everyone has been really supportive. Not that it matters. We're in this." She turns to look at me over her shoulder, and I hold my arm out, inviting her into my embrace. She steps into me, wrapping her arms around me.

"Oh, Monroe, I have something for you. Come with me to the car." Her mom motions toward their car that's a few spots down, and Monroe releases me, following along behind her.

"She's our entire world," her dad says once they are out of earshot.

"Yes, sir." I don't really know how to reply to that. Maybe I should have said she was my entire world, too, but "yes, sir" was the best I could do.

"You're quite a bit older than my daughter."

Well, fuck.

I clear my throat. "Ten years."

"Listen, Legend. I raised my daughter to be a strong, independent woman. I know how stubborn she can be when she sets her mind to something. I'd never tell her who she can and can't date. Mostly because she'd never listen. I like you, but if you hurt her—" He doesn't need to finish. The unspoken words are clear.

"Never." The conviction is my tone is strong. "I'd never hurt her. We've known each other a long time, and it just kind of progressed."

"Don't play with my little girl's heart, Legend Raines."

"No, sir. I would never. If anything, she'll be the one to play with mine." The words ring true, because I can't stop thinking about her since the words first came out of her mouth a week ago tomorrow.

I'm standing stock still, waiting for his reply. What I'm not expecting is for him to toss his head back in laughter. We're talking deep belly-rolling laughter. "That's my girl," he says, clamping a hand on my shoulder and nodding.

"You broke him," Monroe says to her dad. "Why does my boyfriend look so freaked out?"

"Just guy talk, sweetheart. You kids be safe. Monroe, we'll be in international waters, but we upgraded our cell plans. We'll call when we can."

"Love you."

With another round of hugs, we wave them off, and I help her into the passenger seat of my truck.

"That went well." She smiles over at me when I slide behind the wheel.

"Yeah," I agree. "So, where to?"

"Well, how about we just head back to your place to watch a movie? I did tell them I was staying with you."

"My place it is." I don't hesitate, because this is what we signed up for.

Pretending.

Sleeping in the same bed.

Her taking my last name.

It's all a part of the plan.
We've got this.
I think...

MONROE 8

"I'LL GET YOUR DOOR." LEGEND'S voice pulls me out of my thoughts as we park in his driveway. The ride back to his place was quiet, nothing but the low hum of the radio and our own thoughts to keep us company.

A few seconds later, my door is pulled open, and Legend is offering me his hand to help me down. "Thanks." I decide to accept his need to do this. Relationships are about compromise and picking your battles. Just as my mother reminded me. She made sure to tell me those exact words when she pulled me to the car to give me the shirt she picked up for me today while they were shopping.

She also warned me about his age and to not let him force me into anything I wasn't ready for. I assured her Legend was a perfect gentleman, and he is. However, he has been the star of my fantasies a time or two. If I'm being honest, him more so than Lachlan and Maddox. It's the lips that do it for me. They're so damn plump and look so damn soft, and when he smiles—nope. Not going there. Not when I'm about to spend the night at his place.

What was I thinking? Sure, we're going to have to get used to this, but talk about ripping off the Band-Aid. The words were out, and I couldn't take them back. I could have called Emerson or even Forrest and stayed with either of them, and my parents wouldn't have known the difference. However, this is our new normal. We might as well get used to it now. Besides, how bad can it be, sleeping next to Legend Raines every single night?

I'm going out on a limb here and guessing that it's not going to be the worst thing I'll ever have to do in my lifetime. In fact, it might just be one of the best. He's sexy as hell and all mine, for a little while at least.

"Hungry? Thirsty?" he asks as he leads me into his house with his hand on the small of my back.

"I'm stuffed."

"I'm gonna grab a beer. You sure you don't want one?" he asks.

"No, thanks."

"The remote's on the table. Pick us a movie." He moves to the kitchen and pulls open the refrigerator.

"What are you in the mood for?"

"I'm easy. You pick."

"Come on now. I know you like your action films," I remind him.

"Yeah, but my future wife loves her romantic comedies." He takes a seat next to me on the couch. "Don't try to deny it. You and Emerson have made us sit through enough of them for me to know you love them."

"I wasn't going to deny it." I stick my tongue out at him, making him laugh.

Reaching for the remote, I scroll through our options and end up choosing *Oceans 11*. It's one I know we've both seen before, but it's worth another watch.

"Good choice." Legend kicks his legs up on the coffee table and brings his beer to his lips.

"I have good taste. I'm marrying you, after all."

His silent laughter shakes the couch, and my grin widens.

"My girl is smart," he mumbles through his laughter.

Something warm settles in my belly at him calling me his girl so easily. He might not truly be mine, and I might not have his heart, but I have a feeling this little adventure we've found ourselves on is going to be a fun ride.

My eyes pop open when I feel myself being lifted into the air. "I've got you," Legend says softly.

"What are you doing?" I slide my arms around his neck and hold on.

"Taking you to bed."

Even in my sleepy state, his words have my body heating. "I can sleep on the couch."

"Not happening, gorgeous."

When he lays me down on his mattress, it feels as though I'm on a pile of clouds. "Wow, okay, this is nice," I say, snuggling under the blanket to ward off the chill of the air-conditioning.

Legend's soft chuckle has me forcing my eyes open. "Do you want to change?"

"Nah, I'm okay."

"You sure?"

I nod. "I'm sure." I smile up at him. At least I hope it's a smile. I'm too sleepy to really know for sure. However, when he leans forward and presses his lips to my forehead, I feel that.

He doesn't say anything as he stands and disappears into the bathroom. I focus on my breathing to even it out before he crawls into bed beside me and thinks I'm some kind of creepy nighttime heavy breather. It's not me; it's him. I already knew he was a good guy, but I'm seeing a side of him I've never been privileged to witness before.

I like it.

I like it a lot.

When I feel the bed dip, my eyes spring open. I don't roll over to face him. Turns out, I don't have to. Legend moves in behind me and wraps his arms around me. I feel his lips press to the back of my head. “Goodnight, wife,” he murmurs.

I don’t move a muscle. I’m certain he thinks I’ve already fallen asleep. I’ve never slept the night in a man's arms. I’ve never slept next to a man at all. Sure, I’ve had opportunities, but I wasn’t just giving myself to anyone. I’ve yet to meet a man who has earned the right. I didn’t really think about that when I signed up for this.

Not that it matters.

I trust Legend, and a girl could get used to falling asleep like this every night. Closing my eyes, I let the warmth and security of his arms lull me to sleep.

“Morning, gorgeous.” A shirtless Legend smiles as I enter the kitchen. “I was getting ready to bring you breakfast in bed.” He nods toward the two plates of bacon, eggs, and toast on the counter.

“Oh, should I go back?” I point over my shoulder. “I’m down with some pampering,” I toss back at him.

He grins. “Sit your pretty ass down and eat.” He picks up both plates and carries them to the small four-person dining table, placing one in front of me. “Coffee? Glass of milk?” he offers.

“Just water for me. I’m not a big fan of white milk.”

“Just white milk?”

“Yep. I can drink chocolate milk all day long. Oh, and orange juice, but it needs to be nice and cold.”

“I’ll remember that,” he says, handing me a bottle of water from the fridge, taking his seat next to me.

We dig into our breakfast, and I debate on bringing up him taking me to bed last night. I decide against it. No need to make things awkward this morning. “So, I’m going to need to shower and change before going to your parents' place.”

“I’ll grab a quick shower, and then we can go to your place, and I’ll wait for you. You might want to go ahead and leave a few things here. We might end up with more nights like last night, and it's all going to come here, eventually."

"Probably a good idea. At least a toothbrush and a change of clothes."

"I have extra toothbrushes I get from the dentist. I never use them. Mine is electric."

I nod. "Those are the best, but we're not about to be passing those out for free." I laugh. "What should I expect today? Do you think they'll buy that we're really together?"

He nods and wipes his mouth before answering, "Yeah. I've never brought anyone home to them. I'm sure the timing might be a little suspect, but I can just tell them that's part of why I was so pissed about the inheritance. That I was sure I'd found someone, and I hated the rules, and the deadlines that it put over our heads for money. It's not a lie. I hated it and I made sure my parents knew that."

"So, when they ask if we're going to get married?"

"We tell them we're taking it one day at a time. They're already going to know you're important to me by me bringing you home. They know we all spend a lot of time together, so I don't foresee an issue."

"We've totally got this." I raise my hand for a high five, and he smiles, slapping his palm against mine.

I clean up the kitchen while he showers and we head to my parents' place so I can get ready. They left early this morning for their flight, so it's just the two of us. Legend stays in the living room with the remote as I rush upstairs to pack a bag to leave at his place and get ready to meet the parents.

"Yo! Mom, Pops, we're here!" Legend calls out, pushing open the front door to his parents' house. He has his hand clasped in mine as he leads us inside.

"In the kitchen!" his mom calls back.

Legend smiles at me and continues on until we reach the kitchen. His mom is stirring something on the stove while his dad is sitting at the large island. He looks up as soon as we walk in. His eyes go to our joined hands, and when he sees me, his face breaks out into a huge grin.

"Monroe. It's good to see you." He stands and pulls me into a hug. Well, he tries to. Legend still has a tight grip on my hand. "Son, I'm not stealing her away," his dad jokes.

"I'm watching you, Pops," Legend replies but finally releases me. He moves around the island to give his mother a one-armed hug and a kiss on the cheek. "Hey, Mom."

"You're just in time."

"It smells delicious. What are we having?"

"I know it's warm out, but I was craving some chicken tortilla soup."

"You know that's one of my favorites," Legend tells her.

"Monroe, sweetheart, it's good to see you. How have you been?" his mom asks.

"Doing well. This one is taking good care of me." I loop my arm through Legend's and smile up at him. He drops a kiss to my temple, and it's easy to pretend like I'm swooning because I am.

"What about you, Monroe? I should have checked to make sure you like chicken tortilla soup. I can make something else if you'd like."

"I've never had it, but I'm not a picky eater." I wave her off. "It smells incredible. I can't wait to try it."

"No, she's not picky. She just can't decide, so we end up sharing when we go out." Legend looks at me with a fondness in his eyes, and I have to remind myself that he's putting on a show for his family. The look he's giving me is an act, and damn if he's not nailing his role.

"Well, grab a bowl and let's eat." His mother smiles at us fondly, and it warms my heart to know we have their approval. I hate deceiving them, but I keep reminding myself, in the end, it will all be worth it.

"So, how long has this been a thing?" Legend's dad asks. We're still sitting at the dining room table, bellies full from a delicious lunch.

"A few months," Legend answers. "It's complicated, or at least we were trying to keep it uncomplicated, if that makes sense. Our friends are all friends with each other, and now two are married, so we wanted to make sure this was something more before we brought anyone else into it."

"So, you've been sneaking around?" his mom asks, a furrow in her brow.

"Yep," Legend answers.

"Legend!" she scolds him. "I raised you better than that. You need to treat this girl with more respect than that."

"It's fine. We made the decision together." I smile at her. "Legend and I were also friends. It was all unfamiliar territory and boundaries for us, and we just wanted to learn how to navigate that before adding in pressure from friends and family."

"And now?" his mom asks.

"And now she's mine." Legend reaches over and places his hand over mine that's resting on the table.

"Are you hers?" his mom asks.

Legend chuckles. It's a deep sound that wraps around me like a warm embrace. "What's with all the questions?"

"There's a bit of an age gap."

"Have you met guys my age?" I ask her. "All they want to do is party, and—sleep around." The words tumble out of my mouth before I can stop them. "I'm not that kind of girl."

"Oh, honey, no, I wasn't insinuating that you are. There's what? Ten? Eleven years between the two of you?"

"Ten," Legend answers.

"That's a lot of living."

I nod. "I agree, but I'd rather do that living with a man who will stand by my side and help me through it than with one who cheats on me and pushes for things I'm not ready for." I can feel Legend's stare, and I know I've said too much. I let the word vomit commence due to my deep-seated need to defend him.

"Mom, I care about Monroe. I'd never hurt her. You, of all people, should understand that."

"Goodness, I'm sorry," she immediately apologizes. "I've seen Monroe with Emerson so often over the years, and I always just thought of her as so much younger, but I can see just from sitting here with the two of you how much you both care for one another. I didn't mean to insinuate you would hurt her. Your father and I raised you better than that."

"I think what your mother is trying to say is that she was shocked to see that Monroe was the woman you wanted us to meet. In our minds, she was this little girl with pigtails that you and Forrest would bring over with Emerson sometimes."

"We love you, son." His mom speaks up. "We want you to be happy. Both of you. I guess the momma bear in me that always wanted to protect Emerson came out for Monroe as well."

"Don't worry, son. Even though they're married, she's already said that she's going to make sure Roman knows what he has the next time she sees him."

Legend tosses his head back in laughter. "Mom, there's nothing that you could say to Roman that he doesn't already know. He worships his wife and their unborn child. I swear there are literal stars in his eyes when he looks at her." He glances at me. "Right, babe?"

I smile at him. "Those two are made for one another. The love they share is fierce and intense."

"Seems to me like there might be another someone with stars in his eyes," his mom says.

I glance over at her, and she has tears in her eyes as she watches us. "I think it scared me a little to see how you are with Monroe. I've never seen this side of you, Legend. You've never brought anyone home to meet us. And you watch her as if—"

"She's my entire world."

Slowly, I turn my head to look at him. His ice-blue eyes are watching me intently. I don't know what I expect, but it's not him lowering his head and pressing a kiss to the corner of my mouth. It's a small taste of his full, kissable lips, and I already know that it will never be enough.

"I'm sorry. I love this for both of you, and I wish you nothing but happiness," his mom gushes. She pushes back from the table, comes to stand behind us, and hugs us both.

"Love you, Mom," Legend whispers.

"Love you too, son."

"Monroe, I guess it's time we bust out the old photo albums." His dad breaks up the hug fest. "My wife has been waiting for this moment for thirty-one years." He winks at me, and I lose myself in my laughter.

"Oh no, there will be none of that."

"Oh yes, there will be lots of that." I rub my hands together. "Gimme," I say, making his parents laugh.

We spend the next couple of hours talking, laughing, and, yes, looking at Legend's baby pictures. He was an adorable little boy with those bright blue eyes. It was easy to see that he was going to be the heartbreaker that he is today.

We eventually say our goodbyes with plans to get together again soon. As soon as we get in the truck, my cell rings. "Hey, Em," I greet my best friend.

"What are you doing? Want to come over?" she asks as Legend's phone rings. "Who are you with?"

"Legend."

"Are you now?" she says, teasing.

"We had lunch with his parents."

"Meeting the parentals already?" she asks.

"Yep. Had dinner with mine last night."

"Wow. This is really going down, huh?"

"Yep." I keep my answers short. Not that Legend is listening. He's talking to whoever called him.

"You doing okay?"

"Absolutely." I am. It's the truth. It's all going to be fine.

"Well, come over. I know Rome is calling the guys. We thought we could swim, maybe grill out."

I glance over at Legend, and he mouths, "Do you want to go?"

"Up to you," I mouth back.

He nods.

"We'll be there. I need to grab a suit."

"You can wear one of mine. You might as well use them because they're not going to fit me much longer." I hear Roman in the background telling her she's beautiful.

"We'll be there." I hear Legend say.

"We're en route. Can we bring anything?" I ask her.

"Yes, can you stop and pick up a bag of ice for the cooler?"

"On it. See you soon."

"See you soon."

I end the call, as does Legend.

"Do we need to grab anything?" he asks.

"Ice for the cooler."

Legend nods. "You need to swing by your place and grab a suit?"

"Nah, I'll just wear one of Emerson's. Shorts?" I ask him.

"Nah, Rome or Forrest will have some I can wear, or I'll just go in my boxer briefs. Wouldn't be the first time."

He's right, it wouldn't be, but now that he's mine, there's something that feels an awful lot like jealousy that's roaring through my veins at someone else seeing him that way.

"Or not," he says, reading my mind. "I'm new to this relationship thing. Shorts or nothing."

"It's fine." I wave him off.

He pulls into the parking lot of the gas station and turns to face me. "We're in this together, Monroe. I don't want to be one of those married couples who don't talk about things."

He's right. Even though this marriage is for show, we have to live with one another, and we need to communicate. If not, our lives are going to be hell. "I'm sorry. I just... don't like the idea of other women seeing you like that. Now that we're... together."

"I think it's just us, so you and Emerson, but I respect that. I always want you to talk to me, gorgeous." He lifts my hand to his lips and kisses the back. "You need anything?" He nods toward the gas station.

"I'm all set."

"Be right back." He climbs out of the truck, and I watch him as he makes his way inside, grabs a bag of ice, and takes it to the counter. I watch as the woman behind the counter seems to be flirting, but Legend doesn't even crack a smile. That's not like him. He's scowling when he gets back in the truck.

"What's wrong?"

"The clerk was flirting boldly. I told her my girlfriend wouldn't appreciate it. She proceeded to tell me what my girlfriend didn't know wouldn't hurt her. Who does that?" He's clearly upset, and it makes me smile.

"What are you smiling at?"

"My man."

His eyes soften, and he nods before starting the truck and heading toward Roman and Emerson's place.

LEGEND 9

IT'S MID-SEPTEMBER AND HOT as hell. I'm outside finishing up mowing the lawn while Monroe is inside reading. We have plans to go to dinner tonight. She was home alone. Her parents took a weekend getaway, something they do quite often, it seems. Good for them. Emerson and Roman had plans with his parents. When she called and asked if she could come over, I made it clear she didn't need an invitation.

She's going to be my wife. This is going to be her home. We both need to start getting used to that. I told her to pack a bag so she could stay here. I don't like her in that big empty house all on her own. Besides, she's going to be moving in soon. We've touched on the topic, but we have yet to set an actual date or timeframe for when it's going to happen.

I'm just finishing up weed-eating around the mailbox when a black sedan pulls into the driveway. I have no idea who it is, but I follow them up the driveway, weed eater in hand. When the man steps out, he's wearing a suit and thick-framed glasses perched on his nose.

"Can I help you?" I ask. I grab my T-shirt that I took off and shoved into my back pocket because the sweat was making it stick to my heated skin.

"Legend Raines?" he asks.

"That's me. You seem to have me at a disadvantage. Do we know each other?"

He shakes his head and thrusts his hand out toward me. "I'm Edward Mullins. I'm your late grandparents' attorney."

I nod. Not that I needed an introduction. As soon as he said his name, I knew instantly. "What can I do for you, Mr. Mullins?"

"I'm just following up per the content of the will with an at-home visit."

I nod. I'm ready to tell him I'm here and still single, but that's not true. My girlfriend is sitting in the living room, reading. She's there because of the man standing before me and the people he chose to work with. In reality, I know I can't hold that against him. He's just doing his job, and I'm certain he's been paid well to do it.

"Just finishing up. Would you like to come in?"

He nods. "Yeah, just doing a drop-in."

"My girlfriend is inside. Just let me make sure she's decent. We weren't expecting company."

His eyes widen, but he nods and rocks on his heels.

"Have a seat on the porch while I check." I don't wait for his reply. I rush up the steps, abandoning the weed eater on the porch before rushing inside the house.

"What's wrong?" Monroe lowers her Kindle and is instantly on alert.

"Mr. Mullins. My grandparents' attorney. He's here. On the front porch."

"I'm guessing we didn't know he was coming?"

I ignore the way "we" falls from her lips, and what it does to my heart knowing she's freely linking herself with me. We are a united front, and Monroe is all in. "No."

"Good thing I'm here." She flashes me a wide grin. "Are you going to invite him in?"

"Yeah, I told him my girlfriend was inside and I needed to make sure she was decent, since we weren't expecting company."

"Oh, you're good." Her laughter fills the room. "Go, invite him in. We've got this."

I nod and turn back to the front door. I push it open and stick my head out. "Come on in." I wait for him to enter the house and nod toward the recliner. "Have a seat." I move to the couch and sit next to Monroe. Leaning over, I peck her cheek with a kiss. "Gorgeous, this is Mr. Mullins. He's my late grandparents' attorney."

Monroe snuggles up to me, looping her arm through mine. She doesn't seem to mind that I'm hot and sweaty. "It's nice to meet you," she tells him.

"What can we do for you, Mr. Mullins?"

He eyes Monroe before his gaze comes back to me. "May I speak freely?"

"You can. I don't hide things from the love of my life."

Monroe rests her head on my bare shoulder, and I reach down, placing my hand on her thigh.

"You have a year from the date of the letter delivery to get married. It's my job to drop in over that period and your first year as a married couple."

I glance over at the woman next to me. "Not married yet." I wink, and her blush fills her cheeks, and her smile—damn, I love this woman's smile when it's all for me. Who am I kidding? I love her smile anytime, but I want to beat on my chest when I know it's all for me.

"I see. Well, I won't keep you. I just needed to do my due diligence."

"We understand," Monroe tells him.

"I'll be in touch." He stands and sees himself out.

I should have walked him to the door, but damn if I don't want to soak up a few more minutes of being wrapped up in Monroe. "That went well," I tell her. I give her thigh a gentle squeeze.

"We're good at this." She grins and removes her arm from mine.

I feel the loss immediately. "That we are. I need to put the weed eater up. Then I'll grab a shower and we can go get something to eat."

"How long will that be?"

"Fifteen minutes or so?"

She looks down at her Kindle. "Can we make it forty-five?"

"Yeah, gorgeous. Finish your book. We'll go when you're ready." Not able to stop myself, I lean over and place a kiss on the top of her head. She smiles up at me, and I catalog this as another smile that's all mine before forcing myself to head to my room to shower and get cleaned up. I take my time, since she's got a book to finish. I can't help but smile that this is my life now.

I don't hate it.

"What are you having?" I ask Monroe. She's sitting across from me at the small diner here in town. I told her we could go anywhere she wanted, and this is what she chose.

"Waffles."

"Breakfast for dinner. I like it." I smile at her.

"It's not just breakfast, Legend. It's an experience, a party in your mouth, a strawberry masterpiece."

I chuckle at her. "Maybe I should get them too."

"Oh, you should. They'll change your life. How have you lived in Ashby your entire life and never had the strawberry waffles?"

I shrug. "I always go for the eggs, bacon, and toast."

"Not a bad choice, but I'm telling you. Life. Changing." Her smile and enthusiasm are infectious. So when the waitress approaches for our order, I motion for Monroe to go first.

"I'll have the same," I tell her, handing her our menus.

"So, we should talk about the next step."

I nod. "Yeah, moving you in."

"What are you thinking?" she asks.

"Soon. I know you're giving up a lot for me, so the sooner we move this along, the sooner you can get back to your life."

She rolls her eyes, the smile never leaving her lips. "I'm all set, Legend. I told you it's not a big deal. I'm not dating, anyway."

"Why not?"

She shrugs. "The last guy was an asshole. He wanted more than I was ready to give him."

"Did he hurt you?"

"No." She shakes her head as she says it.

I study her eyes, and I'm relieved to see she's telling the truth.

"He got mouthy, but I ended things with him. I know I deserve better. Hell, every woman and man deserves better than to be in a dominating relationship."

"Name and address?" I ask, only half joking, and she cracks up laughing.

"Stop."

"Monroe?" a male voice asks.

I look up to find a guy about her age standing next to our booth.

"Henry," she says stiffly.

"I've called you," he says, not bothering to hide his irritation with her.

"And I didn't answer."

He opens his mouth to speak, but I cut him off. "Legend." I point at my chest. I'd offer him my hand, but I don't like the way he's talking to her. "Monroe's fiancé. You are?"

"Henry. We dated."

I nod. "Thank you."

He furrows his brow. Dumbass doesn't know what he had.

He starts to speak, and again, I cut him off.

"You fucked up and paved the way for me." I reach across the table and lace my fingers through hers. I hold her gaze when I say, "Best damn thing to ever happen to me."

Monroe's eyes soften. I know she thinks I'm just playing the part, but my words ring true. Life with Monroe in it, when she's mine, is just better. I've known her for years, but making this claim on her, it's so much more than I bargained for.

"Yeah, good luck with ice queen," he spits, and turns on his heel to leave.

I stand to go after him, but one word stops me.

"Stay."

I pause and look over at her. "He's not going to talk about you like that."

"We're done. He knows he's got nothing on you. He's going to leave me alone now. You telling him we're getting married was enough. He knows he's lost and that you have something he never will."

"I can't just sit here like he didn't insult you."

Our waitress arrives with our strawberry waffles. "Can I get you anything else?" she asks.

"No, thank you," Monroe replies politely, as if my insides aren't a raging inferno. Our waitress leaves, and she smiles at me, picking up her fork. "Stay and have breakfast for dinner with me. He's no longer a part of my life, and nothing he says is going to change that. His words don't hurt me, Legend. I know the kind of man he is. He showed me his true colors. I just want to sit here and enjoy this meal with my boyfriend."

"This goes against my every instinct."

She forks up a strawberry and reaches her arm across the table, holding it out for me. "Open for me, Legend."

I do as she asks, because there isn't a single thing this woman could ask for that I wouldn't give her, including not going after her piece-of-shit ex. "It's good." I nod.

"It's just you and me, right? We're in this? We have to learn to trust each other."

"I trust you with everything." It's the truth. That's the only way this arrangement can work.

"Then trust me that if you don't hurry up and eat those waffles, I'm going to steal them from you."

I chuckle as I grab my fork and pierce a strawberry. I hold it out to her just as she did me. She grins the goofiest, happiest grin and takes it from me. My cock stiffens as she wraps her lips around my fork.

Never in my life would I have thought that watching a woman eat would turn me on, but I would have been wrong. So. Damn. Wrong.

"So, moving in?"

"Right." I cut off a big bite of my waffle. "I think soon."

"And the proposal?" she whispers.

I wink at her. "I've got it covered."

"You're not going to tell me?"

"Nope. You said this might be the only one you ever get, so you're just going to have to wait and see."

She sticks her tongue out at me, and I wish I were sitting next to her so I could pull her lips to mine and taste it. I'm well aware that's not in the agreement, but fuck me, she makes it hard to not want to kiss the breath from her lungs.

"Okay, well, I guess I should start collecting boxes. I can just bring my clothes and whatnot."

"No."

"No?"

I shake my head. "This is going to be real while we're married. My home is your home. I want it to feel that way. I don't care what you bring or what you change. It's just a house."

"Your house."

"*Our* house, Mo. Bring it all. Do what you want. It's ours for the foreseeable future."

"Are you sure?"

"I've never been more sure about anything in my life."

"Thanks, Legend."

"I'm the one who should be thanking you. I appreciate this, Mo. More than you know."

"You and the guys and Em, you're my people. I'm happy I could help. I can't even imagine how messy this would be for you to have some random woman in my shoes."

"It wouldn't have happened."

"What?"

"It was you or nothing. Em is already taken." I wink at her.

She rolls with laughter, turning heads in the small diner. "Don't let Rome hear you say that."

"He knows I would never."

"You're a good man, Legend Raines."

"And you're an incredible woman, future Mrs. Raines."

"Monroe Raines. I admit, I've said it a few times in my head, trying it on."

"Rolls off the tongue," I tell her.

"It's going to take some getting used to. Is that going to be weird for you? Me having your last name?"

"No." There's no hesitation in my reply. I don't tell her that my cock hardens every time I think about her taking my name. I don't tell her that there have been nights where I've lain awake, staring at the shadows on the walls and thinking about that very thing.

I don't tell her my biggest truth—and fear.

I don't tell her that I want her to be mine.

"What about the wedding?"

"I want it to be perfect. Whatever you want, I want, but it will need to be pulled off quickly so that I'm not tying you up with this forever."

"So, a dress?"

"Yeah, gorgeous, a dress." That's something else I've thought about more than I should have, considering this is an arrangement between friends.

She hasn't asked me about a ring, and that's okay. If she asks, I'll tell her, but I want it to be a surprise. This needs to be real to everyone except for us and our closest friends. What kind of man doesn't buy the love of his life an engagement ring? Not this one.

"I'm stuffed." She pushes her now empty plate away from her.

"You need me to carry you out to my truck?"

"Yes, actually, that would be great." She laughs.

I wave down the waitress, hand her a couple of twenties, and tell her to keep the change. Standing, I offer her my hand and help Monroe out of the booth. When she's standing before me, I bend and pick her up bridal style. She shrieks as her arms lock around my neck.

"Legend," she whispers. "What are you doing?"

"Carrying my girl to the truck."

She relaxes into my hold, and nothing has ever felt more right.

We're back at my place—*our* place—and snuggled up on the couch, watching a movie. Strawberry waffles and a night with Monroe is my new favorite thing.

"I need a snack," I tell her.

She reaches for the remote and pauses the television. "I made you some of the peanut butter fudge you like."

"What?" I sit up and turn to face her. "Where?"

"It's in a container on the counter in the kitchen."

"You made me your peanut butter fudge?"

"I did."

She smiles, and I don't think, I just lean in and kiss the corner of her mouth. It's not a full-on kiss. I'm tempted to kiss the hell out of her, but I've enjoyed this time with her, and don't want to make it weird or scare her off. She's staying here tonight, and I'm looking forward to waking up with her in my arms. We both know that's how the night's going to turn out. Every time she stays with me, that's how we wake up.

Jumping off the couch, I rush to the kitchen. "You want anything?" I call out to her.

"A water and a tiny piece of fudge. I'm still stuffed."

Grabbing two bottles of water and the entire container, because Monroe's fudge is the best, I make my way back to the living room. Monroe hits the play button and we finish our movie. When the credits roll, I look over to find her sleeping.

"Hey." I place my hand on her cheek. "Wake up, gorgeous," I say softly.

Her eyes flutter open. "I'm sorry I fell asleep."

"Don't be."

"You're going to have to tell me how it ended."

"Nope, we're just going to have to watch it again."

"I can't make you sit through it again."

"I'd sit through it a thousand more times if you were next to me." I trace my thumb across her cheek. Her eyes hold mine, and we're both lost in the trance. My heart is pounding, and from the way her eyes are suddenly dilated, I'd say hers is as well. I'm tempted to place my hand to her chest to feel it, but I refrain. Barely.

"Ready for bed?" I finally ask. I know if I don't break this trance, I'm going to do something we didn't agree to. Like kissing her. Not just her lips. I've imagined stripping her naked and exploring her body. I know it's wrong, but I can't seem to stop myself.

"Yeah."

Standing, I pull the blanket off her and lift her into my arms. "I got you."

She loops her arms around my neck. "I know." She kisses my cheek, and I tighten my hold on her.

It takes everything inside me, all the willpower I didn't even know that I possessed, to place her on the bed.

I'm falling hard for her, and I don't think I can stop it.

MONROE 10

TODAY IS MY DAY OFF, and everyone else is at work. Legend won't be home until around seven tonight. Emerson is working, and I assume the rest of the guys are as well. Legend and I decided I'd be moving in with him this weekend. He already gave me the code to the door and he's told me multiple times to make myself at home.

I've washed all my laundry, and I'm pretty much packed up. It's not like I have a lot of furniture to take with me. It didn't take me long to pack up my life in a few cardboard boxes. Instead of sitting around the house, I decided to do a little shopping. It started out just for groceries to make Legend dinner tonight. Then it ended up being... well, more than that.

I bought some organizers for under the master bedroom bathroom sink and grabbed a couple for the guest bathroom as well. Then I decided to get them for under the kitchen sink too. I know Legend isn't going to let me pay rent, so these are just little things I'm doing to make his life easier.

I bought a cart full of hangers because I didn't pack mine, and I know there aren't any in the closet of his bedroom that will be mine. I picked up some body wash for me, and I noticed they had Legend's on sale, so I grabbed some for him as well. When I pull into his driveway, my car is full, and I'm smiling. It feels good to do something nice for him. He spoils me, and we're not even engaged yet.

Using the code to let myself in, I haul everything into the house and get to work. A few hours later, the bathrooms and under the kitchen sink are organized, all the hangers are ready for my clothes to be moved in, and my body wash sits next to his in the shower. Lucky for Legend that I picked up a bottle for him. His was turned upside down and beyond empty. It makes me feel like maybe I'm taking care of him. That's what you do when you're married, right? Support your partner? That includes making sure they don't run out of body wash. I mean, I benefit from that too. Who wants to sleep next to a man who smells?

Glancing at the clock, I see it's almost time for Legend to come home. Rushing to the garage, I throw out all the garbage before starting dinner. We're not having anything fancy, just tacos, but I know he loves them. Then again, Legend likes pretty much anything. I put the hamburger patty in the skillet and get to work on dicing tomatoes. I cheated and bought the lettuce that's already shredded. It saves so much time.

By the time Legend walks through the door at two minutes after seven, dinner is ready, and I feel I've accomplished a lot.

"Welcome home." I smile at him.

He grins widely and doesn't look the least bit upset to find me here.

"Hey. Dinner smells great." He walks to where I'm standing at the small island and slides a hand around my waist, pressing his lips to my cheek. "Did I forget we were having dinner?"

"Nope. I got all my laundry caught up, and I'm packed for this weekend. I went shopping and decided to make you dinner."

"You didn't have to do that, but I appreciate it. I'm going to go wash my hands." He rushes out of the kitchen while I pull down a couple of plates. He's back in no time, and I hand him one. "You first," he tells me.

"You're the one who worked all day."

"You cooked. You eat first."

I stick my tongue out at him, and his eyes heat. I quickly busy myself making my plate. The sexual tension continues to grow between us, and most days I feel like I might combust. He walks behind me and places his hand on the small of my back while reaching around me to grab a soft taco shell. He stays where he is, his hand still on my back, and takes a massive bite out of the plain shell.

"How did you know I was starving?"

"You're always hungry," I tease.

He leans in close, placing his lips right next to my ear. "Yep."

His hot breath fans over my cheek, and instantly, heat pools between my thighs. I shift my stance to ease the ache his hot breath and whispered words cause. He didn't even say anything sexy, and I'm all worked up. I can't imagine how my body would respond if he really tried to lay on the charm. Something tells me I'd be in a puddle at his feet.

Once we both have plates made, we sit at the small dining table and dig in.

"How was shopping?"

"Good. I bought some hangers for the closet for all my stuff, a few organizers for under the sinks, and picked us both up some body wash."

"Shit. I knew I was supposed to stop and get something on the way home. Thank you for that. How much do I owe you?"

"Nothing. It was on sale. I wasn't even sure you needed it until I was putting mine in the shower and noticed yours was turned upside down."

"Yeah, I might have had to add a little water to the bottle this morning," he admits.

"Well, you're good to go."

"Thanks, Mo." There's a softness in his eyes that I've only ever seen when he looks at me. Maybe I wasn't paying attention all these years, but it's a heady feeling to know this man, the life of the party, softens for me.

"What about you? How was your day?"

"Not bad. I love what I do, so there are very few bad days."

"It helps that you also work with four of your best friends. Oh, and that you're the boss."

He chuckles. "That doesn't hurt." He takes another bite and swallows before asking. "So, you're all packed up?"

"I am. I brought a few things on over today. I figured since I was coming over, I might as well."

"I'll help you bring it in."

"I already did. Just a couple of bags of clothes that are on the floor of the closet."

"I'll help you hang them up."

"You don't have to do that. I'll do it once we're done here. It won't take me long. I just assumed getting a head start might be nice. Not that I have a lot to bring. Mostly clothes, toiletries, a few knickknacks, and pictures."

He reaches across the table and places his hand over mine. "This is your home, Monroe. You don't have to ask permission. You don't need to worry about messing with my stuff. What's mine is yours."

"This is temporary."

"You're going to be my wife."

Why does my belly get all fluttery every damn time he says that? "Fine, but if there is something I change or do that upsets you, you have to promise to tell me."

"That's not going to happen." He's steadfast in his answer. He shoves the last bite of taco into his mouth, and I know staring is wrong, but suddenly, everything this man does is sexy, even eating, apparently. "Are you staying tonight?"

"I have work clothes." The truth is, I was hoping he would ask me to stay. No matter how we fall asleep, I wake up with his arms around me, and it's something I've come to crave. I refuse to think about what that means.

He nods. "Stay."

I smile and return his nod before standing to clean up. Legend stands as well. When he walks behind me to get to the refrigerator, his hand trails over my hip. I shiver at the contact.

He's touching me more, and it's something I can't get enough of. Sure, I'm getting the lady version of blue balls, but it's worth it. Every touch sends sparks of desire racing through my veins. I'm doubting my resolve to be able to keep my hands off him before this year is up.

I plop down on the couch and turn my head to look at Legend. "I really didn't think I had that much stuff."

He huffs out a laugh. "It wasn't too bad. It helped that the guys were here. I think we're so exhausted because somebody decided we needed to unpack everything today and break down the boxes."

"Gee, I wonder who that was?" I ask, when we both know it was him.

His laughter fills the room, and I love the sound. "I wanted you here, and I wanted you settled. It's important to me that this is your home." He reaches over and tucks what I'm sure is my wild, haggard hair behind my ear. "Welcome home, gorgeous."

"You're stuck with me now," I tease, because that's all I can do while I'm ignoring the way my heart flutters in my chest at his soft voice and his welcome home. I don't know how, but this place—it feels like home to me.

He feels like home to me.

"Are you hungry?"

"I'm starving."

"Let's order pizza."

"Perfect. I'm going to shower and wash off the day while we're waiting. Let me get you some cash." I start to stand up, and he places his hand on my thigh to keep me in place.

"Not happening, Mo, and you know it. Go get your fine ass in the shower. You want ham and pineapple, right?"

"I'm fine with whatever."

"I know that's your favorite."

"Yeah, but it's not yours."

"You're my favorite." He winks.

"Yeah, yeah," I say, blowing off his remark. What I want to tell him is that he's quickly become my favorite too. Instead, I stand and make my way to our room to shower.

Twenty minutes later, I'm clean and moisturized, my hair is pulled up in a wet, messy knot on the top of my head, and my belly is growling. As I pass the spare bathroom, I freeze when I hear the water running. Slumping back against the wall, I stand motionless as I think about a naked Legend just behind the door.

"Snap out of it," I tell myself, standing back to my full height. I move to the kitchen and grab some paper plates and a couple of beers. We've earned it after today. Once I have everything set up in the living room, I grab the remote and start scrolling for something for us to watch while we eat.

The knock on the door startles me. I jump, the remote flies out of my hand, and I let out a little scream. Why? I have no idea. I guess I was so engrossed in what we were going to watch, and possibly thoughts of a wet, naked Legend just down the hall, that I was lost in my own head. I stand to answer the door just as Legend comes racing down the hall. His hair is dripping wet, as is his body, and he has the world's smallest towel wrapped around his waist. It does nothing to hide his... package.

"What's wrong? Are you all right?" He runs his eyes over me while I stand here still staring at him.

All of him.

He rushes toward me, and as soon as he's close enough, with the hand that's not holding the towel, he cradles my cheek. "Mo, baby, what's wrong?"

Another loud knock sounds at the door. "Pizza."

"You screamed."

I swallow hard and pull in a deep breath, which is a mistake, because, damn, he smells incredible. "The knock at the door. I was zoned out. It startled me." I take a step back and then another. With each step, I start to breathe a little easier.

Another knock.

"The money is on the table by the door."

I nod, turn, grab the cash, and rush to pull open the door. I pay the delivery guy, who's looking at me with an odd expression, and I wonder if my face says, *I just saw my soon-to-be husband, who's my husband in name only, pretty much naked and wet, and he smells better than this pizza you just delivered?*

I sure hope not.

Pizzas in hand, I place them on the coffee table before grabbing my beer, twisting off the cap, and taking a long pull.

"You want another?" Legend asks from behind me.

"Yep," I manage, breathing a little easier now that he's dressed.

I hear him in the kitchen as I busy myself making us both a plate of a few slices of our favorites. "Thank you," I say when he places another beer next to me on the end table.

"You're welcome. Thanks for this." He picks up his plate and starts to eat. "You sure you're okay?" he asks after several minutes of silence.

"Does embarrassed count as fine?" I laugh. "I can't believe a knock at the door startled me so badly."

"What were you thinking about?"

You.

You wet.

You naked.

"I was scrolling, trying to find us something to watch."

"Did you find something good?"

Nothing as good as what my imagination was coming up with, thinking of you in that bathroom. "Not really."

"Hmm." He picks up the remote and begins to scroll. He chooses a series he knows I love that I started a few nights ago.

"We don't have to watch this."

"You love this show."

"I know, but it's kind of a chick flick."

"And you're a chick."

"You're not."

"I'm living with one, one that I want to make happy." He presses the play button and sets the remote out of my reach.

"Thanks, Legend."

"Anytime, gorgeous."

The next thing I know, I'm being lifted into the air. "I can walk," I tell him.

"I've got you." He carries me to our room and places me on the bed. "Here, you can sleep in this." He reaches behind his neck and pulls off the T-shirt he's wearing. "I'm gonna go lock up." He kisses my forehead and leaves the room, closing the door softly behind him.

"I'm in so much trouble," I mutter to myself. Standing, I strip down to my panties and slip his shirt over my head before climbing beneath the covers. I lift his shirt to my nose and inhale.

Damn, he smells good.

A few minutes later, Legend comes back into the room. He turns off the light and makes his way to his side of the bed. I can hear him rustling around before he, too, slides beneath the covers. I'm lying on my side, facing him. He does the same. There's just enough light filtering in through the blinds to make out his form.

"Mo?" he whispers.

"Yeah?"

"I'm really glad you're here."

My heart skips in my chest at his whispered confession. "Me too."

We're both quiet, letting the charged air hang between us. I'm getting ready to turn over to try and put out this invisible fire that burns between us when he moves, and I feel his arms wrap around me.

"Come here," he says softly. He buries his face in my neck, and I place my hand over his that's resting just below my breasts. "Night, gorgeous."

"Night." I close my eyes, and will myself to fall asleep. I can't seem to do it. Maybe it's because of my little nap out on the couch. That's what it has to be. Surely, it's not because of the man holding onto me as if I'm precious to him.

It's not that.

It can't be that.

I'm certain that if I keep lying to myself, I'll start to believe it.

LEGEND 11

IT'S THE SECOND WEEK OF October and the perfect weather conditions for a bonfire. Forrest has been talking about it all week. He's made it clear we're all expected to be there. Not that any of us would pass it up. We're a close group, and we prefer each other's company to anyone else's.

Although, I'd choose my girlfriend over them. Well, my fake girlfriend. Monroe and I have been faking it for exactly a month this week, and things have been going smoothly. She comes to eat lunch with me on her days off, and I drop her off her favorite drink at least twice a week at her office. We've had dinner with her parents and mine a second time, and so far, no one seems to be batting an eye that we're together.

At least, not after my mother's initial shock. She's still apologizing, but she doesn't need to. I understand her concerns. I could imagine if and when I have kids, I'd feel the same way if my son brought home a much younger woman, but in the grand scheme of things, ten years isn't all that much. Not really. We're both legal adults, and we know what we want. Well, we know what we're supposed to tell people that we want.

We've even had a handful of sleepovers before she moved in because that's what would have been expected, and I didn't hate having her in my bed. I still don't. In fact, on the nights when we decided she should stay at my place, I found myself wanting to head home and go to bed just because I knew she was going to be next to me. It's wrong, and I know I'll need to get a handle on it, but first, I need to ask my girlfriend to marry me.

We've talked a lot over the last month, and we decided a month or so is long enough to date in the open. We want to get engaged and be married so we can start this next year of our lives. The reservations I had are slipping away. The more time I spend with her, the more I'm convinced that we can do this. We can be friends who are married in name only and come out of this on the other side unscathed. That doesn't mean that I don't want her. My girl—pretend or not—is sexy as fuck, and the more time we spend together, the more I realize that. The man who gets to call her his for real is one lucky bastard.

Usually, we arrive together, but tonight, I had a stop to make on the way to Forrest's place. *A very important stop*, I think as I pull into her parents' driveway. I promised Monroe that I'd do this the right way, and I'm nothing if not a man of my word. That's why I called her dad earlier and asked if I could stop by.

Grabbing my keys, I decide to leave my phone in the truck. I don't need any distractions for this. Climbing out, I tap my right front pocket and can't help but smile when I confirm the ring box is there.

With each step that carries me to the front door, my nerves start to kick up. What are we going to do if her father doesn't give me his permission? Will she still go through with it? Will I?

No. I don't even have to consider my answer.

If her family is not on board with this, then I'm calling it off. I don't need the money, and it's bad enough we're deceiving them. If they can't tell that she'll be my world during the time we're married and accept that, then this is a no go.

My hand is raised to knock when the door swings open. "Legend. Good to see you," her father greets me. "Come on in."

"Thank you, sir."

He smiles. "Eric." He steps back and allows me to enter the house. He leads me into the living room, and there's no sign of Monroe's mom, but that's okay. I only need one of them here to do this. "What brings you by?"

"I care a great deal about your daughter, sir." I swallow hard. "I love her." There is no point in making small talk. I'm here for one reason, and from the look on his face, he understands.

I hold his stare, willing him to believe me. I might not actually love her, as in she owns my heart, but I do care about her. She's been in my life for a long time, and we've grown really close over the last month of dating.

"Does she love you?"

"Yes, sir." I'm going to hell for this, but I'm committed. Reaching into my pocket, I pull out the ring box and hold it up for him. "I came here today to ask for your blessing. I'd like to ask Monroe to marry me."

He reaches out and takes the box. He whistles. "That's a big rock, Legend."

"It's two carats. The center square diamond is one carat, and the smaller diamonds around it are a carat." I don't know if that's important information, but I'm spilling details, hoping to get his blessing, I guess.

He stares at the ring inside the box for what seems like hours, when I know that's not the case. Finally, when he looks up, a slow grin tilts his lips. "This looks like her," he says, closing the box and handing it back to me.

"Yes, sir. I've searched for a while. I didn't know what I wanted, but I knew that when I saw it, I would know."

"You've lived a lot of life. Ten years more than my daughter. I like you, Legend, and I see how you are with her. Can you promise me not to clip her wings? To let her learn and grow and be the woman she wants to be?"

"Every day. Monroe is... special. She has the biggest heart of anyone I know, and being around her is infectious. I know what I have. I know the honor it will be for her to become my wife, and I promise you I'll never take her or the gift of her love for granted."

"You know, my wife and I had a feeling this was coming. Just seeing the two of you together. You fit."

"Thank you." I swallow back the lump of emotion clogging my throat. I might not be in love with her, but I care about her. I crave every second of time I get to spend with her. And to know that her parents see that, for me to have what I hope is their acceptance, it gets a man in his feels.

"Welcome to the family, Legend. Take care of my little girl."

"Always, sir. Thank you." I expel a heavy sigh of relief, and he cackles with laughter.

"When are you asking her?"

"Soon." Tonight, I think, but I don't tell him that. If I chicken out doing this in front of our friends, I don't want to disappoint him.

"I'll be looking forward to that phone call."

"Thank you." I stand and shove the ring box back into my pocket.

"How did you get her out of the house without letting her know where you are?"

"I made up an excuse of needing to stop at the shop and that I'd meet her at Forrest's place in an hour. I texted Roman to make sure her car was there before coming here, but I should get going."

"You're a good man, Legend."

A heaviness falls onto my shoulders. I hate deceiving him, but we're too far into this to turn back now. "Thank you, sir. I'll see you soon." He walks me to the door, and with a wave, I pull out of the drive.

My mind is racing. Now, I need to ask my girl to marry me.

I'm still wrapping my head around the fact that Monroe is going to be my wife. The drive to Forrest's place is a blur of scenarios and what I want to say. I've never thought about proposing marriage. I thought I would do it someday, but that's as far as it went. Now that the moment is here, I want it to be right. Right for us, right for her. I want the moment to be everything she's ever dreamed of. As she said, this could be her only proposal, and I want her to have the full experience. That's the least I can do.

Making my way around the side of the house, I see everyone already gathered at the fire and a massive pile of wood set off to the side. Drake and his girlfriend, Lisa, are here, as well as Lyra. They're new to our Everlasting Ink family, but they seem to fit in well. Them being here means that Monroe and I have to be on the entire night. Which is fine. We're used to it.

Making my way to where she's sitting, I bend over the back of the chair and press a kiss to the tip of her nose.

She giggles, tilting her head back to look at me. "Hey, babe."

I smile at her. She's taken to calling me babe, and I have to admit that I don't hate it. I've never been with someone long enough to establish pet names.

"Gorgeous." I smile at her. "You need another?" I point to the drink in her hand.

"Yes, please."

I give her shoulder a slight squeeze before heading to the cooler to get her another one of her drinks. When I reach her, I hand it to her. She stands, and I take her seat, pulling her onto my lap. She settles her back against my chest, and I wrap my arms around her. It's easy to be affectionate with Monroe.

"Aw," Lyra says, pointing at us. "I love this so much."

Monroe laughs, and I smile at her, staying quiet. That's not my usual stance. I'm usually loud and laughing and joking around. I'm still that guy, but right now, I'm the guy who holds his girl close.

"Are you not drinking?" Lachlan asks.

"Nah, not when I gotta get my girl home safe."

"You two should stay here," Emerson suggests. "Or with us."

Monroe sits up and turns to look at me. "Are you going to drink with me, boyfriend?" she asks.

Reaching up, I brush her hair out of her eyes. "Is that what you want, gorgeous?"

She smiles and nods. "Yeah, it's been a while."

"I like taking care of you." It's the truth. Something flipped inside me when Monroe offered to marry me. Suddenly, I'm a man with a woman to care for and protect, and I take that job seriously.

"Have a drink with me."

"We're staying," I tell Lachlan, keeping my eyes on Monroe. Her smile lights up her face, and she leans in, placing a kiss on the corner of my mouth.

We've done that a lot in the last few weeks. Forehead kisses, kisses on the cheek, and those that linger just on the corners of our mouths. I've yet to fully taste her lips, and I think it's time I change that. I slide my hand behind her neck and lean in, but I'm interrupted by Maddox, who dangles a beer between us.

Sitting back in the chair, I take it from him, and he smirks. Asshole. Payback is a bitch, and I'll remember this. He knew what I was about to do; hell, I wasn't hiding my intent to kiss her.

Monroe settles back against my chest. She grabs my arm and wraps it around her, and my annoyance with Maddox fades away. How can I think about anything else but her?

As the night moves on, Monroe and I both switch to water. We've had three drinks between us, but we're still staying. No way in hell am I risking her. Sure, it was one drink, and hours have passed, but I would never be able to live with myself if I hurt her or someone else.

Monroe wiggles around on my lap, moving to the opposite side, and pauses when she feels the ring box. I'm cursing myself for not locking it in my truck.

She turns to look at me. "What's that?" she asks.

"What's what?"

I play dumb. I'm not sure this is the right moment to ask her. I glance around the fire and see that Roman has Emerson snuggled up on his lap. Forrest and Maddox are talking about the football game that's on tomorrow and who they think is going to win. Lachlan is half asleep, his chin buried in his chest, arms crossed. Drake, Lisa, and Lyra all left not long ago. It's just the original crew, and none of them are paying a bit of attention to us.

"What's in your pocket, Legend?" Monroe asks. The light of the fire dances in her eyes.

"His pocket rocket," Lachlan mumbles, opening his eyes.

"No. That's much bigger." Monroe waves him off.

She'd know. Every night she's spent in my bed, she wakes up with my hard cock pressed against her ass. The first time, I felt guilty and jumped out of bed to make breakfast. However, the next time, I waited for her to wake up. I wanted to see her reaction to the fact that my body wants her.

That I want her.

She didn't even mention it. In fact, this is the first time she's said a word about it, and the need to kiss her grows stronger by the minute.

My hand moves to cradle her cheek. "That's something I bought for you."

Her eyes glisten with tears. "Show me."

"I was hoping for something a little more romantic," I confess. I trace my thumb across her cheek. Her skin is so fucking soft.

"You're holding me in front of a fire. What's more romantic than that?" Her voice is soft, keeping the conversation between us.

"You really want to do this here?" I ask her.

She bites down on her bottom lip. "We're surrounded by our friends."

"I want it to be a moment you'll never forget. I want you to look back and smile when you think about it. I want you to have everything you've ever wanted." I lean in a little closer.

"You."

"Me what?"

"*You* are what makes it special. The fact that you care about me having a moment to cherish makes the moment, Legend."

I nod and tap her thigh. She moves back to the other side, and I reach into my pocket and pull out the ring box. I tap her thigh again and she stands. I drop to a knee in front of her. My hands shake as I pop open the top of the little black velvet box. Taking her left hand, I poise the ring at her finger.

Finally, I lift my eyes to hers, and they're shimmering with tears. If not for the blinding smile she was giving me, I'd think she was having second thoughts. "You're beautiful."

She laughs and shakes her head.

"You are. You have the biggest heart of anyone I know. Spending time with you is my favorite thing to do. I want that forever." I swallow past the lump in my throat. "Monroe Morrison, will you do me the incredible honor of becoming my wife? Will you marry me?"

She has quickly become my favorite person.

I prefer spending time with her over anyone else.

Her heart is huge, and just looking at her takes my breath away.

"Yes." Her smile is bright as I slide the ring onto her finger. I stand and pull her into a hug, crushing her to me. My heart is racing as if I just ran a marathon, and from the rapid rise and fall of her chest, I'd say she's having a similar experience.

When we pull back, I cup her face in my hands, looking for a sign that this isn't what she wants. She's giving up so much for me. I make a silent vow to give her the world while she's mine.

"You sure about this, baby?" The endearment is one I've never used with her, but it rolls off my tongue with ease.

"Never been more certain," she replies. Her tongue peeks out to lick her lips, and I have to taste her.

My mouth presses to hers. It's a gentle brush of our lips, but it's not enough. I trace her lips with my tongue, and she opens for me. My tongue glides past her lips and against hers with practiced ease. It's as if I've been kissing her for years. This doesn't feel like a first kiss. This feels like a promise of what's to come.

It's not until I hear catcalls and clapping that I pull away from her. Not too far. I rest my forehead against hers, still holding her in my arms.

“They’re never going to let us live that down,” I say once I’ve caught my breath.

“It’s not a crime to kiss your fiancée.”

“You’re going to be my wife.” A thrill rushes through me. She might not be mine forever, but she’s mine for now, and I’m going to have to learn to be okay with that.

“Yeah,” she agrees.

“Let me see.” Next to us, Emerson pulls Monroe from my arms to inspect the ring. “Damn, Legend, you did good,” she says.

The girls laugh, and I know I’m smiling like a fool.

“That didn’t look fake,” Roman says from his spot next to me.

I shrug. “She wanted it to be real. She says that if this the only proposal she’s going to get, she wanted it to be authentic.”

“Is it real for you?”

“Of course it is. She’s going to be my wife.”

“That’s not what I meant, Legend, and you know it.”

“It’s as real as we are making it.” That’s a non-answer, and we both know it. I can’t tell him that it’s real as fuck. When I was down on one knee, I didn’t think about why or how we got there. All I could think about was that my ring was going to be on her finger.

She’s mine.

MONROE 12

I'M STANDING IN FRONT OF the mirror in a room designated for the bride and staring at my reflection when there's a knock at the door. We opted for a small venue on the outside of town for our wedding. I considered getting married at my parents' place but eventually decided against it.

I'm glad I did. The venue is beautiful. Everyone pitched in, and I love the outcome.

"I'll get it," Emerson says, moving toward the door. She opens it just a crack. "Nope. You can't see the bride before the wedding."

"But—"

"Not happening on my watch, Raines."

I laugh when I turn to see Emerson blocking the door with her foot and crossing her arms. Her hand is resting on her baby bump. She's over halfway to her due date, and I can't wait to meet their little one. She had an ultrasound last week, and they found out the gender of the baby, but they're keeping it a secret until the wedding. Waiting just might kill me.

"I need to see my wife."

A shiver races down my spine at hearing him referring to me as his wife. Not quite yet, but in the next thirty minutes, he's supposed to be waiting for me at the altar, which is really an arch of beautiful, fresh flowers my mom and Legend's put together. Those two hit it off instantly, and the wedding took shape just three short weeks after our engagement. Of course, Legend and I knew it was coming, so we'd already been planning. Our parents questioned why so fast, and we simply told them we were ready, and they accepted our answer.

"She's not your wife yet," Emerson sasses.

"Baby girl." Roman's deep voice joins the conversation.

"Rome, they're not married, and it's bad luck for the groom to see the bride before the wedding."

"I'll wear a blindfold," Legend offers.

"Fine. Stay where you are." Emerson closes the door on them and turns to face me with a huff of annoyance. "That husband of yours is a nuisance."

"He's not my husband yet." I toss her words back at her.

Emerson rolls her eyes. "You know what I mean, and now mine is joining forces with him. He wants to see you. Well, I guess he wants to talk to you, because he said he'd wear a blindfold."

I shrug. "That's fine. Send him in."

"I have to find something to blindfold him with first." She rummages around until she ends up pulling the sash from the robe I was wearing before sliding into my dress. "This will do." She slips out the door, and a few seconds later, Legend is stepping into the room. He's got the sash tied around his eyes. He closes the door and rests his back against it.

"Legend?"

"Come here, baby."

I do as he asks and walk toward him. When I'm close enough, I take both his outstretched hands in mine. His shoulders relax, and he exhales once we're holding hands.

"Are you all right? Having second thoughts?"

"No. No second thoughts, and I'm fine now. You?" His voice is soft and a little hesitant. Almost as if he's afraid of what my answer might be.

"I'm dressed and ready to go." I look down at my dress. I admit that I had Legend in mind when I bought it. I can't wait for his reaction.

At that, he smiles. "I can't wait to see you in your dress." He rubs his thumbs over my knuckles before lifting both hands one at a time to press a kiss to the back.

"What's going on, Legend?"

He sighs. "It's been two days since I've seen you."

"I know. It's been crazy getting all the last-minute details ironed out." I stayed at Emerson's place last night. She was insistent that Legend and I be apart the night before. I can't complain too much. I did the same when she married Roman over the summer.

"I missed you. I guess I just needed to make sure you're still okay with all of this."

"Too late to back out now." Not that I would want to. I also don't tell him that I missed him too. I'm already in too deep. The walls around my heart are crumbling, and I need to work harder to keep them in place.

"No, it's not. You're giving up so much for me, Monroe."

"We've been over this. It's a year, Legend. It's going to be fine. We're going to go out there, get hitched, and spend a year together. Everything is going to work out." I pause and then ask, "You still want this, right?"

He nods. "I want to marry you."

His answer is like an arrow to my heart. I shake off the warmth of his words. "Then you better get out of here. I'll be the one in white in case you didn't know."

"I'll be the one who can't take his eyes off you, waiting to make you his."

I laugh at his reply because I can't let his sweet words penetrate my heart. Not now. Not today.

I knew Legend was a great guy. Of course I did. He's the best, but I didn't know the sweet side of him. The side that brings me my favorite drink to work when he has a break in his schedule. The guy who carries me to his bed at night and wraps himself around me after we fall asleep watching movies. The man who tells me he's waiting to make me his. It all feels too real, and I've had to give myself a daily reminder that this is temporary. Still, I don't want to miss this time with him. Nothing can keep me from walking down that aisle toward him.

"You better go."

"The next time I lay eyes on you, you'll be my wife."

"Close enough." I laugh.

"See you soon, gorgeous."

"See you soon." I press a kiss on his cheek and step back. He opens the door feeling his way and slips out.

Before I'm able to catch my breath, Emerson comes soaring back into the room. "He better have kept that blindfold on."

"He did." I can't help but smile at my best friend.

"What did he want?"

I shrug. "He said he missed me." That's not all he said, but that's the part that I picked out of our conversation and pinned it to my heart that's already soft heart where Legend is concerned.

"Aw." Emerson's face softens. "I think he really likes you, Mo."

"Of course he does. We're friends."

"No. It's more than that. I saw him the night he proposed, and I've seen him every day since all of this started, and each time he seems to be.... I don't know. More in tune with you, I guess. I don't know how to explain it."

"We've been spending a lot of time together. That's bound to happen." I turn away from her so she can't see the truth: that it *is* more. At least it feels that way to me. However, it's too late. My best friend knows me better than anyone.

"You're falling for him."

"He's a great guy."

"Monroe."

I don't look at her. I can't. She'll see the truth written all over my face. I am falling for him, and even though I know I should do everything in my power to stop it, I won't. I don't want to.

Pulling in a breath, I turn to face her. "Emerson." I smile sweetly, and she playfully rolls her eyes.

"Talk to me."

"Fine. Yes, I'm kinda sorta falling for him." I expect her to tell me to lock that shit down tight, but instead, she just grins.

"What are you grinning about?"

"I approve."

"Come on, Emerson. You know what this is as much as I do. I might be falling for the guy, but I have zero hope that things will end with us having a happily ever after like yours."

"I have a good feeling about this. You forget that I'm the outsider."

"You're my best friend."

"That's not what I meant. I get to observe the two of you together." She pauses. "I'm glad you went all out for the wedding."

"What?" Her change in topic is giving me whiplash. "Why?"

"Because it's going to be your one and only."

I scoff. "Are you trying to make me a lonely old cat lady?"

"Nope. I just have a hunch."

"Yeah, yeah, we need to get moving." I hear what she's saying. Hell, I feel that connection every time I'm near him, but that's not what this arrangement is supposed to be about. I can't change the rules. If I'm being honest, I'm scared as hell to let my heart think of Legend as being mine for a lifetime.

"You had a hunch too, and look where I am."

"Em, that's different. You only ever wanted Rome, and it was easy for those of us who were paying attention to see that he wanted you just as fiercely."

She taps her temple with her index finger. "Like I said. I've been observing. Now, enough arguing. Let's get you married. Are you ready?"

"Yes." No hesitation.

I'll take what I can get from Legend Raines.

"You look beautiful, sweetheart." My dad leans in to kiss my cheek. "I can't believe my little girl is getting married."

"Dry it up, old man. You're going to make me cry." I lean into him, and he chuckles softly.

"This is what you want, right? I know you love him, and he loves you, but as your father, I have to ask."

How does he know that? Instead of asking, I bite down on my cheek and nod instead. The music starts, and I clear my throat. "You ready for this, Daddy?"

He sniffs. "Yeah. I'm ready."

As I link my arm through his, the double lobby doors open, and we begin our march down the aisle.

The wedding is small, just our friends and close family. Smiling, I scan both sides before I allow my eyes to seek out Legend. He's standing in front of the flower arch our mothers made with Lachlan's help. His arms are at his sides, but when our eyes meet, he fists his hand and brings it to his mouth. His gaze never moves. I'm not sure either one of us blinks as I take the final steps to reach him.

I don't hear what the preacher says, but I do hear my dad say, "Her mother and I do."

Legend reaches for me and helps me take the final step to stand before him. He brings my hands to his lips and kisses them tenderly. "Hey, gorgeous." He flashes me his signature cocky, flirty grin, but there's something else that lingers behind it. The tenderness of the man I've gotten to know so well over the last couple of months.

"Hi," I whisper.

The preacher starts, and I struggle to listen to what he says, not wanting to miss my turn to say my vows, but Legend's heated gaze has me enthralled. Time seems to stand still. I can hear myself talking, but it's as if I'm in a tunnel. Legend slides a wedding band on my finger, and I do the same to him. He kisses my rings, and I'm melting into a puddle of need for this man standing before me.

"I now pronounce you husband and wife. You may kiss your bride."

Legend grins, and he leans in close. "Hi, wife," he whispers.

"Hi, husband."

He takes my face in his hands and lowers his lips to mine. The tenderness in the way he holds me close brings tears to my eyes. His lips are soft as they mold to mine. However, the zap of lust that sparks between us is anything but tender. It's heat and passion. It's all-consuming. My head spins as my body reacts to his lips against mine.

I'm married.

When Legend pulls back, he slides his arm around my waist and holds me close. He presses his lips against my temple as everyone claps and cheers for us. Lifting my head, I smile up at him, and the one he gives me in return lights me up inside.

"Mr. and Mrs. Legend Raines!" Maddox shouts.

We make our way to our small group of family and friends and receive hugs and well wishes. It's everything I could have ever dreamed of for my wedding, including the man who just gave me his last name.

I know it's not real, but today, I'm going to pretend like it is. I'm going to smile and laugh and kiss my husband as much as I can. We're going to dance, drink champagne, eat cake, and celebrate the day.

Our wedding day.

That's not fake. The day, the meaning behind the vows we just took, or the way my heart races every time he looks my way or touches me. That's all very real. I can feel things shifting between us, and I don't know what it means. What I do know is that I crave his touch, even the small ones, and I'm going to spend the next year soaking up as much as he's willing to give.

"Well, we're just a couple of old married folks now," Emerson teases, her hand resting on her baby bump.

"That we are." I smile at my best friend. "Hey, you know what the absolute best wedding present would be?"

"The one I already got you."

"Yes, I love the mixer, but no. I was thinking you could tell me the gender of the baby. I need to shop."

Emerson laughs. "You can wait like everyone else."

"How is that fair? I'm the best friend, the favorite aunt. I should get dibs on gender."

"Trust me, my mom has tried everything to get it out of us too. I like the idea of everyone finding out together."

"Well, when is that going to be?"

"The week you come home from your honeymoon." She wags her eyebrows.

"We're just going for a few days to make it seem legit," I whisper.

"Uh-huh."

She's not convinced, and honestly, I don't blame her. It's hard to be convincing when you don't believe that yourself.

"Nothing is going on."

"The night he proposed, he kissed you like he meant it, like there's most definitely something going on."

"That was the first and last time until today." The memory of our first kiss will forever be cemented in my mind. The reminder of his lips against mine, the way he traced them with his tongue, burns like a beacon in the night. I'll never forget that moment by the fire.

Emerson doesn't get the chance to grill me further because our husbands join us. Roman wraps his arms around her waist and places his hand on her bump. Legend makes a similar move, wrapping me in his arms and holding me tightly.

"What are you ladies talking about over here?" Roman asks.

"Just how we're both old married ladies now." Emerson laughs.

"So, living the dream." Roman kisses her cheek.

"Something like that." Her grin is wide.

"Welcome to the club." Roman makes eye contact with me before he moves on to Legend. "Enjoy it, brother."

Legend holds his fist out for Roman, and they bump knuckles. The statement catches me off guard. Roman knows the real reason behind all of this. Maybe he's just staying in character because of the other guests.

"What time are you leaving for your honeymoon?" Emerson asks.

"We're going to head out in the morning," Legend tells her. "We're there for four days, so we'll be home Wednesday at some point."

"You've got a cabin, right?" Roman asks.

"Yeah, it's on a mountainside," I chime in. "The pictures show it has an indoor pool and a hot tub. It's huge, way bigger than what we need for two people."

Roman shrugs. "It's your honeymoon. It's supposed to be over the top and something you'll always remember."

"See," Legend says, his lips next to my ear. He kisses my cheek, and I melt into him.

"We did the same thing, only in Georgia. Not that it mattered where we were. We didn't leave the house all that much."

"I'll pretend I didn't hear that," Forrest says, joining us. Lachlan and Maddox follow behind him.

We're in a little huddle, our crew. We've all been together for so long that it's nice to know that we'll always be in each other's corner. I try not to think about how the dynamic will change once this year is up. I'm hopeful that it won't. It might take some time to get things back to an even flow like they are now. I'll be forever grateful that Emerson chose me to be her best friend and, in turn, brought these amazing men into my life.

"So, who's next?" Emerson asks.

"What are you talking about, baby girl?" Roman asks.

"To get married. Which of you are next?" she asks Maddox, her brother, and Lachlan.

"Em, you know this is... not real," I whisper to her.

She shrugs. "I'm predicting it's you, big brother," she teases, completely ignoring my response.

Forrest nods. "I'd be down for finding myself a leading lady."

"Leading lady?" Maddox roars with laughter. "Fuck, man, you make us sound like we're seventy."

"I mean, y'all are old-timers," I joke.

"Hey, now." Legend nips at my neck, causing me to squirm in his arms. Not just from the bite but from the heat that courses through my body at the feel of his lips against my skin.

"It's okay, husband. I know the truth hurts." I pat his arm, which is locked tightly around my waist.

He moves his hands to my hips and holds me close. His hard length presses against my ass. I bite down on the inside of my cheek to keep from telling everyone to get the hell out so we can be alone.

"Does this feel like I'm an old man to you?" His words are whispered just for me.

"I might need more proof." I turn in his arms. I'm aware that our friends are standing close and that there's a strong possibility they can hear what we're saying, but in this moment, I don't care.

"You let me know when you're ready, wife, and I'll give you all the proof you need." His words are sealed with a quick, firm press of his lips against mine. The guys all hoot and holler. I bury my face in his chest, trying to get my breathing under control.

I'm in so much trouble.

I want to have sex with my husband.

LEGEND 13

"TODAY WAS A GOOD DAY," I say, reaching over to take my wife's hand. I can't seem to stop touching her. All day, I've cuddled her or kissed her, and now that we're headed home from our wedding reception, I know I have to reel it in, but I can't.

The only not-so-pleasant part of the day—and to be honest, I'm just neutral about it—is the fact that my grandparents' attorney was in attendance. Monroe and I said hello and thanked him for coming, but we otherwise ignored him. I'm not even sure when he left. He was here; he saw the proof with his own eyes that I'm married. I don't have to be friends with the guy.

"It was perfect."

Her wistful tone makes me smile.

I softly squeeze her hand before bringing it to my lips for a kiss. I'm crossing lines, but knowing is not enough to stop me. I want her. It's that simple. For the last few months, we've been dating and sharing a bed where she wakes up in my arms, and now she's my wife. I'm having a hard time remembering that this isn't real.

I was worried that she would get hurt at the end of all of this. In the back of my mind, there was this lingering anxiety that her heart would be broken. Now, I realize it's not Monroe I should have been worried about. It's me. I should have been safeguarding my own heart. Instead, I was too worried about hers, and she slipped her way past my defenses.

My wife has quickly become my favorite person, and I don't know how in the hell I'm supposed to give that up. We have an entire year before that happens. It speaks volumes that we've been husband and wife for a matter of hours, and I'm already dreading the day she walks away from me.

When we make it to the house, I kill the engine and turn to face her. "Stay put."

"I can walk, Legend," she sasses. She tries to act like she's annoyed, but the smile playing on her lips gives her away.

Leaning over the console, I slide my hand behind her neck, guiding her to me. "I know you can, *wife*. But it's our wedding day, and I'm going to get your door." I kiss the tip of her nose, drop my hand, grab my keys, and climb out of the truck.

As I pull open her door, she grins, shaking her head as I reach in and unbuckle her seat belt. "Did I miss the part of our vows that says my husband has to cater to me?" she teases.

"You must have." Before she can turn to climb out, I reach in, scoop her up in my arms, and lift her from the truck.

"Legend!" she screeches. It turns into laughter when I use my hip to close the door and start walking toward the front door. "What are you doing?" She loops her arms around my neck.

"Carrying my bride over the threshold." I wink, and her grin grows even as she playfully rolls those beautiful blue eyes of hers.

"Legend, you don't need to do all of that. Come on, put me down." Her request is stale at best. She makes no move to unclasp her hands that are threaded together behind my neck.

I lean down until my lips are right next to her ear. "No."

I keep making my way to our front door, ignoring her laughing protests. I manage to enter the keyless entry code without putting her on her feet and push open the door so that I can carry my wife inside.

My. Wife.

That's something else I can't stop doing. Referring to her as my wife—in my head and out loud. It's like now that she's mine, I need to let the entire world know it, including her. It's ridiculous, and I can recall a moment not long ago when I gave Roman shit for doing the same thing. He told me I'd understand one day, and that day is finally here.

It hits differently, the feelings of knowing she's now Mrs. Legend Raines. I never would have believed it until I'd lived it.

I kick the door closed, and it makes a loud crashing sound. She jumps, causing me to tighten my hold on her. "Sorry, gorgeous." I didn't mean to scare her.

"You can put me down now." While she says the words, she keeps her arms wrapped around my neck. Again, her words are stale. An empty request that has me holding her a little tighter. She thinks she's supposed to tell me to put her down, but she's perfectly content in my arms.

"Patience, wife." I smile at the beautiful woman in my hold.

She's mine. That's all I can focus on. No one else can touch her or hold her at night while she sleeps. At least not for the next year. That privilege goes to me, and fuck me, but I'm stoked about it.

I'm setting myself up for a crash-and-burn scenario when our time is up, but when I've got her like this, in my arms, holding onto me, smiling at me as if I hung the moon, well, I can't seem to find any fucks to give. I promised her she would be my queen, and for the next twelve months, I intend to show her exactly what that means.

Consequences and pain be damned.

I make it to our room and step inside. It's dark, but I'm able to make my way blindly to the bed and place her down gently before reaching over and turning on the bedside lamp. The first thing I see when the light illuminates the room is my wife's smile. It lights up the room more than the lamp ever could.

"Is this how married life is going to be? You carting me around everywhere?" Her smile is radiant, and her question is one she already knows the answer to.

I shrug. "Probably." I step in front of her and push her long, dark, curly hair over her shoulder. "You're beautiful."

A light pink blush coats her cheeks. "Thank you. You look handsome." Monroe tugs on the hem of my untucked black dress shirt.

I stare down at her, and all I can think about is stripping her out of that dress. That's what a man is supposed to do on his wedding night. I'm supposed to cherish my wife. The need to do that very thing is so strong that it's like a tidal wave of desire pulling me under.

"Let's get you out of the dress." My voice is husky even to my own ears.

Monroe's eyes widen just a fraction, but I notice. I offer her my hand, and she allows me to pull her to her feet.

"Turn around."

She does as I ask, and I move her hair to the left so that I can have access to the zipper. Unable to resist, I lean forward and press my lips to the back of her neck as I start to help her out of the confines of the silky white fabric. I pull nice and slow, wanting to savor this moment. I'm halfway down her back when I realize she's not wearing a bra.

Fuck.

"No bra?"

"N-No. It wouldn't have worked with the low cut of the dress."

Monroe's explanation falls on deaf ears because my wife's tits are bare beneath this thin piece of fabric. I can't be expected to pay attention under these circumstances.

I keep tugging on the zipper, painfully slow, until I reach the end at the small of her back. A white lace thong with *Mrs. Raines* embroidered on the band greets me.

Mrs. Legend Raines.

My wife.

How am I supposed to ignore that? How am I supposed to walk out of this room to give her privacy to change when all I want to do is rip this dress to shreds and feast on her?

I settle for placing my index finger at the base of her neck and leisurely dragging it along the line of the zipper I just lowered. Her skin is soft like silk, and goose bumps break out across her skin. I want to trace each tiny bump with my tongue. When I reach her thong, I slide my index finger beneath the band.

"Are these panties for me?" My voice is gravelly. I can't hide my desire for this woman.

Her chest expands with air. "They were a gift. From the girls at work."

"You didn't show me."

"I-I didn't think you'd see them."

"You make them look sexy."

She turns to look at me over her shoulder. Her electric-blue eyes are dark with desire. "You're making me feel sexy," she murmurs.

Abort.

I need to leave this room. I need to walk away and leave her alone. I'm crossing all kinds of invisible lines with this relationship. I have to remind myself that this is all for show. We're pretending, and apparently, we're damn good at it, because I can feel the need rolling off her in waves.

"Keep them on," I say, my voice gruff. "I like thinking of you sleeping with our name on your ass." I drop my hand and take a step back. My cock throbs against the zipper of my dark dress pants. I want her, but I can't have her. "I'll step out so you can finish."

With that, I turn on my heel and rush out of the room, closing the door behind me. When I'm safely on the other side, I turn and rest my forehead against the door. My hand rests on the handle because the temptation to bust back through this door and ravish her is strong.

It's so fucking strong.

I force myself to turn and walk away. I stalk toward the extra bathroom and strip out of my clothes. They feel way too restrictive. As soon as my dress pants are down and off, I reach into my boxer briefs and palm my cock. Closing my eyes, I can still feel her soft skin beneath my fingers. Forcing my boxer briefs down over my hard-on, I stroke from root to tip. I'm going to hell for this, but fuck, I need some relief. I can't sleep next to her without this.

Reaching into the shower, I turn on the faucet, letting the water warm up before stepping beneath the spray. Bracing one hand on the shower wall, I lower my head and close my eyes. Flashes of my wife are all that I can see. That sexy white dress. Her thong with our name on it.

Fuck, she's gorgeous.

I begin to stroke as I picture her as she made her way down the aisle to me. Her blue eyes were shining like dark blue diamonds. The way she watched me. The way we watched each other as if we were the only two in the room.

I stroke faster.

Harder.

My cock is heavy in my palm as I let visions of her dance in my mind. The entire day was one long session of foreplay. In my fantasy, she's splayed on our bed beneath me. Her perky tits, which I've never seen but don't need much to imagine, are on full display as I thrust inside her for the first time.

That's it.

That's all it takes.

The thought of being inside her sets me off, and I spill into my hand and all over the shower wall. I'm breathing heavily. It's as if I just ran a marathon. Nope, just the best orgasm I've had in far too long, brought on by my own hand while imagining my sexy wife.

Quickly, I clean up and dry off. I realize I don't have any clothes with me. Wrapping a towel around my waist, I open the bathroom door. The bedroom door is open, which means she's ready for bed. I stroll into the room, where the lamp still gives a soft glow. Monroe is sitting up in bed, under the covers. She's wearing one of my Everlasting Ink T-shirts. Since she moved in a few weeks ago, she's been sleeping in my shirts. Why is that so damn sexy? I've seen women in my clothes before, and it did nothing for me.

But when it's my wife? Yeah, that's all kinds of sexy.

Pulling open my dresser, I grab some boxer briefs, drop the towel, and step into them. I hear Monroe's intake of breath, and I smile. I'm glad to see she is just as affected by my presence as I am by hers. Schooling my features, I grab the discarded towel from the floor and take it to the bathroom.

"You need anything before we go to bed?" I ask her, stepping out of the bathroom.

"I'm all set."

I nod and turn the bedside lamp off. It's on her side of the bed, so I crawl over her in the dark, making her giggle.

"We need to get a lamp for your side of the bed," she teases.

"Nah, then I wouldn't be able to crawl all over you each night."

"Is that something you're into?" The room is dark, but I can still hear the humor in her voice.

I move around until I'm beneath the covers and on my side. I pull her into me, and she giggles again. Fuck, but do I love that sound. She rolls over, placing her back to my front, which is fine with me. I align my body with hers, keeping my arm around her.

"I'm into you." My words are soft as if saying them out loud might scare her away. It's too late. The words are out there, and they're the absolute truth. I'm into my wife, which is fucked because we're just supposed to be friends.

She doesn't respond. Not that I expect her to. She also doesn't pull away.

Closing my eyes, I enjoy the feel of her in my arms. Something I get for the next year, and I'm already addicted. My breathing is slow and even, and I can feel myself drifting off to sleep.

"Legend?"

"Yeah?" My eyes pop open, ready to be or do whatever she needs.

"Thank you for today."

"You know I'm the one who should be thanking you, right?"

"You made today special. If this is the only wedding I ever have, I'll know what it feels like."

"What are you talking about?"

"You made me feel cherished. Today was... everything I could have hoped for my wedding day to be. I know this isn't real, but I can't help how I feel."

"You are cherished. I told you that. You're my wife. My queen." I kiss her shoulder. "We're supposed to be pretending, but that part remains true. I'll treat you as such."

"There were moments where I had to keep reminding myself that we were just pretending."

"I wasn't."

"What?" Her body stiffens slightly, and I run my thumb over her arm where I'm holding her. After a few moments, she relaxes into me.

"Pretending. I wasn't pretending. Every single time I touched you or kissed you, I wanted it to happen."

"We're blurring the lines."

"I know."

The silence hangs between us. We're both hanging on the edge of what we agreed on and what we're feeling. The two are on opposite ends of the spectrum, and neither one of us is sure of the path that we should take.

"It was one incredible day. We'll do better tomorrow," she eventually says.

"Yeah," I agree, but I know I'm lying. I don't know how I'm supposed to do better when all that I want is my hands all over her.

I'd never let myself consider Monroe as an option for me. She was my friend. She's a friend of my best friends and my pseudo little sister's best friend. That's all kinds of twisted and complicated. I had her in this box. One that I wasn't allowed to open. She was this insanely gorgeous and fun girl who was way too young for me. She was tucked away in that box securely.

Until she volunteered to be my wife.

That day, the box was opened, and the complications of what I felt for her were set free to bounce around inside my chest and my mind. I don't know how to handle this. I don't know where we go from here. What I do know is that with every minute spent with her, these feelings grow.

We'll go slow. We'll see how we adapt to married life and take it from there. I've never wanted someone like I do Monroe. I've never dreamed of a woman being mine forever.

Until now.

Maybe it was our vows? Maybe it was promising before our friends and family to love and cherish her.

It could just be today.

That's what I tell myself as I close my eyes and will sleep to claim me. When I wake up, things will be back to normal. Monroe will be a friend who's helping me out and also my wife in name only. It's just the meaning of the day. That's all this is. The wedding has me all up in my feels. I let myself get caught up in the moment.

It's a good lie.

Too bad I don't believe it.

MONROE 14

MY EYES AREN'T OPEN, BUT I know I'm in bed alone. I don't feel the warmth of Legend's body wrapped around my own. I stretch my arms over my head and reach over just in case I'm wrong, but the sheets are cold. I fight back the disappointment of not getting to wake up in his arms. Forcing my eyes open, I look at the spot that's his side of the bed and run my fingers over the cold sheets.

Memories of last night, of how he held me. The way he was adamant that he wasn't pretending with me. I should have asked him what was happening between us, but I chickened out. Not only that, but he didn't seem to want to talk about it either. We were both content to be in each other's arms and let the memories of the day surround us.

It's dangerous, but I don't know how to stop it.

I can feel things shifting between us. It's not something that I expected to happen. Legend is a good man, and he's opened up a side of himself I've never seen before. He's no longer just this fun-loving guy who likes to shamelessly flirt with me. He's now the man who worries about my needs. He's the man who, no matter how we fall asleep, ends up wrapped around me sometime in the middle of the night. He's the man who claims he wanted to touch me, to kiss me, who declares he wasn't pretending.

That's a lethal combination that I know I can't fight.

Last night, he didn't even wait for me to fall asleep. He just wrapped himself around me and held on tight. Somehow, in the midst of all the crazy wedding planning and moving in with him, I've come to crave his hold on me.

That's an issue. Because I told Legend this would be fine. I told him we were just friends who would do this wedding thing, stay married for a year, get him his inheritance, and go back to the way things were. The problem is, I know I'll never be able to go back. I'll never be able to forget what it feels like to wake up in his arms. I'll never forget what it feels like to be the center of his world.

That's what he's made me.

My heart leaps in my chest when his figure appears in the doorway.

"Morning, gorgeous. How'd you sleep?" He leans against the frame of the door, arms crossed over his bare chest. His voice is still gruff from sleep, and his hair is rumpled. He's every woman's fantasy, standing there looking like a sleepy, sexy god.

I allow myself a few moments to take in this beautiful man standing before me. My eyes rake over the tattoos on his chest before they come to meet his. "Like a baby."

He grins at my response and takes a step into the room. "I've got breakfast ready, and we need to hit the road if we want to make it to the cabin before noon."

"Do we want to make it to the cabin before noon?" I ask.

He takes a seat on the bed next to me and places his hand on my thigh. "Well, we have the cabin until Wednesday. I thought you'd want to get started on our little vacay sooner rather than later. Besides, it's snowing there, and I want to make sure we have time to stop and get all the supplies we might need in case we get snowed in."

"Good thing there are lots of things to do at the cabin if we do."

He smirks. "I think we'll be able to figure it out, gorgeous." He squeezes my thigh and stands. "Come on, lazybones. We've got a honeymoon to start."

I toss off the covers and quickly pull down his T-shirt that's ridden up. Not that it matters. He slept with his body molded to mine. He's felt my body. What's the harm in him seeing it too?

"You need any help?" he asks. His voice is husky as his eyes stay locked on my bare thighs.

I clear my throat, suddenly parched. "I think I can manage."

He nods, his eyes never leaving my thighs. "You let me know if that ever changes." With that, he turns and marches out of the bedroom.

"Damn," I mutter to myself. I saw it in his eyes. He wanted me to say I needed help. Hell, I wanted to say that I needed help, but I know we can't go there. We can't cross that line. We've been married for less than twenty-four hours, and the temptation to give in to this intense chemistry we have is strong already.

Pulling myself out of my thoughts, I grab some clothes and head to the shower. I rush through the process because I still need to pack. I've been putting it off because what does one pack to go on her fake honeymoon with her husband, who's supposed to be hers in name only but is also the object of her every fantasy?

The struggle is real.

Since I waited until the last minute, I don't have time to keep dwelling on what to take, so I toss in enough clothes to get me through the few days we'll be gone. I also toss in a few additional items that the girls at work gifted me at the bridal shower they threw for me. I don't know that I'll be brave enough to wear them, but I want to be prepared all the same.

"Ready," I say when I set my bag down in the kitchen.

"Your breakfast is cold." Legend grabs the plate of eggs.

"Hey, give that back." I take it from his hands, pick up the fork he set out for me on the counter, and take a big bite. "I love cheesy eggs," I say once I've swallowed.

"I know. I was going to make you some fresh."

"These are fine, Legend. Thank you." I fork up another bite. There's something about adding cheese to eggs that makes them so much better.

He takes the toast from my plate. "At least let me make you fresh toast. I know you don't like it when it's soggy."

I wrinkle up my nose in disgust, and he laughs. "I'm out on soggy bread."

"I know, gorgeous. Sit down and eat. This will only take a few seconds." He busies himself with popping two fresh pieces of bread into the toaster.

"You know, if you keep spoiling me like this, I might not agree to give you that divorce," I tease in between bites of my cheesy eggs. They're cold, but they're still my favorite.

He shrugs.

Shrugs.

What does that mean? He doesn't care if we get divorced? He doesn't care that I won't want a divorce because he's divorcing me anyway? My mind races, and I know I need to just ask him, but I'm also afraid of his answer. While I'm in my head, debating this, he places a plate with two pieces of freshly buttered toast in front of me. He leans in close and presses his lips to my temple.

"Eat your breakfast, wife." With that, he strolls off toward the bedroom.

What just happened?

I'm turned on, heat rushing to my core. It happens every single time he calls me his wife. Why is that so damn hot?

Ignoring my body's need for him, I do as I'm told and eat my warm, buttery toast and polish off the rest of my eggs. I clean up after myself, washing my dishes, since we're leaving for a few days, and no one wants to go home to a sink full of stinky dishes. By the time I'm done, Legend is walking into the kitchen with a duffle bag tossed over his shoulder. He grabs my bag as well.

"I'm taking these out to the truck. Are you ready to head out?"

"Yes. I just need to get my purse and phone."

"Great. I'll be back to lock up. Don't worry if we forget something. We can pick it up when we get there."

He moves out to the truck, and I rush back to our room to collect my purse and my phone, which is still charging on the nightstand. Legend is in the kitchen, checking the back door when I exit the bedroom. He holds his hand out for me, and I take it. There is no one around who we need to put a show on for, but I'm not passing up any form of intimacy with this man.

Not ever.

Our fingers are laced together as we walk out the front door. He locks up and leads me to the passenger side of his truck, pulling the door open for me.

"Thanks," I whisper. I'm still out of sorts over his comment.

Legend's quiet as he waits for me to get buckled in before closing my door. I watch him as he takes his time walking around the front of the truck and opening his door to slide behind the wheel. Reaching over, he hands me his phone.

"You get to be the DJ."

"Really?" I ask, surprised.

"Happy wife, happy life." He grins.

"So, I get whatever I want, whenever I want it?" There is humor in my voice. He knows I'm kidding. I'm not high-maintenance, and I don't expect him to continue to spoil me like he has been since—well, since this charade started.

He keeps his eyes on the road, but I can see his grin. "Yeah, gorgeous, that's exactly what that means." He pulls out onto the road.

"So, if I said we're eating tacos for every meal while we're gone?"

"Good thing I like tacos."

"Too easy. You'll eat anything." I laugh, and so does he. "Okay, what if I said I want a foot rub every night before bed?"

"Done."

"Just like that?"

He glances over quickly before putting his eyes back on the road. "You sound surprised. There is no part of my hands on you that sounds like a bad idea to me."

My heart trips over in my chest. Flirty Legend I can handle. I've dealt with him for years. Sweet Legend, I have no idea what to do with. He has me feeling like I'm a puddle of goo. The swoon this man brings with his words is next level. I'm going to have to harden up. I need to erect some concrete barriers around my heart if I'm going to attempt to make it out of this arrangement of ours unscathed.

Again, the man has left me speechless. Heat fills my cheeks. I'm not usually one to get embarrassed, and I'm not now either, but I am turned on. I ignore his words because how do you respond to that? Instead, I tap the screen of his phone, and my breath hitches when I see his home screen.

"Where did you get this?" I hold up his phone.

He glances over, and the smile he gives me could end wars. Trust me, it's that lethal. "My mom took it. She texted it to me this morning."

I stare down at his phone. It's a picture of the two of us yesterday at our wedding reception. Legend is standing behind me with his arms wrapped around my waist and his head bent next to mine. We're both laughing and smiling. The picture—it's convincing. We look like the epitome of the happy newly wedded couple.

My fake husband made his home screen a picture of us on our wedding day. No one will see his phone but him, and, well, apparently me.

"I love it," I say softly, staring down at the phone in my hands.

"Me too. She's going to print me a copy for my room at the shop."

"You're going to put a picture of us in your room?" That's a big deal. All of his clients and our friends will see it displayed. Our friends know we're pretending, but still.

"Why wouldn't I put a picture of my wife and me in my room?" he asks. His brow furrows as if he's really confused as to why I would be shocked.

"I guess because we're pretending."

"There is nothing pretend about the fact that you just took my last name, Monroe."

This time, it's not just my heart that flips in my chest, but my belly is flopping too. It feels as though there's a swarm of butterflies taking flight. "You know what I mean. We're just pretending."

"Did you pretend to marry me yesterday? I remember very vividly both of us signing those papers and saying, 'I do.'"

"No."

He reaches over, takes one of my hands in his, and lifts it to his lips for a kiss. "Give us some tunes, gorgeous."

I nod, and with one hand, I scroll through his music app and pick a playlist. I settle on country because this man has me all up in my feels. He knows it, too, which is why he changed the subject.

Does he not realize the way his thumb traces over the back of my hand is turning me on? Does he not have any idea what a simple touch from him does to me?

Shut it down, I tell myself.

I push all my thoughts and the desire I feel for this man way down deep. With my free hand, I scroll through the playlist, changing the songs. I sing along and pretend like it's just me in this truck. We have a little over three hours to get to where we're going. I need to come up with a plan of how to resist my husband.

"Wow. The pictures online don't do this place justice." I lean forward to get a better look at the cabin that will be our home away from home for the next few days.

"I bet the view from up there is incredible." He points to the top balcony. It's three floors, and each floor has its own balcony.

"Why did we get such a huge cabin for just the two of us?" I ask.

"It has an indoor pool, a hot tub, a movie theater, games, a pool table, and a whole list of other things to do. I wanted to make sure we didn't go stir-crazy if the weather gets bad and we get snowed in."

"You think that will happen?"

"I'm not sure. I know we're pretty far up the mountain, but my truck is four-wheel drive. Even if we do, we have enough supplies for a week."

"That's why you were tossing all that food into our cart."

He smiles. "Just making sure I'm taking care of you. I have to think of all eventualities."

"I'm a big girl, Legend. Just because you're my husband, it doesn't mean you're responsible for my well-being."

"Okay."

He says it to appease me. We both know he's not going to stop going out of his way to give me what he thinks I want or need. It's a shame he doesn't let others see this side of him. He keeps this sweeter, softer side hidden. The man who is usually the life of the party, passed out on a donut raft, is going out of his way to show me that he's a man of his word. He promised me he would take care of me, and he's taking that promise to a level I never could have imagined.

When he made that promise, I thought he meant keeping a roof over our head while we're married, maybe keeping the oil changed in my car. And while I have no doubt he will do both of those things, I also know he's going to keep making me cheesy eggs and ensuring that I'm not eating soggy toast.

My heart swells and feels as though it's too big to fit inside my chest.

"Come on. Let's go check it out, and I'll start carrying everything in." He holds his hand out for me, and I take it, allowing him to lead me inside.

We go from room to room and floor to floor, checking the place out. It's incredible and far too much for just the two of us. "We should bring everyone back here. Like, a friends' vacation. Do you think you all can get away from the shop for an extended weekend?"

"Yeah, I think we could make that happen. We have Drake and Lyra now to answer phones and keep things running even if we're not doing any ink. We should plan something when we get home. I'm sure Rome and Em would like a short trip before the baby gets here."

"Maybe, or we could plan it for after. I know Em won't want to leave the baby, but they can bring him or her with us. We can all take turns babysitting, giving them a break."

"You plan it and tell me when and where I need to be."

"A girl could get used to getting her way all the time." I laugh.

"Good." He kisses my temple. "Which room are we taking?"

"Um, I don't care. Just pick, and I'll choose from what's left."

He stops walking and turns to face me. "You're my wife."

I smile up at him, holding up my hand and wiggling my engagement ring and wedding band. "I think that's what these mean," I tease.

He bends so his forehead is resting against mine as he places his hands on my hips. "My wife sleeps next to me."

"You want to share a room?" I ask, surprised. It's just us, and this place has—I lost count of how many bedrooms.

"Yes."

"Okay."

"Okay." He lifts his head, but not far because he places a kiss on the corner of my mouth. "I'll go grab our things."

"I-I'll help," I say, trying to recover from what just happened. My heart gallops in my chest, and I can't help but be a little bit disappointed that he didn't move his lips just a little closer so that I could feel his full lips against mine.

"It's cold out, gorgeous. I'll start with the groceries, and you can start unpacking. How's that?"

"Okay."

He smiles. "I'll be right back."

He turns to leave, and I stand here in the hallway, staring after him.

I think I just fell a little bit in love with my husband.

LEGEND 15

"WHAT DO YOU WANT TO do tonight?" I ask Monroe. We're unpacked and sitting on the couch in the main living room of our cabin. After putting all the groceries away, we took a long walk on the trails next to our cabin. Thankfully, they were not covered in snow and ice. We also didn't run into any bears, which I'm also thankful for. When we got back, we made dinner and finally unpacked our bags, which brings us to now.

"Nothing. The idea of getting back in the truck after that drive is not appealing at all."

"Agreed. You want to watch a movie in the theater room? Soak in the hot tub? Go for a swim?" I rattle off a few options that our cabin provides.

"Let's go for a swim. That indoor pool area is cool."

"Let's do it." I stand and offer her my hand. She takes it without question and allows me to lead her to the bedroom. The one I insisted on sharing with her even though there are many others to choose from. "You take the bathroom first," I tell her, releasing her hand and taking a seat on the bed.

She grins and opens the dresser drawer, pulls out her swimsuit, and rushes off to the bathroom while I sit here and give myself a mental pep talk. I've seen her in a swimsuit many times. This time is no different. She's the same gorgeous woman who I've hung out with countless times. The only thing different is that she's now my wife.

The bathroom door swings open, pulling my attention. I damn near swallow my tongue at the sight of her. She's wearing a white bikini that leaves very little to the imagination. Her perfectly round, perky breasts are barely covered by tiny triangles of fabric.

"You're up." She smiles as if nothing is amiss. Can she not see what she's doing to me? Is the desire I have for her not written all over my face?

Standing, I turn my back to her as I reach down and adjust my cock, giving it room in these tight jeans that were not tight before she walked out of the bathroom, looking like a sex goddess. Pulling open a dresser drawer, I root around to find my swimming trunks and turn to face her. I force myself to take one painful step, then another toward the bathroom. I stop next to her and place a kiss on her bare shoulder. "I'll be quick." My voice is husky and filled with my want for her, and even if I wanted to hide it, I wouldn't be able to. Not with how turned on I am from just seeing her in her skimpy bikini.

I've got to get a handle on this desire I have for her.

In the bathroom, I strip out of my clothes and palm my cock. I need relief, but not when she's waiting for me just on the other side of the closed door. Instead, I think of unsexy things like cute puppies and the letter from my grandma that set this entire plan in motion in the first place. When I finally get myself under control, I slip into my trunks, collect my discarded clothes, and open the bedroom door.

"I grabbed us some towels from the other bathroom, just in case. I didn't check to see if the pool area had a supply there already or not." Monroe holds up the towels in her hands as proof.

"My wife is not only beautiful, she's smart."

She playfully rolls her eyes, but the blush that rises from her chest to her face gives her away. Dropping my clothes on a chair, I take the towels from her hand and shove them under one arm while offering her my free hand. She takes it, and I lead us to the downstairs pool area.

"It's not deep enough to dive, but it's something," she says, releasing my hand and stepping into the water. "Oh, it's heated." She laughs. "I don't know why I didn't consider that."

I toss the towels down on a lounge chair and follow her into the water. She drops to her knees in the shallow end, letting the water wash over her, and I can't help but think of how I'm standing before her as her eyes are level with my cock. I'm hard again, and when her eyes widen, I know she sees it.

I drop down next to her, but I'm able to sit on my ass, while Monroe is on her knees. "Makes me feel like a kid," I say, running my hands through the water.

"Yeah," she agrees, tilting her head back. "I can't wait to be an aunt. Too bad my bestie won't tell me if I'm going to have a niece or a nephew."

"When are they sharing?"

"She said after the wedding. She didn't want to take away from that. I tried to tell her we didn't care, but she wouldn't listen."

"You want kids?" I ask. The way her eyes light up when she talks about Roman and Emerson's baby tells me she does.

"I do. Two, at least. What about you?"

"As many as my wife will give me."

Her eyes flare at my words, and what I just said registers in my mind. That leads to me thinking about Monroe being pregnant. Her belly rounded with our baby. Fuck. I can't think about that. I'm already painfully hard, and I know she'd be stunning.

"Race you," she says before she takes off, swimming away from me.

I start after her and grab hold of her ankle as she reaches the edge of the pool. I pull her body into me, her back aligned with my front. I don't hesitate to wrap my arms around her. "Got you," I whisper huskily into her ear.

She turns to look at me over her shoulder, and all I see is desire in her eyes.

I walk us to the edge of the pool and turn so my back is resting against the ledge. "Turn around."

She does as I ask, turning in my arms. I grab her legs and move away from the wall just far enough she can wrap them around me. It's deeper on this end, maybe five and a half feet, so the water almost covers her five-foot-six frame, making it harder for her to stand on her feet while keeping her head above water.

"What are you doing, Legend?" she murmurs.

"I wanted to hold you."

"That's not what we do," she replies, but her arms and legs remain locked around me. She's not trying to get away from me.

"We make the rules."

We're both fish out of water with the situation we've found ourselves in. Neither of us has ever been married, and we've never faked a relationship before. The rules are what we make them.

"Is this a new rule? That you get to hold me?"

Slowly, I nod. "I think so," I finally answer her. "How do you feel about that?"

She wiggles in my arms, and my cock is nestled between her thighs.

"I think that I like this rule," she says, her pupils wide with desire.

"I think that I like you," I tell her, kissing the tip of her nose.

"You're not so bad," she teases, and I pinch her ass cheek, making her squeal and writhe in my arms. "Ouch."

"You're lucky your ass is underwater, or I would have spanked it."

Her eyes widen. "Are you into that kind of thing?"

"What kind of thing is that?" I know exactly what she's asking, but I want to hear her say it.

"You know—being rough. In bed," she adds.

"No, gorgeous, I'm not. At least, I don't think I am. Are you?"

She shrugs. "Never tried it."

"Do you want to?"

"I'm not sure. It would have to be with someone I trust. Someone I know would never hurt me and would stop if I needed to."

"Are we talking about spanking or something more?"

"All of it." She shrugs.

"I'm your husband."

Her smile is soft. "My fake husband."

"Not fake." I hold her a little tighter.

"You know what I mean. This isn't a real marriage. Besides, a man like you has way more experience than a girl like me."

"You calling me old, wife?" I growl.

Her reply is to toss her head back in laughter. "I mean, I wouldn't say old, but you know, you do have ten years on me."

"Does that bother you? That I'm so much older than you?" I don't think it bothers her. She's in full support of Roman and Emerson and their marriage, but I need to know before I take things further with her. I never want to put her in a position that makes her feel uncomfortable.

"No. It doesn't bother me. However, if this were a real marriage, one where you chose me, it might bother you. I'm not all that... experienced." She avoids my gaze and stares over my shoulder.

"Monroe?" I wait patiently, but she refuses to look at me. Shifting to hold all of her with one hand, I use the other to bring her eyes to mine. "There is not one single part of you that could ever disappoint me. Fuck, gorgeous, I'm honored to get to call you mine for however long that might be." I don't want to say our time is limited, because the more time we spend together, and the more I allow my thoughts to drift to what could be, the more I know I don't want it to end. "You're also forgetting something."

"What's that?" She tilts her head to the side.

"I did choose you."

Her lips part. She quickly closes her mouth, then opens it again as if she's going to reply, but words are failing her.

"I wasn't going to do it. I don't care about the money. The idea that my grandparents are controlling me as they did my mother infuriates me. I know it's different, that I got to choose, but it's still a game they're playing, pulling the strings from the grave, and I hated the idea of it."

"Then how did we get here?"

"You offered to help me."

"Legend, I don't understand. There are a ton of women who would be more than willing to step into my shoes."

I nod. "You're right, but I didn't want any of them."

"Are you saying you want me?"

I don't know what I'm saying, to be honest. "I'm saying that until you volunteered, it was a hard no from me. I don't know what it means, but I know that this never would have happened without you. I would have told my grandparents' attorney to fuck off and go on living my life."

"I'm sorry."

"What? Why are you sorry? You're making the ultimate sacrifice for me."

"I feel like I pressured you into this."

"I gave you my last name of my own free will, Monroe Raines." Leaning in, I kiss the corner of her mouth. I know I need to take a step back. I'm about to beg her to let me trace every inch of her skin with my tongue. I'm pushing at the boundaries we've established, erasing the lines that we've drawn.

"You ready for bed?" I ask.

"Yeah."

I nod and carry her out of the pool. I set her on her feet when we reach the lounger that holds the towels and grab one, helping her dry off. "Arms up," I say, and she obeys, allowing me to wrap the towel around her. Quickly, I take another for myself, tying it around my waist. Holding her hand, I lead us back into the house and to our room.

"I'm going to shower," she says.

"Yeah, I'll do that too." I point over my shoulder. "I'll use one of the other bathrooms. I just need to grab a few things."

"This shower is huge. More than enough room for both of us."

I swallow hard as I process what she's saying. "It is a big shower," I agree.

She removes the towel from around her waist and turns toward the bathroom. When she reaches the door, she stops and turns to look at me over her shoulder. "You coming?"

Fuck. Me.

"I'm right behind you." The lines are so blurred at the moment that I can't even see them. I don't know what we're doing, but I do know she feels it too. The connection between us is too strong for her not to. She's the one who invited me to join her. Tearing off my towel and gripping it tightly in my hands, I follow her into the bathroom.

There's a huge walk-in shower surrounded by glass. There are two matching rain showerheads with jets down the wall and a bench along the entire back wall. The room is already starting to fill with steam as I watch my now-naked wife step under the spray.

She's so fucking beautiful.

I can't take my eyes off her as I peel off my wet trunks, letting them fall to the tile floor. Her back is to me when I step inside the shower. Instead of going to her and wrapping her in my arms, I head to the other side and step beneath the hot spray. Tilting my head back, I let the water run over me as I send up a silent wish for patience. My cock is hard as steel, but I'm not in control here.

Monroe has all the control.

When she turns, I let out a sound I've never made before in my life, but damn, seeing all of her like this for the first time is life-altering. I'll never in my entire life forget this moment. Her breasts, a little more than a handful, are round and perky. Her nipples, a darker rose color, match her lips. Her belly is flat, and her pussy—

"You're bare." The words tumble from my lips as my eyes rake over her bare pussy.

"Is that something you like?"

"It's sexy."

"What if I wasn't bare?" she asks, a hint of teasing in her tone.

I'm still staring at the junction of her thighs. "You'd still be sexy." I lift my gaze to find her watching me. Her eyes travel over my bare chest and don't stop until her gaze is zeroed in on my cock. She swallows hard and licks her lips, making my cock twitch.

"Monroe." My voice is gritty like sandpaper. Her eyes snap to mine. We're both standing still, staring into each other's eyes, and I'd give anything to know what she's thinking right now.

"I-I should wash the chlorine out of my hair." She turns so fast, I'm surprised she didn't slip and fall, and reaches for the shampoo bottle.

My fingers ache to touch her. To be the one lathering up her long strands of dark, curly hair. To run my soapy hands all over her gorgeous body. Instead, I collect my own shampoo and finish my shower. I take my time because there is no way I'm leaving this shower without her. I might not be able to touch her, but I can memorize every inch of her. I can catalog the way the soap runs over her body, the way her dark hair caresses her back.

When she's finished, she reaches for the handle and turns off the water. I'm tempted to stay here and rub one out, but the need to be next to her is too strong. I do the same and push open the door. I reach out for a towel and hand it to her. She smiles and wraps her hair in a turban as I reach for another towel and wrap it around her shoulders.

"Thank you."

I nod, snag a towel for myself, and quickly run it over my hair and my chest before wrapping it around my waist. "You need anything from the kitchen?" I ask her. I need to get away for just a minute to get myself under control.

"Maybe a bottle of water. I'm parched." She licks her lips, and I bite down on the inside of my cheek to stop myself from attacking her mouth with mine.

I nod. "I'll be right back." Unable to resist, I lean over and press a kiss to her temple and stalk out of the room, not giving a single fuck that I'm dripping water all over the floor. I stomp down the stairs and into the kitchen. Bracing my hands on the island, I bow my head and just breathe. I'm in over my head here.

I'm drowning.

I'm falling for my wife.

I remind myself that she's ten years my junior and has a whole lot of life to live. Hell, she admitted she's inexperienced, and if she thought that was going to keep me away from her, she's wrong. So damn wrong. It only makes me want her more. I want to show her how good we can be together. I want to— No. *No. No. No.* I need to stop this. I need to remember that she's helping me. I promised her she would be safe with me, and that means I can't seduce her, no matter how badly I want to be inside her.

Blowing out a heavy breath, I grab two bottles of water and head back up to our room. She's already beneath the covers.

"Here you go," I say, handing her the bottle.

She immediately twists off the cap and downs half of it. I look away as her throat bobs with each swallow.

I'm losing my damn mind over her.

Moving to my side of the bed, I open my bottle and do the same before placing it on the nightstand. I move to my dresser, pull out some boxer briefs, and drop the towel, sliding into them. I don't know if she's watching, but I hope that she is. I'm probably going to hell for that, but this game we're playing, it's addicting.

She's addicting.

Walking to the door, I turn off the lights and blindly make my way back to the bed. I climb in beside her, and because I'm a glutton for punishment and can't seem to help myself, I reach for her. She comes willingly, allowing me to curl my body around her.

"Goodnight, gorgeous."

"Night, Legend."

I lie awake, holding her until her breathing is deep and even. Once I know she's settled, I close my eyes and drift off to sleep.

MONROE 16

IT'S OUR LAST DAY AT the cabin. We leave in the morning, and although I've enjoyed our time here together, I'm also ready to go home. Not because I miss my job, or Ashby, for that matter. We've only been here a few days. No, I'm ready to go home so that I can maybe put a little space between me and my husband.

I sleep in his arms every night—not something new for us—but here, in this place, it feels different. He's also still touching me anytime that he can, and last night, he kissed me goodnight. Not just a peck on the lips, "have a good sleep" kind of kiss. No, he molded his mouth to mine and kissed me for what felt like hours before rolling me over, wrapping himself around me, and whispering goodnight.

I'm in trouble.

So much trouble.

I can't resist him. What's worse is that I don't want to. I almost slipped away to call Emerson last night but decided against it. This is something we need to talk about in person. Besides, this cabin may be huge, but it's quiet with just the two of us. I wasn't willing to risk him overhearing our conversation.

"What time do you want to head out in the morning?" Legend asks.

We're sitting on the couch. We just got back after watching a dinner show. "What time do we have to be out of here?"

"Eleven, I think."

I nod. "I'm easy. Do you have clients tomorrow?"

"No. I'm off all week."

That surprises me. "You are?"

"Yeah, when you told me you were taking the entire week off, I did too."

See, this man, he melts my heart. "You didn't have to do that."

"I know, but I thought we could go shopping. Get a few things to make the house feel more like home for you."

"Legend, that's not necessary."

"Maybe paint the bedroom or any other room. It's small, but I want it to feel like yours while you live there."

"I love your house. I wouldn't change a thing. Well, I might buy a throw blanket or two. We keep having to take the blankets from the bedroom." I chuckle, thinking about Legend tugging the blankets out to the living room because he knows I like to be snuggled up.

"We can do that. Who knows? You might see something else while we're out and about."

"That's really not necessary, Legend."

"I need you to feel like you're home."

"I do. You've made me feel welcome. Promise." I smile at him.

He nods. "What do you want to do on our last night?" he asks, changing the subject.

"Hot tub," I say immediately. "We've yet to try it out." Yesterday, we were gone all day. We shopped a little, drove through the mountains, took in a dinner show, and came home and crashed. Well, after he kissed the breath from my lungs.

He nods. "We still have that bottle of wine that the cabin gave us as a wedding gift."

"Yes, please." I stand from the couch. "I'll go change."

"I'll grab the wine and set it by the hot tub, then I'll be up to change too."

"Thank you." I stand on tiptoes and press a kiss on his cheek. The smile he gives me is soft, and if I didn't know better, I'd say it was loving. Rushing up to our room, I quickly change into my bikini and grab a couple of towels before heading to the upper level, where the hot tub sits on the balcony.

When I open the bedroom door, I bump into Legend. His hands land on my hips as he steadies me.

"Yikes. Sorry about that." I smile up at him.

"You good?"

"I'm good. Just ready to enjoy our last night here."

He nods. "I'll be there in a minute. I poured us both a glass of wine."

"Best husband ever." I wink at him, and he chuckles.

I move to step around him and squeal when his hand connects with my ass. I stop and turn to look at him over my shoulder. He shrugs and disappears into our room. With my ass, which is stinging from his hand, and my pussy craving more of him, I make my way to the upper level, toss the towels onto a chair, and sink into the water, grabbing my glass of wine from the cupholder on the side.

This is the life.

I hear Legend as he joins me, but I keep my head tilted back and my eyes closed. "We should get a hot tub," I tell him.

He chuckles. "You think so?"

"Definitely. But I get visitation rights when you divorce me." My stomach twists at the thought of no more nights sleeping next to him. I keep reminding myself that's our future, no matter how knotted with anxiety it makes me.

He's quiet and doesn't respond to my joke. I peel open one eye and lift my head just enough to see him. He's staring at me with an intensity that has my body heating.

"Let's not talk about divorce on our honeymoon."

"Fine, fine," I tease. "Thanks for the wine." I take a long sip from my glass.

He reaches for his own and drains it before picking up the bottle, refilling his glass, and moving toward me to top mine off as well.

Instead of going back to his side of the hot tub, he settles on my side. I'm stretched out, so he pulls my feet onto his lap and begins to massage.

"A girl could get used to this," I tell him.

"Good."

I don't have to look at him to know that he's smiling. We talk about anything and everything. Being with Legend is easy. He's laid-back and fun to be around. He's been more serious lately, but I can only imagine the stress of marrying me to get his inheritance. It's not fair—the steps he's had to go through to make it happen—but I'm glad I could help him.

I don't know how much time has passed, but the enormous bottle of wine is now empty, and my fingers are pruned. "I'm starting to look like an old woman." I hold my hands up to show Legend as I giggle. Definitely too much wine.

He grins. "You'll be sexy no matter how old you get. Besides, you're married to an old man."

"You're not old."

"When I'm fifty, you'll be forty."

"And?"

"You'll leave me for a younger man."

The breath leaves my lungs. He's talking like we'll still be married in twenty years. "I'd never leave you," I tell him. Reaching over, I run my fingers through his hair, pushing it off his forehead.

He grabs me around the waist and pulls me to his lap so that I'm straddling him. "Because you're my wife," he says, resting his palm against my cheek. "We said vows."

"I remember."

"Can I tell you a secret?"

We've both been drinking. Our inhibitions have melted away, and we're both more loose-lipped than we would be without the alcohol in our systems. "You can tell me anything."

"I really like kissing my wife."

"Yeah?" I croak.

"Can I tell you another secret?"

"I'm listening." I place my hands on his shoulders.

"I don't think I would if it wasn't you."

"You don't think you would what?" I ask, even though I'm pretty sure I know what he means. My heart certainly thinks so as it beats double time inside my chest.

"Like kissing my wife if you weren't my wife."

"Come on, Casanova. We need to call it a night." I carefully stand and climb out of the hot tub, reaching for a towel. Legend is right behind me. This moment is too real, too raw, and I don't know how to handle it. I want things with him that weren't part of our deal, and I refuse to make this harder on either one of us.

I can do this. I can avoid handing my heart over to my in-name-only husband on a silver platter. I just need to keep repeating that in my head until my heart gets on board.

"We can clean up out here before we leave tomorrow. Let's get you inside." He quickly closes the cover to the hot tub and, with his hand on the small of my back, he leads me into the cabin.

We don't speak as we make our way to our room. Once inside, Legend closes the door behind us. He snakes an arm around my waist and pulls my back to his front. He buries his face in my neck and inhales deeply. "You feel it, too, right?"

I don't have to ask what he's talking about. We've been dancing around this chemistry for weeks. "I feel it too," I whisper.

Legend clutches my towel, which causes it to fall to the floor. He then drops his own. I stand still, not sure what he's doing, but I'm on board for whatever happens next. I remain still, eyes closed, just—waiting. For what? I'm not sure. But whatever it is, I don't want to miss it.

His finger slides beneath the strap of my bikini. He traces from one side to the other. Goose bumps break out on my skin, and it has nothing to do with just coming out of the hot tub.

It's Legend.

I focus on breathing when I feel the strap give way, and my top loosens.

"Arms up, gorgeous."

I don't hesitate to do as I'm told and lift my arms over my head, letting the bikini top fall to the floor. My arms drift back to my sides as I wait to see what's next. I'm here for whatever it is. I don't have to wait long before Legend cups my breasts with his large, calloused hands.

Tilting my head back, I rest it against his shoulder as he plays with my nipples, pinching and rolling them between his fingertips. "Oh," I moan, because damn, that feels good.

The desire in the air is so thick, I can almost taste it, but we both remain quiet as he continues to explore me. My eyes remain closed, and I'm enjoying every minute of my fake husband's hands on me.

All too soon, his hands drop to my waist. I lift my head, not sure what's happening next, when he drops to his knees. He places a gentle kiss on the small of my back before he slides an index finger under the waistline on both sides and pulls. My bikini bottoms pool at my feet. Without being told, I kick them to the side, making him chuckle. The deep, husky sound goes straight to my core.

His hands roam as they trace over the backs of my thighs. When I feel his lips press onto my ass cheek in a soft kiss, I turn my head to peer down at him.

"Did you just kiss my ass?" I ask.

"Baby, I want to kiss every inch of you."

I swallow hard. I want to scream, "Yes, please!" but all I can do is nod, unable to find my voice.

He stands and kisses my bare shoulder. "Come lie down with me." He places his hand on the small of my back and leads me to the bed.

I sit down, very aware that I'm naked and he's not. Not that I need to worry for long, because Legend makes quick work of his trunks, tossing them through the bathroom door. He palms his cock and strokes himself with what looks like a firm grip. I can't take my eyes off him.

"Lie back for me."

I scramble to press my head on the pillow and wait for his next instruction. He moves toward the dresser and pulls out one of the red long-stem roses sitting in a vase. At first, I thought the cabin rental place had given them to us until I read the card with Legend's familiar scrawled handwriting, *Happy honeymoon, love, L* on the card.

Love, L.

Legend sits next to me on the bed. "Your skin feels like silk," he murmurs as he traces the rose over my breasts.

I take in a ragged breath at the soft feel of the petals against my skin.

"You're blushing, baby."

"I—this is new for me."

His ice-blue eyes soften. "Do you want me to stop?"

"No," I rush to say. "Please... don't."

He nods. It takes everything I have to remain still while he traces the rose all over my naked skin. When he gets to my pussy, he taps the rose lightly, and I moan.

"What are you doing to me?" This shouldn't be turning me on, right? Slapping my pussy with a rose?

"I know you're concerned about our age, about my experience versus yours. You've hinted at it a few times. I'm showing you that none of that matters when it's me and you." He leans over and lightly traces a hard nipple with his tongue before his eyes meet mine. "Everything with you feels like the first time to me, Monroe."

"You've been at this a lot longer."

He shakes his head. "Not this. Never this. I've never desired anyone the way I do you." He tosses the rose to the floor and settles on the bed next to me. He props himself up on one elbow while staring down at me.

"Why did you stop?"

"I need to make sure this is what you want."

"I want you."

"We've both been drinking."

"I know what I'm asking."

"Do you? Because we're married, gorgeous. For the next year, you'll be sleeping next to me every night. This... tonight, it could change things between us."

"Maybe we should just add to our agreement," I suggest.

"I'm listening."

"We're married. We're both going to be faithful because that's who we are. Maybe while we're married, if we have an itch, we ask the other one to scratch it."

"You got an itch, baby?" he asks, humor in his tone.

Instead of answering with words, I grab his free hand and place it over my breast. He immediately squeezes gently before rolling my nipple between his thumb and index finger. "I do," I finally say.

"You want this? You want me?"

"So much." I should be worried about the fallout. The consequences of blowing up the lines that have clearly been drawn, but at this moment, all I can think about is Legend and his hands and his mouth all over me. I don't know if this is a one-time thing. I don't know if I'll ever have this chance to be with him like this again, and when I tell you that you don't pass up a chance to be worshipped by Legend Raines, I mean it.

I'm still at the beginning stages, and I know one night with him, having all of him and his attention, is going to be life-changing.

Legend doesn't need further instruction. He moves to settle between my thighs and starts kissing me. I wrap my legs around him, needing him inside me, but he's stubborn and way bigger than me, so he doesn't even move when I apply pressure with my legs.

Instead, he pulls his lips from mine and smiles down at me. "Patience, wife."

Heat floods between my thighs, and if I weren't so turned on and out of my mind with need for him, I might be embarrassed. "You're teasing me."

"No, baby. I'm enjoying you. There's a difference."

"Feels like teasing." I pout.

"Let me have this?" His words come out as more of a question than a statement. He's looking at me as if I'm his entire world, and all I can do is nod. My heart pitter-patters into a fast beat inside my chest because I want to be his.

I don't want to pretend.

I nod my agreement, and relief washes over his face. Did he think I would say no?

I don't have time to dwell on it before his mouth crashes with mine. His kiss is hungry and demanding as he pushes his tongue past my lips.

"Legend."

"Yes, wife?"

"I want you."

"Fuck." He rests his forehead against mine. "You're making it extremely difficult to take this slow."

"Who says we have to go slow?"

"It's our first time together."

"Fast or slow, I'll never forget it. We've been dancing around this—whatever it is, attraction or desire or whatever you want to call it—for weeks." I raise my hands to cradle his cheeks. "I need you."

He drops a hard kiss on my lips and climbs off the bed. I'm ready to ask where he's going when I see him pull open his dresser drawer and grab an unopened box of condoms.

"Were you a Boy Scout, Legend Raines?" I tease.

He stalks back toward the bed, a foil packet in hand, and the look he gives me can only be described as smoldering.

"Not a Boy Scout, but I wanted to be able to protect you if we got to this point."

"And you," I remind him.

He nods, putting the corner of the packet into his mouth and tearing it open. I watch with rapt attention as he rolls the condom over his hard cock and climbs back onto the bed. He runs his fingers through my folds. "So wet for me."

"Yes. You," I say, lifting my hips, needing more.

"I don't want to hurt you."

"You would never hurt me, Legend."

"I need you to come first."

"No. I want to come with you inside me."

"Baby." His eyes soften.

"I want my husband inside me." I don't know what makes me say it, but the feral look in his eyes tells me he likes it.

"You want your husband's cock?" he asks as he settles between my thighs. He holds his weight on one hand while lining his cock up with my entrance.

"Yes, please."

"Say it."

"I want my husband's cock. I want you."

"Fuck." He pushes his hips forward and doesn't stop until he's all the way in. His eyes are squeezed closed, and his jaw is clenched tightly.

"Legend?"

"You feel like heaven. I need a minute, or this is going to be over before we're started."

I lock my legs around him, holding him against me. "Take me," I whisper.

His eyes pop open. "You don't know what you're asking for."

"I do. I'm asking for you. Don't hold back. I feel it, too, Legend." I place my hand over his heart and can feel its heavy beat. "We've had weeks of foreplay. We both need this. Take me."

"Hold on to me."

I do as he asks. I slide my hands beneath his arms and grip his back. As soon as he feels my grip, he pulls out and slams back in. I dig my nails deeper into his skin, lock my ankles together, and hold on for the ride. I can already feel my orgasm building.

"I'm close." My words are breathy.

"I feel you, baby. Fuck, I'm not going to last with your pussy squeezing me like a fucking vise."

He rocks into me, and like a tornado whipping through the sky, my orgasm crashes over me. Wave after wave of pure bliss like fire coursing through my veins. It's the most intense pleasure I've ever felt in my life.

"Fuck!" he roars, stilling as he loses himself to the very same pleasure. He's breathing heavily, as am I.

I release my death grip on his back, certain I left a mark, but something tells me he's not going to care.

He pulls out, tosses the condom into the trash can near the bed, and pulls me into his arms. His heart is racing, our skin is slick with sweat, and I'm the most content I've ever been. He holds me like I'm precious, which is how I always feel when I'm with him.

Eventually, we both catch our breath, and I can't help but ask, "When can we do that again?"

He chuckles and holds me a little tighter.

LEGEND 17

MY WIFE IS A FUCKING smokeshow. Seriously, I can't take my eyes off her. We're all at Forrest's place for New Year's Eve. She and Emerson, pregnant belly and all, are dancing in the middle of the living room. They're wearing silk pajama pants, and long-sleeved shirts. Apparently, Emerson wasn't feeling like dressing up, and since we were staying in, my wife decided it was a pajama party.

Before you ask, yes, that means all of us. There isn't a single thing on this earth that Roman and I would say no to when it comes to our wives. The same goes for Forrest, Maddox and Lachlan. Well, they can't say no to them either. Basically, we're a bunch of tatted-up, muscled pushovers when it comes to the women in our lives.

The pajamas aren't sexy, but my wife could make a feed sack look good. Her hair is pulled up in a messy knot on the top of her head, and she looks like she's ready for bed. Maybe that's my turn-on. I know at bedtime, I get her in my arms, and more nights than not, we scratch our mutual itch. The same one we scratched on our honeymoon and have yet to discuss. We're both avoiding it, but I know eventually, we're going to have to talk about it.

"How's married life?" Roman asks.

I've been standing here, propped against the wall, watching the women like some kind of creeper, but I can't seem to help myself. I want to be where she is. "Can't complain. You?"

"Fucking fantastic. Can you believe I'm going to be a dad?"

I clap my hand on his shoulder. "A damn good one too. When are you finally going to tell us what you're having?"

"We told my parents and Forrest earlier today."

I don't take offense. Forrest is Emerson's brother and her only family, since their parents are pieces of shit. "So, spill the details."

"Yeah, we have a plan," he says as he walks over to the speaker and turns down the music. The ladies are laughing and smiling as they move to face him. "Ready, baby girl?" Roman asks Emerson.

Her eyes light up, and she nods. She rushes toward him, and he kisses her softly with his hand on her belly before leading her into the kitchen.

"What's that about?" Monroe asks. I hand her my bottle of water, and she takes it, drinking greedily. "Thank you," she says when she's done.

I take the bottle from her and finish it off. "We were talking about the gender of the baby, and he said they had a plan and walked away."

She grabs my arm and shimmies around with a giant smile on her face. "Are they finally going to tell us?"

Her eyes light up, and I want nothing more than to kiss her, so I do. I lean in and peck on her soft lips. Everyone here thinks we're still pretending. I'm not, and I'm pretty sure she's not either. "I don't know, gorgeous, but I think so."

She beams. "Legend! I'm so excited. Do you know how hard it's been to shop for them, not knowing the sex of the baby?"

I laugh and slide my arm around her waist. "No, but I'm guessing hard?"

"So hard," she says dramatically.

"Well, I know you've all been waiting—" Emerson smiles at her best friend. "—Monroe," she teases. "We told Forrest and Rome's parents earlier today, but we also wanted to share with all of you. We went back and forth on having some fancy gender reveal party, and at the end of the day, we just decided to take the easy way out."

She turns to look at Roman, and he places a small cake on the counter. It's a round cake with several layers, and it's decorated in pink and blue and says Happy New Year.

"How did I not catch onto that?" Monroe asks.

Emerson laughs. "I don't know, but I'm glad you didn't. We had this cake made, and the inside color will reveal the gender."

Roman steps behind her, wrapping his arms around her waist and resting his hands over their baby. "Ready, baby girl?"

"Actually, I want Forrest to do the honors."

"Me?" Forrest asks, not able to hide the surprise in his voice.

Emerson nods. "Yes, you." Emerson nods toward the knife lying on the island next to the cake.

I watch as Forrest clears his throat, finishes off his beer, and tosses it in the trash before going to stand at the island. Roman isn't drinking in solidarity with his pregnant wife. My wife isn't drinking in solidarity with her best friend, and me? Well, I'm not drinking because we're not staying here. We're going home where I can hold my wife in my arms and scratch our mutual itch, which means I'm making love to her until the sun comes up. I can't think of a better way to ring in the new year. Sure, she could have driven us home, but I want to be sober for what I have planned for us.

Forrest, Lachlan, and Maddox are all drinking, but they're all taking it slow. It's been a chill night with friends, and I can't think of a single thing I would have rather done, unless you count staying at home in bed with my wife.

Forrest rubs his hands together, leans over, kisses his sister on the cheek, and then picks up the knife and cuts into the cake. As soon as he pulls out a slice, showing a bright pink center, Monroe cheers and wraps her arms around me. I'm already holding her, but I hold her a little tighter. She pulls away, wiping at her tears as she rushes to her best friend and crushes her in a fierce hug.

Lachlan and Maddox shake Roman's hand while Forrest digs into the first piece of cake. Since he already knew the gender, I'm certain he had his own one-on-one time with the couple to congratulate them.

I step up next to Roman and pull him into a hug. "Congrats, brother." I'm surprised at the emotion in my voice. We might not be blood related, but he's my brother. They all are. His daughter will be my first niece, and I'm excited as hell about it. Maybe not as excited as my wife is, but still excited.

"Looks like you're going to have two baby girls," I tease Roman.

He smiles broadly. "Yeah. A girl dad." He laughs. "I hope you and the guys are ready to be the big, intimidating uncles."

"I'm all over that shit," Forrest says with a mouth full of cake. He swallows. "She's going to have an army behind her."

"Damn right," Roman agrees.

"Come on now," Monroe says. "You're going to have to give her room to make her own decisions and her own mistakes."

"That's where Aunt Monroe comes in," Emerson tells her. "We need to keep these five in check. And when the rest of you get married, I'm recruiting your wives as well."

I give Emerson a mental fist bump. She's talking like Monroe and I will remain married, and I could hug the hell out of her for that. We've only been married for two months, and with each passing day, I can see a future for us. That should scare me, but it doesn't. We don't talk about it, but I can feel it with every touch, with every look we share.

Monroe feels it too.

I know we need to talk about it, and we will. However, we're still in the honeymoon phase. We have several months before any decisions need to be made. We're just going to ride this out, and my hope is that she'll be so wrapped up in me like I know I will be wrapped up in her that she wants to forget about the divorce and we can live happily ever after. I'm dreading our one-year anniversary. The day we're scheduled to meet with my grandmother's attorney. It's still months away, and already, the thought of asking her for a divorce haunts me. I can't imagine a life where Monroe isn't mine.

I'm fucked.

"How about a game of Monopoly?" Roman suggests.

We guys snicker because he knows damn well we all get frustrated with how long that damn game takes, but Emerson loves it. He's whipped, and he's damn proud of it.

"Yes." Emerson turns in his arms and kisses him. "Set it up. I'm going to dish out the rest of this cake."

"Sure thing, baby girl."

They don't confirm that we all want to play. They know we will. That's just how we roll. The guys and I filter into the dining room to clean off the table, and then we set up the game while Monroe and Emerson dish up slices of baby pink cake.

If you'd asked me last New Year's Eve how I'd be spending this one, this would not have been on my bingo card, but that's okay. I wouldn't trade this night or how things have turned out the last few months for anything.

"Ten, nine, eight...," we all start to count.

I slide my hand beneath the table and place it on Monroe's thigh. She glances over at me, just as I hoped that she would. I lean in close. "Three, two, one. Happy New Year, wife." I don't give her a chance to say it back as I kiss her softly. It's not how I really want to kiss her, but I know we're pretending.

We're supposed to be pretending.

Our friends have seen us together enough to know that things are changing. I want them to know, but until we talk about it, I can't devour her like Roman is Emerson.

"My sister," Forrest coughs, and we all laugh.

"Happy New Year, husband." Monroe winks, and my cock twitches in my pajama pants. She doesn't refer to me as her husband often, but damn, when she does, it turns me on like nothing else.

It takes us another hour to wrap up the game. Emerson is the victor, as she usually is.

"You ready to head home?" I ask Monroe.

"Yes." She covers her yawn with her hand. "I'm exhausted. I can't do this late-night stuff anymore." She laughs.

"Aw, Mo's married to an old man, so now she's acting like him," Lachlan teases.

"Trust me, there is nothing old about my husband," Monroe fires back, and I want to beat on my chest like a caveman because her words tell our friends everything we haven't said. If they've been wondering if we're sleeping together, now they know. I'm actually surprised none of the guys have come out and asked me. I guess they're staying out of it. For now, anyway. I'm sure that comment opened up a can of worms that I won't be able to escape.

"Interesting. Tell us more." Lachlan grins.

Maddox smirks.

"We're going home. Forrest, brother, thank you for having us." I stand and offer Monroe my hand. "Rome, Em, congrats on the baby girl. I can't wait to meet her."

"Thank you," they reply at the same time.

"Ready?" I ask Monroe.

"I just need to get my coat and purse."

"They're by the door." With my hand on the small of her back, I lead her to the door. I help her slip into her coat before I put mine on, and I carry her purse for her. When we get outside, I see it's snowed more than I thought it was going to. Without thinking, I bend and lift her in my arms, making her laugh.

"What are you doing?"

"Carrying you to the truck."

When I get to the door, she pulls it open, and I set her in the seat. "Oh, heated seats. Remote start for the win. I didn't even see you hit the button."

"You were too engrossed in the game."

"She always wins," she grumbles good-naturedly.

"Buckle up, gorgeous." I hand over her purse, kiss her soft lips, and shut the door, jogging around to the driver's side. Pajamas do zilch to ward off the chill of the night air. Sure, they're warm and cozy in the house, but they have nothing on the cold Tennessee weather.

The drive is short but filled with my wife's chatter about how excited she is that Emerson and Roman are having a little girl. "I'm so happy for them," she says from her seat beside me. "They fought so hard to be together, and now they're starting their own family. I feel like Em is living one of our romance novels."

"I always thought Forrest would be the first one of us to get married and start a family."

"Right? I can see that too. I knew Em was into Rome, so I paid attention, and it was easy to see she wasn't alone. I knew it would all work out for them. I hoped it would, anyway, but this baby girl, she's a plot twist I didn't see coming, but they're both so happy."

I park the truck and turn off the engine before turning to face her. "Do you want kids right away?" It's something we've touched on, but it's been more of a casual conversation. She wants to be a mom. She's already told me that.

"Am I that obvious?" She laughs. "Please don't think I'm going to trick you into a pregnancy. I promise that won't happen. But yeah, Em and I always talked about our kids growing up together, and she's gotten a head start on me. She's been my best friend since we were in kindergarten. It would be nice for our kids to be close as well."

I want to tell her that we can start tonight. We really need to talk about this, about us, and what we both want. I need to give it some more time, though. I need her to fall for me. *Really* fall for me so that she wants to be mine forever.

"Stay put," I tell her, reaching for my door and climbing out of the truck. I rush to her side, and she's already got her door open. I lift her into my arms, and her giggle makes me smile.

"You know, you're going to spoil me so much, it's going to be hard for my next husband to fill your shoes."

My gut twists. The thought of someone else having these moments with her sets a fire roaring through my veins. I don't know what this feeling is. Is this love? Is it infatuation? Whatever it is, I know that if she walks away, she'll leave me broken and scarred, and I'll never be the same.

I put her on her feet when we reach the front door. Once it's unlocked, I usher her inside. I don't bother turning on the lights; instead, I lock up behind us and lead her through the dark house to our bedroom.

"The fun thing about a pajama party is that we're already ready for bed," she says as we enter our bedroom. I will never again think of this room or this house as just mine. It's ours.

"Hmm," I say, pulling her into my arms and kissing her neck. "I still think we should get undressed."

She tilts her head to the side, and I take full advantage as I trace the slender length of her neck with my tongue. "I-I think I agree. I mean, we are overdressed," she replies. Her voice is breathy and filled with need. "I might need some help."

"What kind of husband would I be if I didn't help my wife with her every need? Do you have any other needs you need assistance with tonight, wife?"

"I have an itch."

I smile against her soft skin at the base of her neck. "Tell me where, gorgeous."

"Everywhere. Too many clothes," she mutters.

Her hands move between us, and in seconds, she has her pajama top off and somewhere on the floor.

"Here?" I ask, cupping her breasts through her bra. Reaching behind her, I work the clasp of her bra. I take my time dropping one strap and then the other from her shoulder before removing it from her body.

"Legend."

"Tell me."

"Your mouth."

"You want me to suck on these tits?" I test the weight of her breasts in the palms of my hands.

"Please."

"Since you asked so nicely." Bending, I guide a hard nipple into my mouth and suck gently. She moans—a sound that is delivered from deep in the back of her throat. It urges me on, knowing that I'm giving her pleasure. I nip and suck and lick, soothing the ache with my tongue.

She grips my back, digging into my shirt. I long to feel her nails dig into my bare skin.

Releasing her nipple with an audible pop, I stand upright, pull my shirt over my head, and rid myself of my bottoms and boxer briefs in one swoop. I capture the opposite nipple in my mouth and lavish it with the same attention.

"Legend."

"What do you need?"

"You."

My heart hammers in my chest. I should tell her she has me for as long as she wants me, but I can't do that. Not while we're naked together. That needs to be a conversation for when we're not in our bedroom bathed in darkness. I need her to be able to see my face, to see the sincerity in my words. I don't want her to think it's the heat of the moment that's fueling my declaration to her.

"You have me." It's the best I can do without saying too much.

"I need more."

Dropping to my knees, I place a gentle kiss on her belly. "Like this?"

"Lower." She grips her bottoms and pushes them past her hips, boy-short panties and all.

I kiss just above her pussy. "Here."

"Legend." She groans. "You're teasing me."

"Does my wife want me to lick her pussy?" I ask.

She inhales sharply. "Yes. That."

"Say it."

"Lick me there."

"Come on, gorgeous. If you want my mouth on this pussy, you have to tell me." I don't know why, but I need to hear her say it.

"Lick my pussy, husband."

My cock is weeping from her words. I grip the backs of her thighs and rest my forehead on her belly. I need a minute before I embarrass myself and come just from those four words. She gave me more than I was asking for. When I think I have a semblance of control, I stand. "On the bed, baby."

She climbs onto the mattress. I blindly feel for her legs, grip her ankles, pull her to the edge, and drop to my knees.

"Look at you, so wet for me," I praise as I lift her legs over my shoulders and do as my wife demands and lick her pussy. I feast on her, massaging her clit with my tongue. She writhes, lifting her hips, burying her hands in my hair. When I push a long, thick digit inside her, she moans, and her legs lock around my head so tightly that I couldn't move even if I wanted to.

I don't want to move. I want to lap at her, devour her as she comes on my tongue. I don't stop until she's calling out my name. Her pussy grips at my finger like a vise, and I can't stand it. I need to be inside her.

Standing, I lift her into my arms. I balance her with one hand. Not that I need to do much. She's wrapped her arms and legs around me like a monkey. Lining my cock up at her entrance, I push in.

Home.

I have never felt this level of belonging like I do when I'm inside her.

When I'm inside my wife.

When she pulses around me and her eyes roll back into her head, it only takes a few deep, hard thrusts, and I'm coming with her. Inside her. We gave up condoms a few weeks back. We were out of them and so worked up, but then she told me she was on the pill. I'll never forget that night. The first night ever being inside a woman with my bare cock. It's fitting that it was with my wife. She might not have been my first sexual experience, but she's the first one who meant anything to me.

I carry her into the bathroom and turn on the shower. I take my time washing every inch of her before quickly drying us both off and carrying her back to bed. I hold her naked body next to mine, knowing that this is what I want my forever to look like.

MONROE 18

SOFT MUSIC AND A HEAVENLY smell that has my stomach growling greet me as soon as I walk in the door. Today is Valentine's Day. We both had to work, so we decided a quiet night in was how we would celebrate. If anyone asked, we told them we had a romantic dinner planned at home. That's our story. But from the low lighting, the music, and that delicious smell, my husband has made it our reality.

Carefully, I set my bouquet of roses that Legend had delivered to me at work today on the table before kicking off my shoes. I toss my purse and keys beside the flowers and go in search of Legend. I find him in the kitchen, pulling something out of the oven.

"Something smells good."

He glances at me over his shoulder. "Hope you're hungry."

"What are we having?"

"Baked steak, mashed potatoes, and corn casserole."

"My mouth is watering."

He laughs, but I'm not joking. It smells incredible, and I'm starving.

"How was your day?"

"Good. Long." I don't tell him that I didn't sleep well because I couldn't stop thinking about him and us and how time seems to be passing us by in the blink of an eye. This year is going to be over before we know it, and I'm not ready for that. Most nights, I can turn it off, but last night, I just couldn't stop thinking about how my life will be without sleeping next to him every night. I'm already addicted.

"Thank you for the flowers. They're beautiful. Did you have a good day?"

"You already thanked me, baby. It wasn't too bad. I started a sleeve for a new client. It's a tribute to his late wife. He's adding bits and pieces of memories and things they loved together."

"Aw, really? I love that so much. Will you take a picture for me when it's done?" Legend is crazy talented, and I'm proud of him for how hard he works. Hell, I'm proud of all of the guys. They've built their business from the ground up and made a reputation for themselves. I can't wait to see how they grow once they get their new facility.

"You know I will. I keep pictures of all of my work."

"Thank you for making dinner. What can I do to help?"

"You can set your gorgeous self at the table. There's a bottle of wine already there. Pour us each a glass while I make our plates."

"You're spoiling me, Legend Raines."

He looks up, his eyes soft. "I wouldn't have it any other way."

He goes back to dishing up our food and has no idea that he just made my belly flutter. I've come to realize that I enjoy all sides of this man. The happy, fun, flirty side, the sweet, caring side, and his dirty-talking side when we're in bed together. Basically, I'll take Legend any way I can get him.

Shaking out of my thoughts, I move to the small dining room table in the kitchen and pour both of us a glass of wine. "More roses?" I eye the bouquet in the center of the table. These look exactly like the dozen that were delivered to my work today, which are now sitting in the hallway.

"Of course. Nothing but the best for my Valentine," he replies huskily.

Is there anything this man says or does that doesn't turn me on? If there is, I've yet to find it. He sets a plate in front of me and one for himself before taking a seat. We talk about our days and how Roman already has an infant car seat and hospital bag in both of their cars.

"He's going to be such a good daddy."

"Yeah, he's stoked. He's nervous, but he's pretty damn excited."

"Emerson is too. I think it's more not knowing what to expect with the delivery. I'm sure the next one will be easier for both of them."

"You think they'll have more?"

I nod. "I'm certain of it. As long as they are able to and everything goes well with this one."

"I can see it." He nods, and a small smile tugs at his lips as if he's picturing Roman and Emerson surrounded by their future kids.

The food is delicious, and the company is even more so. It's the perfect low-key stay-at-home night, and I have my husband to thank for that.

"That was so good," I tell him after cleaning my plate. If I wasn't so stuffed, I'd go for seconds.

"I hope you have room for dessert." He stands and takes our plates to the sink, coming back with a cake carrier. He pulls off the top, and inside is a homemade chocolate cake.

"You baked a cake? Did you not work today?"

He laughs. "Nope, but I had my mom bake my wife a cake."

"Really?" Tears well in my eyes instantly.

Legend places the cake on the table and falls to his knees next to me. "What's going on in that pretty head of yours? Why the tears?" He brushes away a lone tear with his thumb.

"I can't believe you did all of this for me. We were just going to chill and say we had a romantic night in. You didn't have to make it a reality. And the cake. Legend, you had your mom make me a cake."

"I was never not going to celebrate my wife on the one day a year that was created just for that."

"It's just another day."

"Not when I finally have someone to celebrate with."

I place my hands on his cheeks. "You make me feel things."

He nods. "I know, baby. You make me feel things too." He leans in and presses a soft kiss to my lips. "Come on." He stands and offers me his hand. "We can have cake later. Right now, we have a date in the living room." He leads me to the living room and motions for me to sit. I do as I'm told while he reaches beside the couch. He pulls out a soft, plush blanket and drapes it over me.

"This is new."

"Yeah. I know how you like to snuggle. This one is bigger than the other one. We can both cuddle under it." He takes a seat next to me and lifts his arm. I don't hesitate to burrow up next to him, sharing the blanket. The lights were already turned off from him setting the romantic mood. He cues up a movie, and I smile when I see it's *The Notebook*. One of my all-time favorite movies.

"You sure you want to watch this with me? You know I cry at the end every single time."

His answer is to reach over, grab a box of tissues, and place them on his lap. "Nowhere else I'd rather be."

That's how we spend the rest of our night. His arms wrapped around me as we share the new throw blanket he bought and watch one of my all-time favorite movies. As predicted, I bawl my eyes out at the end. Legend pulls me onto his lap and wipes my tears once the credits roll. That only serves to make me cry harder. Legend continues to hold me, running his hand up and down my back to soothe me until my tears slow.

"You want cake, or are you ready for bed?"

"Bed, I think. We can save the cake for tomorrow."

That's all he needs to hear before he's standing, lifting me into his arms, and carrying me off to bed. We go through our routines of getting ready, then slide beneath the covers. Legend is wrapped around me like he is every night, but my heart is still in tatters from the movie, and my mind is still processing this perfect night he planned for us.

In the quiet of the room, I whisper. "Legend?"

"What's up, gorgeous?"

"You make me want things we didn't agree on."

"So it's not just me?" he asks, holding me tighter.

His reply makes this easier. "Will you make love to me?"

He immediately rises up, and with the light of the moon spilling through the bedroom blinds, I can make out his figure. "I'd never turn down the chance to make love to my wife." He kisses me so softly, it's as if he thinks I might break. Every touch of his calloused hands is soft as a feather as he roams them over my body.

Legend makes love to me, just like I asked him to. It feels different and special. It's unlike any other form of sex and intimacy I've ever experienced.

My heart feels so full it could burst.

Is this love?

Does he feel it too?

I'm warm and snuggled in our bed. It's late March in Tennessee and still chilly. Not that I have to worry about that at night with my husband. He keeps me warm. Just like now. I'm in that state of half awake and half asleep. It's Saturday, and I had planned to sleep in, but my body is trained to wake up early. I don't know what hour it is, but I know it's not time to wake up. Not today.

My phone rings, causing me to jolt. I fumble to reach for it on my nightstand as Legend's phone also rings. I feel the bed dip and know he's also reaching for his.

Fear grips me. Something is wrong.

"Hello?" I answer.

"Mo."

"Emerson? What's wrong? Oh my god, are you in labor? Is she coming?" I sit up in bed, suddenly wide awake.

"We're on our way to the hospital. My water broke."

"What do you need?" I toss off the covers. "I'm on my way."

"Nothing. You don't have to come. It's just Rome and me in the delivery room. We don't know how long this is going to take."

"I'm coming. Do I need to stop by your place and pick anything up?"

"No." My best friend laughs. "You know Rome has me covered. I just wanted to tell you."

"How are you this calm?" I ask her as I scramble to pull clothes out of my dresser.

"Because, Mo, I get to finally meet my daughter."

Tears well in my eyes. "I love you, Em. I am so happy for both of you. I'll be there, okay? If you need me, I'll be waiting for you. I can't wait to meet your daughter."

"T-Thanks, Mo. Love you," she replies, choked up.

"Love you too. I'm on my way." I end the call and toss my phone on the bed while tearing off Legend's shirt I was sleeping in. I'm rushing to put my bra on when I feel hands on my hips.

"Take a breath, Mo," Legend says from behind me. He places a kiss on my bare shoulder. "Let's get dressed, and we'll head to the hospital."

"Who called you?"

"Rome."

"I need to get there."

"We will. Let's finish getting dressed, and we'll head straight there. We won't leave until you're ready."

"You don't have to. She's my best friend. I appreciate you wanting to go with me, but you can go back to bed."

"Roman is one of my best friends, and Emerson is like a little sister to me. Of course I'm going to be there."

I can hear the hurt in his voice.

Turning in his arms, I wrap mine around his waist and hold him, resting my head against his bare chest. I let the steady beat of his heart calm me. "I'm sorry. I didn't mean to insinuate that you weren't welcome. Just that you didn't need to go because we're married. That's all. I know you care about both of them too." I lift my head and look him in the eyes so that he can see the sincerity in mine. "I'm sorry."

"I do want to be there because they're both important to me. This is my niece who's being born." His mouth tilts into a grin. "But, even if I didn't know them and had never met either of them, I would be there. You're my wife, Monroe. As your husband, I want you to lean on me, and I want to support you in everything."

I nod and place my head back on his chest. I don't know what else to do. It's either hide or blurt out that I'm falling in love with him. I'm no longer questioning if this is love. I know that it is. I know that my heart will always belong to him, and when I have to walk away from this man, I will never be the same.

"Come on, baby. Let's get dressed. We'll hit a drive-thru and take some breakfast for the guys. I have no doubt the rest of them are already on their way to the hospital too. None of us can wait to meet our niece." He kisses the top of my head before releasing his hold on me.

"Thank you, Legend."

"Anytime, wife." He winks. It's sexy and such a Legend move, and just like that, I'm going to need to change my panties before I finish getting dressed.

We've been here all morning and afternoon, but we all refuse to leave. Emerson has been in labor for going on twelve hours, I think. Honestly, I've lost track of time. Thankfully, the waiting room is comfortable. I'm currently lying on one of the small couches with my head on Legend's lap. My husband went to the gift shop earlier and bought a blanket for me to cover up with. The gesture brought tears to my eyes. I don't know if it's because of where we are and the news we've been waiting on or just because it's him.

As the weeks pass by, Legend doesn't seem to care that our friends see how close we've become. We're supposed to be pretending, but he treats me as if I'm precious to him, no matter where we are. That includes when we're with our friends. Emerson tells me that this is going to work out between us. She has a gut feeling that Legend is my forever. I want to believe her, but I'm also scared that on our one-year anniversary, this all just goes away.

Poof.

Gone.

I'm staring at the television with no sound as Legend combs his fingers through my hair. When the sound of multiple phones getting messages alerts us, I sit up, pull mine from my pocket, and smile as tears fill my eyes.

Roman: *It's a girl! Mom and baby are doing great. Em wants a little time, and then we'll invite you all back.*

Happy tears overwhelm me, and I turn to see Roman's mom crying with a smile so big on her face that it could light up the darkest of nights. His dad's grin rivals his mom's as he pulls her into his arms.

"I'm an uncle." Forrest sits in his chair, smiling down at his phone.

"We're all uncles," Lachlan reminds him.

Forrest nods, still smiling.

"You good, gorgeous?" Legend asks me.

"I'm good. I can't wait to meet her." I wipe my eyes, feeling silly for crying.

Legend takes over, smoothing his thumbs over my cheeks. "Aunt Monroe." He smiles. "Is it safe to say we're going to be babysitting a lot?" he asks.

"I've already told Emerson I want on the list. I guess I should have made sure you were okay with that. I can keep her at their place."

"Of course I'm okay with it. It's our home, baby. Ours together."

I feel more tears well, but I blink them away. "Rome's parents will probably fight me over it." I laugh.

Legend chuckles. "Probably, but I know they've been traveling a lot like your parents, so my guess is that your shot at keeping our niece is pretty good."

Everyone is suddenly wide awake, laughing and talking. When another message comes through from Roman telling us we can come to the room, we all go at once. We ignore the nurses' two-at-a-time rule and make our way quietly down the hall. We're all going to sneak in because we're all eager to meet her. They can kick us out later. Rome's parents and Forrest are already back there, which we understand, but I'm ready to meet baby girl.

When we walk into the room, my emotions flood me. "Em." My voice cracks as I place my hand over my mouth. "She's beautiful."

"Thank you," Roman says, and everyone laughs.

"Can I hold her?" I can't take my eyes off the tiny bundle wrapped in pink in Forrest's arms. He carefully hands her over to me, and my heart melts. "You precious thing," I whisper. I look up and meet my best friend's eyes, which are also filled with tears. "What's her name? I can't keep calling her 'thing.' It's creepy." I laugh as I wipe at my tears with one hand, holding on tightly to this tiny baby girl with my other.

"Her name is Lilly Monroe Bailey," Emerson tells me. She's smiling and crying at the same time.

My heart hammers so hard, I'm afraid I might be having a heart attack as I try to process her words. My best friend named her baby girl after me. This tiny, precious human has my name, and I'm so honored and touched and full of love for this little girl, my best friend, and her husband that I'm overcome with emotion.

"What?" I finally whisper. "You named her after me?" Even I can hear the awe in my voice. If it weren't for the hammering beat of my heart in my chest, I might think I was dreaming, but the overwhelming feeling tells me I'm wide awake.

"You're my best friend." Roman clears his throat. "My best *girl* friend," Emerson amends, and the room laughs. "I love you.

You've been there for me through so many struggles and were my biggest supporter when me and Rome first got together."

I look down at the slumbering baby in my arms. "Hi, Lilly. I'm your aunt Monroe, and I love you so much."

Eventually, Lachlan pries Lilly from my arms, taking his turn. All of the guys, even Drake, take turns holding her while Lisa and Lyra have to beg for their turns.

"She's already spoiled," Roman says, kissing the top of Emerson's head. He rests back against the bed, wrapping his arms around her. He's wearing a silly, happy smile.

Glancing across the room, I lock eyes with Legend. I can't quite describe the look on his face.

He mouths, "Are you okay?" and I nod. His answering smile is comforting.

In my head, I'm trying not to imagine this moment as if it were he and I who just had our first baby. I can see it all as clearly as this moment.

Suddenly, it's all I want.

I wonder if I can convince my fake husband to be mine forever so we can share moments like these together.

If only I was brave enough to tell him that I'm in love with him.

LEGEND 19

I CAN'T STOP STARING AT her with baby Lilly in her arms. She's smiling through her tears. She glances over at me and playfully rolls her eyes when I wink at her. She's a fucking vision. So much so that I can see this as my future. My future with her. Today, this moment brings a clarity I didn't realize I needed. I take that back. I knew I needed it. I've been hiding from it, hoping that I could control it.

I can't control it.

I don't want to control it.

I want her.

Just her.

My wife.

I want this moment for her.

For us.

I just fell in love with my wife.

MONROE 20

"LOOK AT THAT SMILE. YOU love your aunt Monroe, don't you?" I ask baby Lilly.

"That's gas," Forrest replies.

"He's right," Lachlan agrees. "I was holding her the other day, and she was laughing and smiling. Then the worst smell came out of her. How can something so damn cute reek that bad?"

"She's a baby, not a thing."

Lachlan waves me off. "You know what I mean."

"At least she didn't shit on you," Maddox tells him.

"Watch your mouth around my daughter," Roman tells him.

"She's too little to understand."

"My little ladybug is a genius," Roman says.

"A little genius who loves her aunt Mo."

"Are you corrupting my daughter?" Emerson asks, joining us. She places a big bowl of potato salad on the food table. "Are we ready to eat?" she asks Roman.

We're all at their place, celebrating Memorial Day. As soon as I walked through the door, I made a beeline for baby Lilly, and I've been holding her hostage ever since.

"Your wife is a baby hog," Forrest grumbles.

"You should have one of your own," Legend tells him.

"I'd need a wife, hell, a girlfriend, even, for that to happen. You have one. Why don't you have your own so your wife will let me have my niece?"

I still, waiting to see what Legend will say. I keep my eyes on Lilly while I'm mentally saying, *Yes, Legend Raines, I'll have your babies.*

I'm losing it.

Legend looks over at me with a smirk on his face. "What do you think, wife?"

That thing my belly does, you know, like there's a swarm of butterflies flapping their wings a million miles a second, appears. Just like it seems to do most days in the presence of my husband. "I think Forrest needs to chill. He lives next door. He gets to have her all the time."

"But not today," Forrest counters. He crosses his muscular arms over his chest.

Forrest is an attractive guy. He could have any woman he wanted. Hell, they all could. I know he's been lonely since Emerson moved out, but he's lucky. She didn't go far. He can walk across his yard and see his sister, his niece, and one of his best friends anytime he wants to. That's why I'm hogging this precious little girl today.

"I think it's my turn." Legend reaches over and pulls Lilly from my arms. "Aunt Mo and Uncle Forty need to share, huh, sweetheart?" he asks her.

I watch as Legend coos and cuddles Lilly, talking to her softly as if she understands every word. Why is a man holding and loving on a baby so sexy? Why can't I stop thinking about Legend holding *our* baby? It's becoming a problem. Lilly is nine weeks old, and every single time that he's held her since she was born, that's where my mind goes.

"Let's eat." Roman stands. "Legend, you want me to take her?"

"Nah, man. You eat. We're good, aren't we, Lilly bug?"

It's endearing how he started calling her that. Roman calls her his ladybug, and Legend modified it a little. It's adorable. It's not just Legend. All the guys have started calling her that. Four men, all sexy as hell, fawning over this baby girl would make any woman near them ready to reproduce.

Everyone starts making their plates. I make two, one for me and one for Legend. Taking my seat at the table, I slide his plate in front of him.

"What's this?"

"I made you a plate."

He leans over and pecks my lips. "Thank you, baby." His words are soft, but I know our friends hear him, and there's no way to disguise that kiss.

"Hey, I just realized it's been six months." Emerson beams.

She winks at me, and I give her a subtle nod of thanks for pulling the attention away from Legend and me. I jump right in, hoping that everyone will let the kiss and the comment pass without questioning us. We've been able to skate by so far with all the touches and kisses.

"What will be six months?" I ask my best friend.

"You've been married six months."

"I guess time flies when you're having fun." Legend smiles at me, then goes right back to cooing at the baby.

"It doesn't seem that long at all," I say, because with each passing day, I'm closer to losing him, and it seems the days are getting shorter and shorter as we get nearer.

"Six months to go." Legend says it almost as if he, too, is counting down the days. I wish I was looking into his eyes to get a good read on him, but he's purposely giving all his attention to baby Lilly.

"So, what is this?" Maddox asks. He waves his fork, pointing it at me and then Legend. "We still pretending?"

"We?" Legend asks.

Maddox waves him off. "You know what I mean."

"There is no we. There is me and my wife."

"See!" Lachlan points at Legend. "I told you, Mad. He's hooked."

My face heats. Not that I care that they know I have feelings for Legend. I'm pretty sure everyone at this table already has me figured out. But I hate the thought of Legend being put on the spot. This is not how I want my husband to tell me his feelings haven't changed and that in six months' time, we're getting divorced.

I don't even like to think about the D-word these days. I'm in a heavy state of denial and avoidance. I'm just not ready to lay all of my cards out on the table. We're good where we are. We're steady, we're happy, so why ruin that before we have to?

"You know what this is," Legend tells him. "Of course I'm hooked on her. She's my wife. I live with her, sleep next to her.... We share meals together. Whatever else this is or isn't is between us."

"Leave them be," Roman speaks up. "It's none of our business. When they want us to know, they'll tell us." He gives Legend a look. One I can't describe. From the corner of my eye, I see my husband nod.

"Can I have my niece now?" Forrest asks. The table erupts in laughter, and the tension and awkward moment are put behind us.

Legend kisses Lilly's cheek before passing her off to Forrest. His hand immediately goes to my thigh under the table as he eats with one hand. It's obvious, and I see our friends giving us curious looks. Maddox and Lachlan are smirking like they have secrets that only they know about.

I pretend like nothing is happening and continue to eat my food. The conversation changes to the new shop, and I'm reminded of how we got into this situation. The guys all deserve the best, and Legend getting his inheritance will help all five of them, as well as my best friend and her daughter. Even if my heart gets broken in the end, it will all have been worth it. I can say, ahead of the pain I know that's coming my way, I would do it all over again if given the chance.

Today was my day off. I work four ten-hour shifts. My day off rotates each week, but I love having a day off during the week to run errands. The first thing I did this morning was go to the grocery store before it got packed. I came home, unloaded everything, and started cleaning and doing laundry.

Legend is a pretty clean guy. He picks up after himself, and he's not afraid to jump in and help clean the house. I did some deep cleaning today. I scrubbed both bathrooms from top to bottom, as well as wiped down the cabinets and the walls in the kitchen before cleaning the counters and moving on to the floors. I've done five loads of laundry, most of which were bedding, and I think I'm more exhausted than if I'd been at my day job all day.

I've also got roast potatoes and carrots in the Crock-Pot. What we don't eat tonight, I'll turn into vegetable soup for tomorrow night. The weather is warm, being late in the middle of June in Tennessee, but homemade vegetable soup is my favorite. I make it just like my mom does. She uses a can of spicy vegetable juice and a can of regular. It's not hot, but it gives it a nice flavor. I've never made it for Legend, but so far, I haven't found anything that man won't eat.

I'm in the kitchen, grabbing bowls, when I hear the front door open. When I turn to say hello, Legend is standing there with a white box and a small gift bag in his hands. "What's all this?" I ask him.

"Can't a man spoil his wife?" His grin is infectious.

"You spoil me enough."

"Never." He places the white box down on the counter. "This, my darling wife, is a homemade cinnamon streusel cake. I picked it up at the bakery in town." He hands me the small gift bag. "This is for you."

"Legend, you have to stop doing this." He's constantly dropping treats off to me at work, buying me blankets because he knows I love them and you can never have too many. I've lost count of the number of times he's given me flowers.

His reply is to bend his head and kiss me. "Thank you for making dinner. It smells great."

"Stop ignoring me."

"I'm not ignoring you. You didn't ask a question. You made a statement that I don't agree with. I'm not engaging in that argument."

"I'm here because I want to be." That statement holds more meaning than he will ever know.

He loops his arms around my waist so we're standing chest to chest. "And I spoil you because I want to."

"How are you still single?" I ask him.

"I'm not." His smile leaves his face. "I'm happily married."

"You know what I mean."

"I was waiting for you." His lips land on the corner of my mouth.

"You're going to be a tough act to follow, Legend Raines."

"What if I told you I wanted to be your only act? In fact, what if I told you I'm not acting at all?"

My breath stalls in my lungs before I pull in a deep breath. "W-What are you saying?" My hands are sweating, and my knees are weak. Is he saying what I think he's saying?

He lifts me to sit on the kitchen island and steps between my legs. His hands are braced on either side of me as he leans in close. "I'm saying that I can't imagine being married to anyone else. I'm saying that the thought of another man getting his hands on you makes my blood boil." He lifts those solid, calloused hands and cradles my cheeks. "I'm saying that I'm in love with my wife. I'm not pretending, Monroe. I haven't been for a long damn time."

I bite down on my bottom lip to keep the happy tears from rolling down my cheeks. I swear this man has made me an emotional basket case in the time I've spent with him. Who knew one person could shed so many tears of joy?

With his thumb, he gently tugs, releasing my lip from my teeth. "Tell me what you're thinking?"

"I love you too," I blurt. I inwardly cringe because he gave me this sweet speech, and all that I can manage to do is blurt out the words. However, the slow, sexy smile he gives me tells me he's okay with the outcome.

"Yeah?"

I nod. "I've been trying to prepare myself to bring it up, but I didn't want to cause problems when things were going so well. I wasn't sure how you felt, and I was worried that this happy little bubble we've been living in would be broken."

"Do I not show you every day how much you mean to me?"

"You do, but it's been that way since we started this arrangement. By the time we reached our wedding day, I forgot we were pretending."

"What are you saying, Monroe?"

"Nothing." I shake my head and look over his shoulder at the cabinet as if it's the most fascinating thing I've ever seen.

"Baby." He grips my chin and turns me to face him. "Tell me." There's so much hope in his eyes, and what I now know is love shining back at me, that I tell him the truth I've been keeping to myself since this all started.

"I wanted to marry you. Not because I was helping you but because of the man you are. If I'm being honest with myself and with you, I was already half in love with you, if not all the way, but in denial the day we said our vows."

"Everything you just said, I feel it deep in my soul. I love the life we're building together. I want this life with you. I don't want a fucking expiration date because my love for you will never expire." With that, his lips crash with mine.

I lean into the kiss, giving him all of me. The pressure on my chest, of constantly worrying about the heartbreak that I was certain would come, is gone.

Legend, my husband of convenience, is in love with me.

He pulls his mouth from mine and starts trailing kisses down my neck.

"Does this mean we're not getting divorced?" I ask.

He stops and lifts his head. "You're not allowed to say that word."

I smile and slide my arms around his neck. "I've spent months wanting to tell you how I feel. Now that it's out there, I want to make sure there are no misunderstandings." I know what he said, but I just need to hear it clearly because forever with him is almost too good to be true.

"No divorce." He furrows his brows at the word. "Forever, baby. You and me."

"Forever."

His hands are everywhere as he devours my mouth. "Did you wear this dress for me?" he asks through his kisses.

"I wore it because it's cute, and it's summer and hot as hell."

"*You're* hot as hell." He slides his hands up beneath my dress. "Lift."

I do, one side and then the other so that I'm no longer sitting on the material.

"Arms up."

I follow his command and lift my arms, letting him pull my sundress off me.

"You're so fucking beautiful." He kisses my bare shoulder as he reaches behind my back and unclasps my bra, letting it fall to the floor.

"Legend."

"Wife?"

"We're in the kitchen."

"Our kitchen."

"This is where we cook."

"And this is where I'm going to fuck my wife. Don't worry about the counter. We can clean it." He runs his hands over my hips until he reaches the thin strip of fabric around my waist. "How attached are we to these panties?" He's gripping the sides so tight, they could snap, and I feel a rush of heat between my thighs.

"Not attached." I shake my head with the words because I don't want there to be any confusion. Panties can go. I just need him to not stop touching me.

The next thing I know, I hear ripping fabric. My legs go back around his waist, and he lifts me from the counter with one arm while the other tosses my now-ruined panties to the floor.

"Perfect." He licks his lips.

"You're overdressed, husband."

His nostrils flare. "Say it again."

I know what he wants, and while I don't say it nearly as often as he does, it seems to have the same effect on him as it does on me when he refers to me as his wife. "You're my husband."

"Fuck yes, I am."

A hard peck to my lips, and he steps back and peels his shirt over his head before quickly removing his jeans and boxer briefs.

"Much better." I'm leaning back on my hands casually, as if I don't have a care in the world, when in fact I know we are most definitely going to have to sanitize this island, and not just because my bare ass is sitting on it.

He grips his hard cock and strokes. "Scoot to the edge." His words are a demand more than a request, but I'm happily willing to comply.

I move to the edge, my ass practically hanging off. "Now what?"

"Wrap those sexy legs around me."

My legs instantly wrap around him, and he rubs his cock over my pussy. "You hear that? You hear how wet you are for me?" he asks.

"What are you gonna do about it?" I'm taunting him, but he's teasing me, so we're even. I'm aware I sound like a child, but damn, I want him inside me.

"I'm gonna fuck my wife. We're gonna eat whatever it is that has our home smelling almost as good as you do. You're going to open your gift, and then I'm going to carry you to our bed and make love to you until the sun comes up."

I lock my legs at the ankles and pull him closer. He aligns himself at my entrance and pushes inside me.

"I was beginning to think you were all talk," I say, tilting my head back and enjoying the stretch of him being buried deep.

He smiles. "Hold on." He moves my arms to wrap around his neck. The next thing I know, he's lifting me and stepping away from the counter. "Bounce on *your* cock, baby."

I don't need to be told twice.

I begin to move, and we both moan. He grips my ass cheeks and assists with lifting me and dropping me back down on his cock. My body tightens around him with every thrust. The fire in my core intensifies until it crashes into me like a hurricane hitting the shoreline. It's intense and overwhelming.

"There you go. Squeeze my cock." He moves us to the wall, pushes my back against it, and hammers into me repeatedly. Aftershocks of my orgasm race through my veins as he calls out my name, spilling inside me.

We're both still and panting before Legend carries me back to the island and sets me down, his cock still buried inside me. Reaching over, he grabs the small gift bag and hands it to me.

"I thought we were going to eat first?" I tease, all too comfortable still being connected to him this way.

"Just open the gift, gorgeous."

I take the bag from his hands and pull out the tissue paper. I don't know what I was expecting, but a new Kindle Paperwhite wasn't it. "You bought me a new Kindle?"

"You mentioned your battery wasn't staying charged the other night."

Placing the bag and my gift on the counter, I grip his shoulders and pull him close. His cock twitches inside me, and I raise a brow.

"That's what you do to me."

"Thank you for my gift." I kiss him softly. "I love you," I say against his lips.

"I love you, Monroe Raines."

We stay in the kitchen, naked, just kissing and enjoying the fact that we're both in this. We're in love, and we're married, and we're not allowed to say the D-word.

We eventually clean up and sit down to eat our dinner, and as soon as we're finished, my husband keeps his promise and makes love to me until the sun comes up.

LEGEND 21

IT'S NOON BY THE TIME I get to the shop. I'm working late tonight. A longtime client booked this date months ago. He needs to do later in the day because he works third shift. I don't mind it.

Of course, at the time, I didn't realize how much I'd enjoy going home to my wife. I smile when I think about how I had her bent over in the shower this morning before she left to meet Emerson for breakfast. We've gotten used to showering together, and even though she tried to sneak out of bed and let me sleep in, I joined her a few minutes later.

There will never be a time when my naked wife will be within reach that I won't be right next to her. I'm addicted to her. I'm pussy whipped, heart whipped. I'm soul whipped, and any other kind of whipped you can think of, sign me up if it means life with Monroe.

If the guys could read my thoughts, I'd never hear the end of it. That's not exactly true. Roman would have my back. He's all the above for his wife too.

One day, when they all fall ass over heels in love, they'll understand.

"All right, man, what's with the cheesy smile?" Forrest asks.

I don't even bother trying to school my features. "Just in a good mood."

"I call bullshit. You've been extra smiley the last few months, but the last few weeks have been on another level. You're like happy-go-lucky Legend on steroids."

I laugh. "Just living the dream, brother."

"This have anything to do with your wife?"

"It has everything to do with my wife." I've not confessed to any of the guys that my marriage is real and permanent. I don't know why. I guess I just wanted to stay in my happy love bubble with Monroe.

"What's up?" Forrest asks.

"What? Can a man not be happily in love with his wife?" I ask.

"Whoa." I turn to see Lachlan standing behind us. "You just dropped the *L* bomb."

"I'm aware."

"Mad! Rome!" Lachlan calls out for the other guys. I knew this was coming when they found out. Not that I care. We give each other shit on a daily basis. It's our love language. At least, that's what my wife calls it.

Maddox and Roman come strolling into the break room.

"How are you all not with a client right now?" I ask them.

Roman shrugs. "Just worked out that way. My next is in fifteen minutes." He turns toward Lachlan. "What's up?"

"Legend is in love."

Roman smiles. "She know?"

"Yeah, she knows."

"So, what's that mean?" Forrest asks.

"It means I'm married to the love of my life." I smile wide because damn if it doesn't feel good to say that out loud.

"And the deal?" Maddox asks.

"The deal is that Monroe is my wife. She will stay that way until I take my last breath." My tone gives them zero chances to doubt me and my love for my wife.

"Damn," Lachlan mutters. "We lost another one."

The guys all laugh, and I join them. "Trust me, man, it's not something to run from."

"There's got to be something to it. These two have been smiling so fucking big, we could turn down the lights and save on the electric bill," Forrest jokes.

"Married life is fan-fucking-tastic," I tell them. "Going home to her is... everything."

"Aw, Legend, do you love my bestie?" Emerson asks.

All heads turn to see her standing in the doorway to the break room. I can tell by the sparkle in her eye that she already knows the answer, but I give her one anyway.

"Yep," I confess.

"Where's ladybug?" Roman asks, stepping next to his wife before pulling her into his arms and kissing her.

"His wife stole her from me." Emerson points at me.

"I didn't steal her," Monroe says, stepping into the room. "I'm just borrowing her for a little while. Right, Lilly bug?" she asks the drooling baby in her arms. She snuggles her close, and I'm telling you now, that's going to be us sooner rather than later.

"Hey, gorgeous." I go to her and slide my arm around her waist. I drop a kiss on her lips before doing the same to the top of Lilly's head. "What are you ladies getting into today?"

"Girls' day is off to a good start. We had breakfast, then took this little cutie for her checkup, and next, we're going to get some lunch."

"And what would a girls' day be without visiting our favorite guys?" Emerson adds.

"But I'm your absolute favorite, right, baby girl?" Roman asks his wife.

I block them out and bend my lips to my wife's ear. "Missed you."

She smiles up at me. "It's been a handful of hours."

"Too long."

Lilly reaches out and pats my face, giving me a toothless grin.

"Come here, you." I take her from Monroe and blow kisses on Lilly's bare belly where her little shirt has ridden up. She cackles with laughter.

"You need one," Roman says, reaching for his daughter. Her smile widens when she sees her daddy, and he takes her from my arms.

"Whenever my wife tells me we're ready." I look down at Monroe, who's staring up at me with a soft expression on her face.

"By the look you two are sharing, I'd say the Everlasting Ink family will be growing soon."

"We did always say we wanted our kids to grow up together," Emerson speaks up.

"We've been married for a hot minute." Monroe laughs off their remarks.

"These two didn't even need to be married." Lachlan points to Roman and Emerson.

"Don't remind me," Forrest mutters.

"We should start a betting pool," Maddox suggests as he reaches into his back pocket and pulls out his wallet. "I got twenty, it will be before your first anniversary." He tosses a twenty-dollar bill down on the table.

"Wait, we need to write this down." Forrest pulls his phone out of his pocket and starts typing away. "I'm going with by the end of the year." He places his phone on the table while he tosses his own twenty out.

"You know we're standing right here." I laugh. I really do love these assholes.

"You want in?" Lachlan asks.

"Hey!" Emerson protests. "That's cheating."

"Are you getting in on this?" Monroe asks her.

"Damn right I am." She turns to Roman, who still has Lilly in his arms. He shifts slightly, and she pulls his wallet out of his back pocket. "What date do you want?" she asks him.

Roman looks up at me and shrugs. "I'll take Halloween."

"Thanksgiving for me." Emerson tosses two twenties onto the table.

"I'll take Christmas," Lachlan says, adding his twenty.

"What happens when none of you win?" Monroe questions.

"Then we all get our money back," Maddox answers.

"I think *we* should get it," Monroe challenges him.

"No way. You have control over who wins."

"So what if it's before all of your dates?" she counters.

It's wrong that I'm getting turned on by listening to my wife challenge our friends about when we're going to get pregnant. However, I can't seem to help myself. I move to stand behind her, pulling her back to my front to hide what this conversation is doing to me.

She rubs her fine ass against my hard cock. She knows me too well. I'm sure she also knows that if she doesn't stop wiggling around like that, I'm going to take her to my room, close the door, and get started on that baby she's talking about.

"No dice, Mrs. Raines," Lachlan chimes in. "If none of us wins, we get our money back."

"I have a better idea. If no one wins, we put the money in Lilly bug's piggy bank," Forrest suggests.

A chorus of voices saying, "Done," echoes around the room. We are all definitely on board for spoiling our niece.

"Sorry to interrupt," Lyra says, knocking on the frame of the break room door. "Roman and Legend, your next appointments are here."

"Thanks, Lyra. We'll be right there," Roman tells her.

She nods and turns to go back to the reception desk.

"I'll walk you out to the car," Roman says, guiding Emerson by the small of her back, baby Lilly still in his arms.

"I'll be right there," Monroe tells them.

"I won't be home until around eight or so. I have this small piece, and then the sleeve I'm starting comes in at three."

"I'll make something easy for dinner for you to heat up."

"No, I'll just pick something up on my way. If you're okay waiting until then?"

"That's fine. We're going back to Emerson's later to do some scrapbooking. I'm sure we'll be snacking because that's what we do." She grins, and I lean down and kiss the smile on her lips.

"Be safe, gorgeous."

"Always."

"Love you."

Her arms wrap around my waist as she hugs me tight. "I love you too."

"Yep, another one down." Maddox chuckles.

"Get to work," I toss over my shoulder with no heat in my words. Lachlan, Forrest, and Maddox leave us alone.

"So they know?"

"Yeah, they know. Not that they were surprised. Sometimes, I think they know me better than I know myself. Forrest called me out on my extra-smiley demeanor."

"Em and I had a very similar conversation at breakfast."

I kiss her temple. "I need to get to work." With her hand in mine, I lead her to the front desk where Lyra is sitting. My next client stands when he sees me. I watch as he roams his eyes over Monroe. She's wearing a pair of short khaki shorts, which make her tanned legs look like they're ten miles long, and a tight white tank top. He takes a second pass, and I feel my blood start to boil.

"When you're done eye fucking my wife, we can get started." I cross my arms over my chest and glare at him.

"Legend!" Monroe gasps.

Snagging my arm around her waist, I move her to stand in front of me. I slide my hand behind her neck and kiss her. Not just some generic peck on the lips. I trace her lips with my tongue, demanding she open for me. She does instantly. When I pull away, we're both breathing heavily.

"I love you."

Her eyes soften. "I love you, too, caveman," she teases.

"Only for my wife." One more quick peck and she's turning and walking out the door. My client doesn't turn to watch her go. Smart man. "Ready?" I ask him. I can be reasonable. I'm not about to throw hands because he looked at her. At least not today. I'm in a hella good mood, and I got to see my wife when I wasn't expecting to, so he's lucky.

"Meant no disrespect," he says once he's in my chair.

I nod. "Let me get your stencil and place it, and you can tell me what you think." I should tell him it's not a big deal, but he was eye fucking her, and as her husband, that's a very big deal to me. I accepted his no disrespect, and he'll know in the future that she's mine, and he needs to treat her as such.

"Take a look," I tell him once I have the stencil placed.

He stands and heads toward the mirror. "Perfect." He sits back in the chair, and I get to work.

It's Friday night, and I'm sitting on Roman's couch, with baby Lilly. I'm holding her hands while she's standing on my thighs and bouncing up and down on her little legs. "She's getting stronger," I tell Roman.

"Yeah, she is. That's her new favorite thing. She could do it for hours."

"Well, Lilly bug, you're in luck. Your mommy and Aunt Monroe are downstairs, scrapbooking, so I have a feeling I'll be here for a while."

She coos and laughs as her little legs bounce away.

"Man, you made a cute kid," I tell him.

He laughs. "She looks just like her momma."

"I can see a little of you in her too."

"Yeah, Em says she has my moodiness."

"No," I say dramatically, making faces at her, and she grins. "You're not moody like Daddy, are you?" I ask her. "Hey, I've been meaning to ask you. Do you have the number for the realtor that sold you this place?"

"Yeah, I think I still have it in my phone. You looking to move?"

"We're going to have to when we start a family. My place is a one-bedroom now. I thought about adding on, but the lot's not big enough for that, and I want to have room for the kids to play in the backyard."

"You guys trying?"

"Nah, not yet, but I want to be ready."

"You know, I was talking to the guy across the street the other night when I was taking the trash cans to the curb. They're getting ready to put their place on the market. If you can get to him before he signs, you could avoid the realtor fees and save some money."

I let that sink in. I can imagine the smile on my wife's face when she realizes that she's going to be living across the street from her best friend. This is a great neighborhood. Forrest made sure of that. He wanted Emerson to have a safe place to call home. Everything that was the opposite of what they grew up in.

"Which one?" I stand, place Lilly on my hip, and walk to the windows. Pulling open the curtains, I peer out the window.

"That one." He points to the large two-story across the street.

"Damn, how big is it?"

"Five bedrooms. Not sure about the rest. Come on. Let's go knock on the door." He reaches down and grabs a binky for Lilly. I'm guessing it's just in case, because this little girl is cooing happily as she runs her fingers through my beard. He pulls open the door and motions for me to go ahead. "You want me to take her?"

"Nope. I'm soaking up all the Lilly bug time I can get." I kiss her chubby little cheek and bounce her on my hip.

We step up onto the front porch, and Roman knocks.

The door is pulled open a few seconds later to reveal a smiling older gentleman with gray hair. "Roman, nice to see you."

"You too, Gerald. This is my friend, Legend. He and his wife are looking for a bigger place. I told him about yours."

"Well, come on in. I'll show you around."

"Thanks." I follow them inside, and Roman reaches over, taking Lilly from my arms. "Sorry to barge in on you like this."

"Oh, no trouble at all." He walks us through the downstairs, which consists of the living room, dining room, family room, master bedroom, office, kitchen, and laundry room.

"The basement is finished with a walkout patio. Come on, I'll show you." We follow him down the stairs, and the open space is perfect for entertaining. There's a storage room, a small kitchen, and two additional bedrooms down here. "The wife and I had four kids, and we always had a few extras hanging around."

"Why are you selling, if you don't mind me asking?"

"This place is just too much for us. Our kids are married with families of their own, living all over the United States. We want to downsize, buy an RV, and travel around, stopping to see each of them as we go."

"Living the dream." Roman smiles at him.

"The missus and I sure seem to think so. Come on, I'll take you upstairs."

With each step we take, I can see Monroe and myself living here. The upstairs has an open balcony sitting area, four bedrooms, two bathrooms, and a laundry room. This doesn't include the space in the basement.

"We had this house built, and with two daughters, we knew the boys didn't have a chance, so we had two bathrooms put in. The laundry room was my wife's idea. Walking upstairs to switch the kids' laundry was a lot easier than packing loaded baskets up and down the stairs. When the kids got older, she taught them to do their own. It's one of my wife's favorite things about this house."

"You have a beautiful home, Gerald. Would you mind if I ran across the street and brought my wife over to have a look? I think she's going to fall in love with it."

"Sure." He reaches into his shirt pocket and pulls out a small spiral-bound notebook. "The wife and I crunched some numbers last night. This is what we're thinking." He flips open the notebook and hands it to me.

"That's a good number." I nod at him. "If she loves it like I'm sure she will, since her best friend—and two of mine—live right across the street, we'll take it. I'll go to the bank on Monday."

Gerald chuckles. "Well, all right then."

"I'll be right back."

Roman nods and turns to start chatting with Gerald. I rush downstairs and out the front door.

"Mo!" I call as soon as I enter the house. I walk to the basement steps and open the door, calling down to her again. "Monroe, get your gorgeous ass up here." I hear the ladies laughing and footsteps.

"What's going on?"

"You ladies need to come with me. The house across the street is for sale. Rome and I just took a tour."

"Who's buying a house?" Monroe asks as she starts to climb the steps.

"We are, baby. We can't start our family in a tiny one-bedroom. This place is incredible, and you'd live right across the street from Em."

Her eyes are bright as she processes what I'm saying.

"Gerald and Helen's place?" Emerson asks. She's right on Monroe's heels as they step into the living area.

"Yep."

"Mo! That place is massive and so pretty. Come on." She grabs Monroe's hand and pulls her out of the house and across the street.

"Wow." I hear Monroe say as we step up onto the porch. "I guess I never paid much attention to this place."

Emerson knocks, and Gerald calls for us to come in. I take Monroe's hand and lead her over to him. "Gerald, this is my wife, Monroe. Monroe, this is Gerald. He and his wife are looking to downsize."

"It's so nice to meet you," Monroe says politely.

"You too. Come on, let's take that tour."

Gerald leads the four of us, five if you count Lilly, through the house again, and I know she loves it. I can tell by the smile on her face. An hour later, after Gerald has pointed out every aspect to the ladies, I pull Monroe off to the side.

"Well?"

"Legend, this is... more than I ever could have dreamed of. Can we afford this?"

"We can. Gerald and I already talked numbers. I've invested a lot of my money, and I do well at the shop. Besides, we'll also be able to sell my place and replace the cash we use for the down payment."

"You want to do this? You want to buy a house with me?"

"Of course I do. Our babies need their own rooms."

She launches herself at me. "I love it. I want it."

I chuckle. "I knew you would once I saw it. Come on, let's go talk numbers."

Thirty minutes later, I have Gerald's number and a promise to call him after I talk to the bank on Monday.

"This is really going to be our home?" Monroe asks as we follow Roman and Emerson back to their place.

"Yeah. We get to live across from our best friends, and our kids will be raised together. Just like you wanted."

"You do know we're not pregnant, right?" She grins up at me.

I wink at her, and she shakes her head. Once we get the house bought, I'll start convincing her it's time to start our family. Not that I think it will take much convincing. This is what we both want. We're building our forever.

MONROE 22

I PLOP DOWN ON THE couch next to Legend and place my feet on the coffee table. "We're going to need more furniture."

He laughs. "That we are. Welcome home, baby."

"I can't believe we live here."

"You know the best part about this house?" he asks.

"The master is on the first floor, so the kids won't be able to hear us when you ravish me?"

He points an index finger at me. "That is an excellent point, but no, I was going to say that when we're at Forrest's or Rome and Em's, and we're drinking, we don't have to drive home or stay with them. We can just walk across the street and sleep in our own bed."

"Good point. I like that we'll be able to host too. All the pressure won't be on them."

"I don't think they see it as pressure. I know Forrest bought his place for Emerson, and he was good with all of us hanging there. I also know that Roman and Emerson are fine hosting as well, especially since they have Lilly. She can be snoozing away in her own bed, and they can be with us, just hanging out."

"Yeah, I guess when we have kids, that will make things easier for us too."

"We should work on that." He winks. "At least get a few hundred practice sessions in."

"Oh, you think so?"

"Definitely." He reaches over and tugs me onto his lap.

"We have boxes to unpack, and tomorrow is Forrest's Labor Day cookout."

"I wish we could have gotten the keys a little earlier so we could have celebrated here."

I look around the room at all the boxes. "Yeah, we're not ready for that."

"Agreed. When's the next holiday?"

"Halloween."

"We'll have to have a Halloween party."

"Or we could have our one-year anniversary party."

"That one. I choose that one. I'm down for any kind of party that celebrates you being my wife." He buries his face in my neck, and all I can do is close my eyes and soak up the moment.

There's a knock at the door, and Legend yells for whoever it is to come in. We're too exhausted to move right now.

"Hey, hey!" Emerson says.

"In the living room!" I call out.

"We went home and made lunch, and I brought some for you all. I know you don't have groceries or anything, and I'm sure you're exhausted after moving everything in today."

"I love you."

Emerson just laughs. "Don't go professing your love for me just yet. It's chicken salad sandwiches and chips. Nothing fancy."

"It's food." I stand, and Legend playfully swats me on the ass. I turn to give him hell, but his words stop me.

"Love you."

"You can't sweet talk your way out of this. That hurt." I'm lying. He barely tapped me.

"I guess I need to kiss it better," he tells me.

"And on that note, I'm out." Emerson places the bag on the kitchen island and makes her way back to the front door. "Call us if you need us."

"I think I can handle this on my own, Em," Legend calls back.

"Too much information, Legend. Too much." Her laughter fills the entryway and dies down as she exits the house.

"You're so bad."

"Let's eat so I can have dessert."

"Did she bring dessert?" We both know she didn't bring dessert and what kind of dessert he's talking about.

"You, gorgeous."

"We have to unpack."

"We will. After we each have lunch and I get my dessert."

"I guess I'll take one for the team."

I yelp as he lifts me into his arms, tosses me over his shoulder, and stomps off toward our bedroom. The guys helped him put our bed back together before they left. I was able to find the sheets and blankets, so it's made, but that's the extent of our unpacking.

"I thought we were going to eat lunch."

"I changed my mind." He tosses me onto the freshly made bed, and I laugh as I bounce across the mattress.

"We have so much unpacking to do."

"We'll get there. It's all about priorities, baby."

I shake my head with a smile pulling at my lips. "The responsible thing would be to start unpacking."

"No, the responsible thing would be for me to remind my sexy wife that she's all that matters. Everything else is just noise."

He's hovering over me, arms braced on either side of my head, smiling down at me. I place my hands on his cheeks and stare him in the eye. "I love that I get this side of you. A side I never knew existed. I love that we have fun together, and well, I just love you. My heart races anytime you're near. I think about you all the time, and you're the first person I want to call to tell you about my day."

"This is me with you, Monroe. It's the version of me that I give to you as my wife, my love, my everything. This version of me is yours and no one else's. It didn't exist until the day you said you would marry me. At that moment, I felt the change. The idea that you would be mine, even for a predetermined amount of time, created the me that is your husband. Only ever yours." His lips drop to mine, and I open for him.

I don't care about unpacking. Sure, it needs to be done, but at this moment—connecting with my husband and christening our new home together—these moments are the ones I live for. The world won't stop spinning if we spend a few hours enveloped in a freshly made bed in our new bedroom.

Legend leans in closer, pressing his lips to mine. I wrap my arms and legs around him and manage to flip us so that I'm straddling him and he's lying flat on the bed. "What if I want my dessert first?" I ask him as I reach for the waistband of his jeans and pop the button open.

"You know I can't say no to you."

"Good." I shimmy back and unzip his jeans. "Lift that ass for me," I say, barely able to hold back my laughter as I try to be him.

He chuckles but does as I ask. He kicks at his jeans and boxer briefs once I have them over his hips, and they fall with a loud thump to the hardwood floor.

Knowing I need a better angle, I climb off the bed. "Move to the edge," I tell him as I begin to lower to my knees.

"Wait." He reaches behind him and grabs a pillow, placing it on the floor.

"Always taking care of me." It's a good thing he loves me. I don't know how I would ever live without this man in my life.

"Until my last breath."

Kneeling on the floor next to the bed, I'm nice and comfortable on the plush pillow. I wrap his cock in my hand and stroke him a few times. "You can lie back and relax."

"No way. I'm not missing a single second of your lips around my cock."

"It's not like it's the first or last time this will ever happen."

"Don't care. I'm not missing it." He quickly gathers my mass of hair and pulls it to one side. "That's better."

"So you want to see me do this?" Fisting his cock, I bring it to my lips and lick the tip as if it were a lollipop.

"I want to see it all, Mrs. Raines."

"Will that ever stop turning me on? Hearing my married name?"

"It's your name. Period. You are Mrs. Legend Raines, Monroe Raines, for the rest of your life."

"Can I tell you a secret?" I ask him. I swirl my tongue over his cockhead while I wait for him to answer.

"Baby, you can tell me anything."

"It would have always been you, even if you didn't love me back. I never would have taken another man's name. Deep in my soul, I knew I would have always been yours." I look down at his cock that twitches in my hand and see gathered precum. The time for talking is done. I have to get to my dessert.

I lick him clean before taking him to the back of my throat.

"Fuck." He pants, his grip on my hair growing tighter.

I stroke him while bobbing my head, taking him repeatedly into my mouth. Just like all the times before this, with him, my body reacts. It's a heady feeling to know that I'm turning him inside out with pleasure.

"Mo, baby, I'm gonna come," he tells me.

I don't stop. I keep lapping at his cock like it's my last meal.

"You have to stop."

I don't. I keep going.

He tugs on my hair, and the next thing I know, he's roaring my name as he spills down my throat. I swallow. For the first time in my life, I take everything. He's never let me do this before. He always insists he pulls out, but this time, for whatever reason, he lets me take all of him. Something I've never done. Giving this man, my husband, another first.

"Come up here." He places his hands under my arms and lifts me. He lies back on the bed and settles me over the top of him.

His arms are wrapped tightly around me, holding me close. "That was... intense," he says.

I try to roll off him, but his grip is tight. I stop trying and relax into his hold. "A first for me."

"Fuck." His cock twitches between us.

"Already?" I lift my head, and he shrugs.

"That's what you do to me. To know that I'm the first you've ever taken that way." He shakes his head. "Never in my life did I think a woman could undo me like this, but you, my wife, you know how to bring me to my knees with my need for you."

"I hope that never changes."

"Never." His voice is adamant.

We end up climbing under the covers and taking a nap, and when we wake up, we shower, then start working on unpacking. In my books, there couldn't have been a more perfect first day in our new home.

"What are they doing down there?" Emerson asks.

"I have no idea." We're sitting in the living room. I'm holding a slumbering Lilly while we get caught up. Roman and the guys went down to the basement when everyone arrived, and they've been down there all afternoon. "I think he might be putting together his man cave. I know some furniture he ordered online was delivered this week."

"That explains it. It was like that when Rome was building his too. So, how are things? The two of you seem to be getting along rather well."

"Perfect, Em. There is this entire new side of him that he keeps hidden away. When he pulls out that side of him, I melt every time."

"I see it. He's different with you. He looks at you as if you're a treasure."

"Oh, you mean how Rome looks at you?"

She laughs. "We're lucky."

"So lucky. I never could have imagined when I offered to help him that this is how it would turn out. That we'd fall in love and want to stay married. It's surreal, but I've never been happier."

"I had hoped. There was something about the way he looked at you that night. You offered, and it was as if he'd never seen you before or something."

"Who would have thought this is where we would have ended up? Married to best friends, living across the street from one another."

"We had it all planned out."

"I know, but for it to actually come true. And we never said we would marry best friends, just that we would live next to each other and raise our kids together."

"So, the marrying best friends part was a perk." She laughs. "We're still missing a piece of the puzzle. Have you all talked about kids?"

"A little. Nothing like when we want to start trying, just that we both want them."

"When do you want to start trying?"

"Soon, I think. We have this huge house to fill, and really, not having room would have been an issue, but that's taken care of."

"How are you all settling into the house?"

"There's so much space."

She laughs as the guys step into the room. "There you are. We thought we were going to have to send a search party," she teases.

"We're done," Maddox tells us.

"What were you doing down there?" I ask.

"I have a surprise for you." Lachlan clears his throat loudly, and Legend rolls his eyes and laughs. "Fine. *We* have a surprise for you."

"Much better." Lachlan nods.

"What is it?" I ask.

"Come with me."

"But Lilly bug is comfy."

"You're a baby hog, anyway." Forrest sits on the couch next to me, and I sigh as I hand over the precious baby girl.

"Y'all just need to have your own," Roman grumbles, sitting on the love seat next to his wife.

"We're working on it." Legend winks.

He's not lying, but he's also not telling the truth. We've mentioned it but made no plans, and I'm still taking my birth control. I take his hand, and he leads me downstairs to the basement.

"Okay, if there is anything that you don't like, we can change it. I copied Emerson's with Roman's help."

"What?" I ask as he walks over and opens the door for one of the basement bedrooms. He turns on the light and we walk inside. "Oh, my word. Legend? You made me a scrapbook room?"

"Yes, and you even have a little reading nook over there in the corner. I figured if I was getting a man cave with a pool table and poker table, you deserved a little slice of space just for you as well."

"I thought you were working on the man cave?"

"I know. And I will, but I wanted to do this for you first."

"Husband of the year. I can't believe you did all of this." I take in the cabinets, the large table, and the lighting. He even set up my supplies.

"I wasn't sure how you wanted everything organized, but you have plenty of space to move everything around and add as much as you want."

I turn, and he's standing right there. I wrap my arms around him, holding on as tightly as I can. "I love this. I love you so much. Not because of the things you do for me but because you want to do them. You've given me so much of you that I'm not sure I know where you end and I begin."

"We don't. We're one. There is no you and me, baby. There is only us."

"Is it wrong that our friends are upstairs, and I kinda want to christen my new scrapbook room?"

His head falls back in laughter. “Not at all. If that’s what you want, I’ll make it happen.” He wags his eyebrows.

“Let’s table that. I need to show Emerson.” I let go of him and rush out the door until I reach the bottom of the steps. “Emerson!” I call up. I wince because I forgot Lilly was sleeping.

She appears at the top, wearing a smile. “Do you love it?”

“You knew?”

“Yep. They wanted to make sure it was the right style.”

“Yes, I love it. Thank you. Get down here so I can pass out hugs.”

“Let’s not get rowdy,” Legend teases. “Your hugs are mine.”

“You’re going to have to share them tonight. All of this earns every single person in this house a bear hug.”

“Fine.” He sighs, but the smile on his lips tells me he’s happy.

I’m deliriously overjoyed. This man, my husband, he’s my everything. When everyone gets downstairs, I pass out my thank-you hugs, and I file this moment away as another memory shared with the people I love the most.

We eventually make our way back upstairs and order pizza. It’s another night filled with great friends and the man I love more than anything—definitely one for the memory books.

LEGEND 23

ARE YOU SURE YOU DON'T want me to stay home?" I ask Monroe.

"Go." She waves me off, her voice raspy. "I'm just going to stay here in bed all day, coughing my head off. There is nothing that you can do."

"I think we should take you back to the doctor. It's been six days of antibiotics, and you're still not any better."

"I'm supposed to be taking them for ten. I have four days left. If I'm not any better when they're done, I'll go back. Promise. Now, go before you're late for work. That will put your entire day behind."

"Fine," I grumble. I hate that she's sick, and there isn't anything I can do to make it better. It's eating away at me. "If you need anything, you call me. It's an early night at the shop for me, so I won't be late."

"I'll be fine, babe. Love you," she says as she lapses into another coughing fit.

Standing from where I'm sitting on the edge of the bed, I grab a cough drop and open it before handing it to her.

"Love you too." I bend and place a kiss on the top of her head. With each step that carries me out of our bedroom and to the garage, I feel worse about leaving her. I know she's right. There isn't anything I can do to make her better. I just hate it.

By the time I make it to the shop, I'm kicking myself in the ass for not canceling my client load for today when I thought about it last night. I might not be able to make her feel better, but I could be there, too, just in case.

"Morning, Legend," Lyra, our receptionist, greets me.

"Morning."

"Wow, what's up? Are you sick or something?" Maddox asks.

"No. I didn't get much sleep. Monroe is still sick. She coughed all night long, and I kept waking up to make sure she didn't need me."

"Aw," Lyra coos. "Look at you being a good husband."

I ignore her comment. I'm not in the mood to defend how much I love my wife. There isn't anything I wouldn't do for her.

"Damn, she's been sick forever," Maddox replies.

"About two weeks now. She's been on antibiotics for six days, but I can't see any kind of improvement. I made her promise me she'd go back to the doctor when she finishes this round if she's not any better. I know these things take time, but damn, I really thought that with antibiotics, she'd be okay by now."

"She has bronchitis, right?" Lyra asks. "I know that can be brutal, and the cough can linger for a while."

"That's what they told us at urgent care, but I think she's getting worse, not better."

"She might need a stronger antibiotic or a different course."

"Yeah. I just want her to heal. I hate seeing her like this."

"Let me know if I can do anything." Maddox tells me.

"Thanks, man. Is it just us today?"

"Yeah. Lilly has a checkup, so Rome took the day off, and Lachlan and Forrest are both working Saturday."

I nod and head to my room to get ready for my first client of the day. While I'm setting up, my phone rings. I rush to pull it from my pocket, thinking it might be Monroe. "Hey, Mom."

"How's Monroe feeling?"

I smile because my mother and my wife have grown close. "She's not any better. I tried to convince her to let me stay home and take her back to the doctor today, but she's determined to finish her antibiotics, and then, if she's not better, she'll go back."

"Well, sweetheart, she might have a point. I hate that she's not any better, but sometimes these things take time."

"I know. I just hate feeling helpless."

"How about I make her some of my homemade chicken soup?"

"Yeah, I think she'd like that. I can swing by after work to pick it up."

"No. You go on home. I'll bring it to your place around six."

"Thanks, Mom. Love you."

"Love you too."

I shove my phone back into my pocket and smile for the first time today. My mom's chicken soup is so good. I know Monroe hasn't had an appetite, but there is no way she can turn that down.

Lyra brings back my first client, and I get lost in my work. Four hours later, I'm wrapping up with the guy in my chair. "Lyra will cash you out and go over aftercare instructions. Thanks for coming in."

"It's dope," the kid tells me. "I'll be back for more. I want a sleeve."

"Sounds good. Lyra can take care of that too."

He nods and rushes out the door. He's twenty and well on his way to being ink addicted. Nothing wrong with that. In fact, it's good for business.

Grabbing my phone, I call Monroe to check on her.

"Hey," she croaks.

"How you feeling?"

"Same."

"Did you eat something?"

"I had two pieces of toast. I'm not hungry."

She already knows I'm going to tell her she needs to eat.

"My mom called to check on you. She's going to make you some of her homemade chicken soup and bring it by tonight."

"That's sweet of her. She doesn't have to do that."

"She volunteered, and trust me, her soup is so good, it could change lives."

She laughs, which sends her into a coughing fit, making me feel bad for trying to cheer her up.

"You need me to come home?"

She sighs. "Legend, I'm okay. I'll see you when you get home tonight."

"Do you need me to stop and pick anything up?"

"I don't think so. You've been stockpiling things you think I might need for the past two weeks."

She's not wrong. "Well, if you think of something, call or text, and I'll bring it home."

"Thanks, babe."

"Love you, Mo."

"I love you too."

Damn, this day can't be over fast enough.

My last client of the day isn't even finished paying, and I'm out the door. I'm anxious to get home to check on Monroe. It's just before five when I'm pulling into the garage. The house is quiet as I head toward our room. I can hear the shower running. That's a good sign that she felt strong enough to get out of bed and shower. Stepping into our room, I debate on stripping down to shower with her, but I know she's not feeling well. I'll just keep her company until she's done. Then I'll help her dry off and put her back in bed or carry her out to the couch until Mom gets here with dinner.

When I push open the bathroom door, my heart stalls in my chest. "Monroe!" I call out to her as I drop to my knees. She's lying on the floor, naked. The shower is running, the steam from the hot spray filling the room. That's a good sign the water is still hot, so she couldn't have been lying here long.

"Baby?" I touch her forehead, and she's clammy and burning up. I don't know if that's from the steam in the room or if she's running a fever. Bending my ear to her mouth, I can hear that she's breathing, but it's a very shallow breath.

"Fuck." I scramble to pull my phone from my pocket and dial 911. "My wife," I say as soon as they pick up, not letting them start their spiel. "I just got home, and she's collapsed on the bathroom floor." Tears prick my eyes, but I fight them, not letting them fall. I need to be strong for her.

"Sir, can you tell me your address?"

I rattle off our address.

"Can you tell me if it looks like she's taken anything?"

My eyes scan the room, even though I know she didn't. "No. No, she's been sick. I should have stayed home with her today." I reach down with my free hand and grab hers, and it's ice-cold. "H-Her hands are cold, and her fingertips are blue."

"What about her lips?"

I glance at her lips. "Blue too." I don't know how I missed that. "I don't know how her hand is cold. She was burning up when I touched her forehead. I mean, the shower is on, and the room is steamy, but I don't think that's why. Hurry! Please hurry. You have to help her."

"Sir, we have an ambulance en route. Please stay on the line."

"Monroe, baby, please wake up. Please." I lean down and kiss her cold lips. I don't give a fuck if I get sick. "Her color is off too. She looks almost ash-like." I try to give the woman on the line as much information as I can.

"Sir, the ambulance is one minute out. Is your front door unlocked?"

"No. I don't think so."

"Can you go unlock it?"

"No. I can't leave her."

"Sir, we need to be able to get into your home to help your wife. Can you run and unlock the door for me?"

"Fuck." I bend down and kiss Monroe's cold lips. "I'll be right back, baby. I promise. I'll be right back." This time, I can't stop the tears as they start to fall. I scramble to my feet and race out of our bedroom and down the hall to the front door. I unlock it and swing it open, letting them know to come on in. I turn and race back to the bathroom as fast as I can, dropping to my knees. "I'm here," I tell her, stroking her hair out of her eyes. "Wake up for me, baby." I reach up, yanking on the end of her robe to pull it off the hook, and I lay it over her. I don't want anyone seeing her like this, but I'm too afraid to move her to dress her.

"Sir, did you get the door unlocked? The paramedics are there."

"Y-Yes. The door's open."

What's taking so long? I called what feels like half an hour ago. I know, in reality, it's been a matter of minutes, but they need to get here. My thoughts are interrupted by shouting, asking where we are.

"In here!" I call back. I hang up the phone and shove it back into my pocket. I hear feet rustling, and then three paramedics rush into the room. They surround us and start working on her. One of them pulls her eyelid up, and her eye rolls into the back of her head.

"Be easy with her!" I shout, fear pushing my panic forward.

"Sir," the female paramedic addresses me, "we're doing our jobs. We're going to help her, but you have to let us. I'm going to need you to step back."

"No. No. I can't leave her. I never should have left her."

"Legend?"

I look up to find Roman standing in the doorway. His eyes are wide and filled with worry as he takes in the scene around us.

"Come on, man. Let them do their job. We'll stand right here." Roman grabs my arm and tries to get me to stand.

"I can't." I jerk my arm to break out of his hold. "Don't take that off her. She's naked," I tell the paramedics, completely losing control.

"Legend." Roman is closer now. He wraps his arms around me from behind and drags me away from her.

"No. Rome, no. She needs me. I can't leave her. She needs me. Mo!" I call out.

"Listen." His voice is stern. "She needs them. They need to have room to work on her. This is their job, man. Let them do it." He hugs me from behind, his arms locked around mine, holding me in place. "Take a deep breath."

"I can't breathe without her." More tears fall as I watch the love of my life unconscious on our bathroom floor.

"I know." His voice cracks. "Tell me what I'm seeing, Legend. What's going on?"

"I found her. She's been sick. I should have stayed home. She told me not to, but I wanted to be here. Rome, they have to help her. You have to help her!" I call out to the three paramedics, who continue to work on her.

"What did she take?" One of the male EMTs turns to ask me.

"Nothing."

"We need to know if she took something. It could mean life and death for her."

"Nothing." Anger swells in my chest. "She's not a fucking drug addict. She's been sick. All that she's taking is the antibiotic they gave her at urgent care," I spit back.

"How long ago was that?" the other guy asks.

"Six days ago. She's not getting any better. I tried to get her to go back, and she said she'd finish her ten days of meds, and if she wasn't better, she would go back then. She told me to go to work. I should have stayed home. I should have fucking been here." I slump back into Roman's arms.

"I got you, brother," he says, his voice raspy with emotion. "I got you. She's going to be okay."

"She has to be. Please, help her." This time, my cry for help is weak at best. I feel the defeat, and the heaviness of the moment seeps into my bones. I can't lose her. Please, God, let her be okay.

"We can't wait until we get to the hospital. We need to intubate now," one of them says.

"Pushing IV fluids," the female paramedic calls out.

"BP is dropping," the other informs them.

"Pushing RSI," one calls out.

"Do it now," the female demands.

I open my mouth to demand they help her—even though that's exactly what they're trying to do—but no words come out. All I can do is watch in horror as they stick a tube down her throat. I try to break out of Roman's hold again, but his grip is too tight.

"They're helping her breathe, Legend. They need to do this to help her. Just stand down, man. Let them do their job." Roman's voice is calm, but I can hear the strain in his words.

"I love her."

"I know you do. We all do, but you have to let them do their job. That's what Monroe needs right now."

"What did you give her?" I ask, finding my voice.

"Medication that helped us intubate her," the female paramedic answers, not once stopping what she's doing.

"Oxygen is better," one of the guys says, and he sounds relieved.

"Why won't she wake up?"

"Sir, we're doing everything we can," the woman says gently.

"We need to take her in now." They move quickly yet carefully, wrapping her in a warm blanket and transferring her to the gurney.

"I'm coming with you."

"You can come, but you're riding up front."

I nod stiffly. I'll do whatever I have to do to stay with her. "Fine." I turn to look at Roman.

"Go. I'll call the guys and your parents and have Emerson call her parents."

"Thanks, man." I follow the paramedics out of the house, knowing that Roman will take care of locking up, and if he doesn't, oh well. Nothing matters right now but Monroe.

When we get to the emergency room, it's a flurry of activity. They take her through a set of double doors while I'm stranded at the desk, checking her in. "Can I see my wife now?" I ask the receptionist.

"I'll put you in a private family waiting room, and the doctor will be in to talk to you."

"I want to be with her."

Her eyes soften. "I know, but you need to let us help her right now. The doctor will be with you soon." She nods, and I follow her down the hall to a room.

It's not all that big, but it is private. I pace back and forth, waiting for someone, anyone, to come in and tell me how she is.

The door opens, and in rushes Roman, Emerson, baby Lilly, and my mom. "Mom." I break when her arms wrap around me. I squeeze her tighter than I know I should, but I need to be grounded. "She won't wake up," I say, and I hear a sob.

I look up to find Emerson handing Lilly to Roman before rushing toward me. I pull away from my mom and catch her in my arms. We're both sobbing. "She has to be okay, Em. She has to be."

"She's a fighter," she whispers.

When I release her, we both wipe at our eyes as her parents enter the room. I tell them what I know and hold her mom tightly against me. Roman's parents show up and offer their support. They leave with Lilly just as Forrest, Lachlan, and Maddox join us.

I go through it all again, telling them what I know, and they all reassure me she's going to be fine. I wish we knew that for certain. They weren't there. They didn't see her blue lips or grip her cold hands. They didn't see her eyes roll back into her head or watch the paramedics shove a tube down her throat so that she could breathe easier.

"I'm looking for the family of Monroe Raines," a tall guy wearing a white coat with salt-and-pepper hair says, stepping into the room.

"I'm her husband; these are her parents, her brothers, and her sister." There's no point in going through the dynamics of our friends. We don't have time for that.

"How's my daughter?" her dad asks.

"Can I speak freely in front of the room?" the doctor asks.

"Yes," I rush to answer. "How's my wife?"

"I'm Doctor Hamilton. Your wife is stable, but I need to ask you a few questions."

"Go ahead, Doctor," Monroe's mom replies softly.

"How is your marriage?"

"Perfect," I answer immediately. "What does that have to do with my wife's condition?"

"It's protocol to ask these types of questions."

"They're happy," Emerson speaks up. "Anyone who knows them knows they're happy."

Doctor Hamilton nods. "Was she taking anything that you're aware of? Has she been acting funny or outside of her usual demeanor?"

"No. She was taking the antibiotics that were given to her six days ago at urgent care, but they didn't seem to be helping. My wife is not a drug addict." I'm pissed off, and I don't care who knows it. My tone is more asshole than anything, and right now, I don't give a flying fuck.

The doctor looks me up and down as his eyes flash to the other guys.

"What? You think because we have tattoos, we're immediately into something illegal? Let me tell you something. My skin and what I decide to do with it is my choice. Why don't you stop being so fucking judgmental and go do your job and take care of my wife?"

"You don't know us," Monroe's dad speaks up. "But I can assure you these men are honorable, and I know my daughter. She's not using drugs."

"You have to understand we hear this same story with almost every case, and it's about fifty-fifty that we're being told the truth."

"That might be, but this time it's fact. Now, are you going to tell us what's wrong with my daughter, or do we have to demand a new physician?" he asks. He steps beside me, placing his hand on my shoulder while sliding his arm around his wife's waist. We stand together as a solid unit, fighting for our girl.

"Tell me a little about her illness," the doctor asks.

"She's been feeling bad for going on two weeks. Six days ago, she went to urgent care and was diagnosed with bronchitis. The meds they gave her didn't seem to be helping, but she was determined to finish the prescription before going back. She's had low energy and a deep, raspy cough. She gets out of breath easily, so she's not been moving around a lot. She's young and healthy and vibrant when she's not sick."

The doctor nods. He taps on the tablet in front of him and reads the screen before looking up at us. "We're still waiting on the toxicology report. Not that we don't believe you, but it's protocol. She's had chest X-rays and a CT scan, and we're just waiting for radiology to read them. She's intubated, which means the tube in her throat is helping her breathe. Mr. Raines, it's my understanding you were the one to call 9-1-1."

"Yes."

"Five more minutes, and we would be looking at a very different outcome. She wouldn't have made it, according to her vitals that were documented by the paramedics. You saved your wife's life tonight."

He goes on tapping at the tablet in his hand as the breath leaves my lungs, and I drop down to a chair, burying my hands in my hair.

She would have died.

If I'd waited to leave work even a second longer. If I would have stopped to get her flowers like I sometimes do, I would have lost her. Tears leak from my eyes, and a sob gets caught in my chest. I hear the doctor asking about allergies and other medical history, but I can't pull myself out of my own grief to answer. Luckily, Emerson and her parents pick up the slack for me.

I feel a presence in front of me. Looking up, I see Forrest standing there with tears in his eyes. He drops to his knees and pulls me into a hug.

"I got you, brother. I got you." His hug is firm as we both cry. Him for the little sister she is to him, and me for the love of my life.

We compose ourselves, and Forrest stands, taking the seat next to me as I tune back into what the doctor is saying. I need to keep it together for her.

“Her fever is high, 103.4. We’re running tests and cultures to rule out every possibility,” the doctor explains.

“When can I see her?” I ask. Even I can hear the brokenness of my voice.

“We currently have her in a medically induced coma. She’s on a strong level of IV antibiotics, fluids, and anti-viral medications. Her blood pressure was extremely low, so we’re giving her medication for that as well. We’ll know more when all the tests have come back.”

“When can I see her?” I ask again.

“We’re moving her to the ICU, where she can be closely monitored. Normally, it's two at a time, but we can do three as long as you agree to not get in the staff’s way. We want her better as badly as you do, and you need to let us do our jobs.”

“Understood. I just need to be with her.”

“Visiting hours—” he starts, but I cut him off.

“I won’t be leaving her side until she walks out of this hospital. I don’t know who I need to pay or what needs to be done to make that happen, but I won’t leave her.”

Doctor Hamilton sighs. “You can stay, but the first time you interfere with her care, I’ll have you removed from the grounds.”

I nod. I’ll bite my tongue and keep my mouth shut as long as she’s being taken care of.

LEGEND 24

FINALLY, WE'RE ALONE. AFTER HOURS of encouragement and their failed attempts to get me to do the same, I convinced her parents and mine to go home to sleep in their own beds for the night, with my promise to call if there are any changes. Our friends have done the same. The lights are off in her room, but there is still a glow from all the machines she's hooked up to.

I haven't left her side since they brought me to her room, and I won't. I don't leave this hospital until she does. Quietly, I lift my chair, place it closer to the bed, and gently take her hand in mine. Her fingers are still cold, but not like they were before. Her color is better. She doesn't look as ashen. Her lips and her fingers are still a darker color than they should be, but they are no longer blue.

"You're making progress, gorgeous," I tell her. I bend to kiss the back of her hand, mindful of all the tubes and wires. "You scared me today. You're still scaring me. When I saw you on the bathroom floor, my heart stopped." I feel the tears start to build, and it's just me and her in this darkened room, so I don't bother to stop them. "I need you to open those pretty blue eyes for me, baby. I need to see you." I kiss her hand again and rest my forehead on the bed. I know that she's not going to wake up. They have her in a medically induced coma, but if she's listening, I need her to know I'm here and fighting for her to come back to me.

I've never felt that level of fear in my entire life. I never want to experience it again. I lift my head again to watch her. The gentle rise and fall of her chest, even knowing it's a machine that's causing it, soothes me. She's still here. She's still fighting.

"I can't live this life without you, Monroe. I know you're sick, but please, baby. Please fight to come back to me. I need you. We have so many plans. We have that huge house to fill with our babies. We have lots of barbeques to host in our backyard, and we promised we'd grow old together. I'm going to need you to keep that promise.

"I wish I could hold you. If I wasn't afraid of hurting you or getting kicked out, I'd climb into that bed and pull you into my arms. I'm so sorry I didn't stay. I knew how sick you were. I should have been there. Fuck, I could have been too late. Five more minutes, and I could have lost you." Sobs rack my chest as I let my fear wash over me.

I've never felt this kind of fear. My mind won't stop racing. She has to come out of this. She has to be okay. I need her to be okay. We still have so much left to do, so much life left to live together. I close my eyes, resting my head on the bed, holding her hand in mine while trying to stay calm. Eventually, sleep claims me.

The next thing I know, a nurse is in the room with us, switching out her IV bags. "Sorry to wake you," she whispers.

"How is she?"

"Vitals are good. She's a fighter."

I nod. "You hear that, gorgeous? You're a fighter." I stand and place a kiss on her forehead before taking a bathroom break. When I come out, the nurse is gone, but there's a blanket and a pillow laid out on the lounge chair on the opposite side of the bed that weren't there before.

"I'm right here, baby. I'm going to lie down, but I'm with you, okay? I'm not leaving without you. I love you with everything inside me, Monroe Raines." I kiss her cheek this time and settle on the lounge chair. It's uncomfortable, but as exhaustion weighs down on me, I drift off to sleep.

When I wake up the second time, the sun is starting to rise. I sit up, wiping my hands over my face. I check on Monroe, but there doesn't seem to be any change. She's still hooked up to these machines that are keeping her alive, with a tube down her throat. There's a lump in mine, but I swallow it back. I need to be strong for her.

I stand and make my way to the bed.

"Morning, baby." I kiss her cheek. "Love you," I murmur as the door to her room opens.

In walks Dr. Hamilton. "Good morning, Legend."

"Doc," I greet him.

"I've been looking over her vitals from last night. She's stable, which is a good thing. Later on today, we're going to do a wean test."

"What's that?"

"We're going to turn down the machine and see how she does with breathing on her own."

"Is that safe?"

"Yes. It's a crucial test to gauge how her lungs are healing." He pulls up the chair and sits. "We got the test results back."

"And?"

"The toxicology report was negative."

"Told you."

He nods. "I know. I meant no offense, I assure you. It's protocol. There are so many families who come in just as adamant as you were who have no idea their loved ones are taking drugs."

"I understand. I could have handled it better," I tell him.

He waves me off. "You'd just witnessed something very traumatic. It's in the past. Now, the chest X-rays and CT scans, along with the cultures and other workup we've done, show she has viral pneumonia."

"She was on antibiotics."

"She was, but they were not the right antibiotics."

"I knew I should have made her go back," I mutter.

"From what I can see from her urgent care notes, she did have a classic case of bronchitis. She was treated appropriately. However, this is just one of those things that can happen. Pneumonia can come on out of nowhere with these kinds of illnesses. Chances are, if you had brought her in, we still would have admitted her for IV medication and fluids, as she was dehydrated."

"But then she wouldn't be here, lying in a hospital bed with a tube and a machine breathing for her."

"We don't know that for sure. Don't beat yourself up about this, Legend. You saved her. Five more minutes, and we wouldn't be having this conversation. Remember that. You saved your wife's life."

"I'd give mine for hers if I could."

"We're going to get her healthy and back home to you."

"You can't make that promise."

"You're right, I can't. However, I can look at her stats, and I can have faith in my team and the science behind the medicine. Sure, that's not always enough, but your wife, she's a fighter."

"She is." I nod my agreement.

"We'll be in later this afternoon for the wean test. If that goes well, we'll move her to a step-down unit, and if she continues to do well from there, you'll eventually be able to take her home."

"When will she wake up?"

"We still have her in a medically induced coma. If she passes the wean test, we'll stop those medications, and as they wear off, she should wake up."

"Should?"

"The human body is often a mystery. That's how it should work, and I'm hopeful that's the result we will get."

"What should I expect when she does wake up?"

"She's going to be very groggy and in and out of consciousness. She'll be sleeping a lot, but as time goes by, the grogginess will pass, and she will be more clear-minded and alert. She's going to have a sore throat for a few days from the tube, and her voice may reflect that."

"Thank you, Doctor."

He nods and leaves just as quietly as he entered.

"You hear that, baby? We're going to see if you can breathe normally without the machine. You get to show these people you're a fighter."

Grabbing my phone from the charger that Emerson picked up for me in the gift shop, I fire off a text to our parents. I take my time, making sure I give them every detail the doctor just told me. Then I copy that exact message and send it to our friends. Once I have everyone updated, I move to the chair on the other side of the bed and hold my wife's hand, willing her to open her eyes.

"I'm here, Mo. I'm here, and I need to see those baby blues. Please come back to me. I need you."

"So, what does that mean?" my mother-in-law asks. "She failed the wean test, so what's next?"

"It's not uncommon. We'll try again tomorrow. Her vitals continue to improve, her fever has broken, and her blood pressure is stabilizing. It's still a little low, but that's to be expected."

"When do we try again?" I ask.

"If she continues to stabilize, we'll try again tomorrow."

"So, she won't wake up before then?" her dad asks.

"No. We're keeping her in a medically induced coma until we can wean her off the machines."

"Thank you, Doctor." He nods and excuses himself.

"Legend, why don't you run home and shower and take a nap? We'll stay with her," Heather suggests.

"I appreciate that, but I'm not leaving this hospital without her."

"Son." Eric places his hand on my shoulder. "We won't leave her."

"I know you won't. But I can't either. If I could, I'd take her place. I wouldn't hesitate to take this from her." I turn to face my in-laws. "Your daughter is my everything. When I said my vows, I meant every word. In sickness and in health. She needs me. She needs to know that I'm here fighting for her. I can't take the chance that she needs me and I won't be here. I should have stayed home yesterday. I knew she wasn't getting better. I tried to convince her to let me take her back to the doctor, but she was being stubborn. I should have tried harder." My voice cracks. "I can't live without her." Thoughts of what I could have done differently swirl in my mind. I know I can't go back and change the decision to leave her. I'm struggling to let it go. Maybe when she wakes up, when I see those pretty blue eyes and hear her voice, I'll be able to push it to the back of my mind.

Heather pushes past her husband to hug me tightly. "She loves you so much. She knows you're here for her, and this isn't on you. These things happen, Legend. There was nothing you could have done. I talked to her yesterday morning. She told me how you'd been taking care of her, and she had to force you to go to work. You can't shoulder this blame."

"I just need her to wake up. I need her to show me those pretty blue eyes and smile up at me like she always does. I need her to tell me I'm being irrational. I need her to take a full breath on her own because I don't feel as though I've taken one myself since I walked into that bathroom."

"I love the way you love our girl," Heather whispers.

"Damn proud to call you our son," Eric agrees.

"She's so damn easy to love." I smile through watery eyes.

"Your friends are out there and want to say hi. Your parents too. We're going to step out and let them have a turn. We'll go and grab some food. Can we get you anything?" Heather asks.

"I don't have much of an appetite, but thank you."

She gives me a hug, and they're out the door.

"Did you hear that, gorgeous? There are so many people here to see you, wishing for you to get better."

A soft knock on the door, and my parents enter. As soon as I see them, tears well in my eyes again. "Hey."

"How you holding up, son?" Dad asks me.

I shrug. "She's got another day of this." I go on to explain the wean test and how she failed and that we can try again tomorrow. "She's strong. The doctor says her vitals continue to get better, so he's hopeful that she can pass the test tomorrow."

"What do you need?" my mom asks.

"Her. I just need her."

They spend about fifteen minutes or so with us before saying they're going to my place to clean so that when she does get to come home, the house is free of germs. I thank them and give them both a hug before they go.

"Can we come in?" Emerson asks, peeking her head in the door.

"Yeah. Baby, Em and Rome are here." I'm talking to her like she can hear me. I don't know if she can, but if there is even a slim chance, I need her to know I'm still here. I'm still fighting this fight with her.

"Her parents filled us in."

"Tomorrow." I nod. "She'll pass tomorrow." I'm putting the positivity out into the universe, not only for Monroe but for anyone or any power that might be able to help my girl breathe on her own. My cell phone rings, and I reach for it on the bedside table. I see my grandmother's attorney's name on the screen, but I silence the call.

"We can stay with her if you need to take that," Emerson offers.

"Nah. It's the attorney."

Emerson's eyes grow wide. "Oh shit. The meeting. Tomorrow is your one-year wedding anniversary. I'm sorry. With everything going on, I forgot."

"It's fine."

"What are you going to do?" Roman asks.

"I'm going to sit my ass in this chair until I'm allowed to take my wife home. I don't care about the money. I never did. All I care about is her. As far as I'm concerned, the money can be donated. It won't make my wife better any faster. It won't help her breathe on her own again. I have no use for it."

My phone rings again, and it's the same number. I stand and walk to the corner of the room. "Hello."

"Mr. Raines, it's Edward Mullins. I was calling to confirm our appointment tomorrow. We're still meeting at your new home, correct?"

"No." I take a deep breath to calm my nerves. He doesn't know where I am. "There will be no meeting. I'm unable to make it."

"Legend, you do understand—" he starts, but I cut him off.

"What I understand is that my wife is lying in an ICU, fighting for her life. What I understand is no amount of money can heal her. What I understand is that I can't live this life without her. I can live without five million dollars. So, no, Mr. Mullins, we won't be meeting tomorrow."

"I'm sorry to hear about your wife."

"Thanks," I mutter. "I need to go." I end the call and slide my phone into my pocket. "I fucking hate this. I hate seeing her like this. I hate that I feel helpless."

Emerson comes to me and wraps me in a hug, and I hold on to her as tightly as I can. "She loves you so much, Legend. She's going to come back to us."

"I need her to. We have plans. Babies, and barbeques, and growing old together. She has to beat this."

"She will," Roman says, placing his hand on my shoulder. He grips it tightly, lending me his strength. "She just needs time to heal."

After a few minutes, Emerson pulls away. "The others are anxious to come and see her. Drake and Lyra have both been checking in as well."

"Tell them thanks."

"We're going to stick around for a while. We'll come back in and say goodbye before we leave."

"Love you, man." Roman pulls me into a hug.

"Love you too."

They leave, and I take my seat next to the bed. Monroe's hand is finally warm in mine. Hope swells inside me. "You're getting better, baby. Your hands are warm. Your color is better. Just keep fighting. I'm right here. I'm with you every step of the way. Just keep fighting."

MONROE 25

I CAN FEEL HIS HAND in mine. I try to squeeze, but nothing happens.

"Just keep fighting."

I know that voice. Legend wants me to fight. I'm trying, but I can't move, and my eyes won't open. It's dark, and my chest hurts.

"Just keep fighting."

I'm trying. I want to scream, but the words won't come.

I try again, but darkness claims me.

LEGEND 26

"FUCK YES!" I CHEER, AND the doctor and nurse both laugh. I should feel bad, cussing in front of my mother-in-law, but I can't seem to find the will to care. I rush to the side of the bed and take her hand in mine. "You did it, baby. You passed."

"We'll remove the tube and monitor her closely. As long as she stays stable, we'll move her to a step-down unit."

"And when will she wake up?"

"We'll stop the meds. It will take several hours, even days. Every patient is different, but as well as she's done over the past forty-eight hours, I'm hopeful that in the next ten or so hours, she'll start to be more alert."

"Thank you, Doctor," Eric tells him. I can hear the emotion in his voice. It's been a tough couple of days.

He and Heather move to the opposite side of the bed. "Our girl is a fighter," Heather says.

"She is. You're doing so well, baby. Just keep fighting. You've got this, and I'm right here." I pick her hand up and bring it to my lips. "I love you so much, Monroe." Tears prick my eyes, but I will them not to fall. She's getting better. She passed the test, and she's breathing on her own. She's fighting to come back to me. I know she is.

"Your mom and I cleaned the house and washed the sheets, and this afternoon, we're making meals to stock the freezer. We'll be back to check on her and you in a few hours."

"Thank you for everything." I smile at them.

They both give me a hug before they leave, and I sit down in the chair as close to the bed as I can get without actually lying in it with her. "You're doing so well, baby. Breathing on your own again. Keep it up, gorgeous. We're going to get you out of here and home and in our bed. I love you. I can't wait to see those baby blues."

I rest my head on the bed, still holding her hand, and drift off to sleep.

My eyes pop open when I feel her hand flex in mine. I sit up and see the most beautiful sight in the entire world. "Hey, baby." My voice cracks. "Good to see those pretty blue eyes."

"W-What?"

"Hold on. Let me get you a drink." I pour her a glass of water from the pitcher on the table and hold the straw to her lips. "Slow," I tell her as she drinks greedily.

"What happened?" She winces. Her voice is raspy, and it's obvious her throat is sore.

"I'll tell you everything, but let me call the nurse so they can come and check you over." I lean over and kiss her lips before pressing the call button for the nurse. I can feel the heavy weight of worry lift from my shoulders.

She's going to be okay.

Not a minute later, the nurse bustles into the room and smiles when she sees Monroe awake. "Your husband was right. You do have pretty blue eyes. How are you feeling?"

"Okay. Better than I remember. What happened?" she asks as she reaches for her throat in obvious discomfort. I wish I could take that pain for her.

The nurse continues to take her vitals while all I can do is hold on to her hand and stare at her beautiful blue eyes. The worry of whether I'd ever see them again is gone, and relief has taken its place. However, it's also stolen my ability to speak. I can't seem to find the words to tell her how it felt to find her, to see her lying in this bed, uncertain of when or if she would come back to me. I know the doctors had her in a medically induced coma, but she was out the entire time since I found her. It was always in the back of my mind: what if they were wrong?

Taking a deep breath, I calm myself and begin to fill her in on the last couple of days. "You gave us quite the scare."

"I'm sorry you had to find me like that."

"I'm not. They said if I would have been just five minutes later, you might not have made it."

"I'll send the doctor in," the nurse says.

"I missed you," I tell her, pulling her hand to my lips for a kiss.

"I heard you."

"You did?" My pulse races at her confession. "I wasn't sure, but if there was a chance, I needed you to know that I was here."

She nods. "I tried to reach out to you, but I couldn't."

Fuck. I'm so glad I stayed. I'm glad she knew I was here even if she couldn't tell me. "It's okay, baby. You're here, and you're going to be okay. I love you so much, Monroe."

Her entire body seems to relax at my words. "I love you too."

With hands that are still trembling with both relief and elation, I send a text to our parents and our friends. Sliding my phone back into my pocket, I tell her about everyone who's been coming to see her. I tell her about our parents cleaning the house and stocking our freezer for when she comes home.

She drifts in and out of sleep, but I don't let myself get worked up about it. The doctor warned me this might be the case. I'm perfectly content to sit here with her, holding her hand until she wakes up again.

"Have you been here the whole time?" Her voice pulls me from my thoughts.

Leaning forward, I press my lips to her hand, which is still entwined with mine. "Yes."

"You look exhausted."

"Thank you." I smile at her. "You look beautiful."

She rolls her eyes. "We're already married, Legend. I'm certain beautiful is not how I look at the moment."

"You're always beautiful to me."

Her gaze softens. "You should go home and get some rest."

"No way. I'm not leaving here unless you're with me." The words are barely out of my mouth when the doctor comes in with good news.

"Your vitals are excellent. We're preparing a room for you now in the step-down unit. Congrats, Mrs. Raines, you're leaving ICU."

"Thank you, Doctor." I stand to shake his hand. "When can I take my wife home?" I thought that the weight of worry was gone, but his words are what finally lift the heaviness from my chest.

"She'll spend another night just so we can monitor her and get another day of IV antibiotics. She'll need to eat, drink, and use the bathroom on her own. If she's doing all that, and there are no setbacks, you should be able to take her home tomorrow. I'll make rounds around eight, and if she does well overnight, we'll start the discharge process."

"Hear that, baby? You keep kicking ass, and we'll bust you out of this joint tomorrow."

The corner of her mouth lifts in a smile, and my heart squeezes in my chest.

She's going to be okay.

MONROE 27

"ARE YOU SURE YOU DON'T need anything?" my mom asks.

"Mom, I'm fine. I promise. Legend is taking good care of me."

"Oh, I know that." She waves her hand in the air. "That man loves you."

"Yes, that man does," Legend says, walking into the room. He places a bowl of his mom's chicken soup on the table next to me. "She made a fresh batch."

"She told me on the phone earlier. You all have to stop spoiling me."

"Never gonna happen, gorgeous," Legend says, kissing my temple.

"Well, we're going to get out of your hair. Legend, you let us know when you're going back to work. Your mom and I already decided we'd take turns keeping Monroe company," Mom tells him. I don't know how they're missing work, but I know there's no point in arguing with them over it. They'll be here regardless.

"I don't need—" I start, but they both give me a "don't argue look," so I give up.

"You're weak, baby. The doctor said you have to take it easy. Your body is still healing."

"Okay," I agree because I know they need this more than I do. I'm feeling so much better. My throat is a little sore, and I'm weak, but the doctor assured me that as the days pass, it will get better too.

"Love you guys," I tell my parents. They both bend to give me hugs, refusing to let me move off the couch. This is my first day home, and while I appreciate the company, I'm ready to just snuggle with my husband.

"Come here." Legend pulls me onto his lap and snuggles me. "Fuck, baby. I missed you. I've never been more scared in my life."

"I'm sorry."

"You have nothing to be sorry for. I'm just so fucking relieved to have you here in our home, in my arms."

"This is where I always want to be. It's not why we started and not how this story was supposed to end. I like this ending better."

"I can't do this without you, Monroe. I can't live this life without you."

"I love you." He leans in and kisses me. "I'm tougher than I look," I tease, trying to make light of the situation.

"My wife's a fighter." He kisses my cheek when there's a knock at the door. He sighs. "You are so damn lovable, everyone wants to check on you. It's going to be hours before I get you all alone."

"You have me forever, Legend."

"Damn right I do." He lifts me off his lap and gets up to answer the door.

I hear the door open and then, "What are you doing here?"

I stand because I don't know anyone that my husband would be asking that question of. Not in that tone of voice. I make it to the entryway. "Who is it?"

"My grandparents' attorney, Mr. Mullins."

I can feel the color drain from my face. "Legend. What day is it?"

"Our anniversary was two days ago."

"No. Oh, no. Legend. I'm so sorry."

He turns toward me, pulling me into his arms. "No. That money wouldn't have done a damn thing to bring you back to me. I don't care about the money, Mo. I never did. You're all I need. We'll figure out a way to expand, and if we don't, that's fine too. We're all doing well for ourselves where we are. We'll level up when we can. No amount of money was worth leaving your bedside."

"Do you mind if I come in?" Mr. Mullins asks.

"Of course," I answer. Legend scowls, but I ignore him. "Come on in and have a seat." I turn and start walking toward the living room. My husband refuses to release me, so he's headed that way, too, and I assume Mr. Mullins is following. Legend gets me settled on the couch and covers me up with one of the many blankets he's bought for me before sitting next to me.

"There has to be something we can do. I was in the hospital."

"I know. I talked to your husband."

"Can we submit medical records or something?" I ask.

"Baby, we don't need that money."

"I know, but you were going to expand the business. It's your inheritance, Legend, and you're losing it because of me."

"I don't give a fuck about the money. Do you hear me? All I need is you, Mo. Nothing else matters."

"If you don't mind, I'd like to read you something." Mr. Mullins reaches into his briefcase and pulls out a folder. From inside the folder, he pulls out a small stack of papers. He clears his throat and begins to read.

"'In the event that my grandson has proven beyond the shadow of a doubt that he married for true love, his inheritance is to double to ten million dollars. This is to be kept quiet, as we need to be absolutely certain. Knowing about the additional funds can make anyone a good actor. As our trusted legal counsel, this decision will lie in your hands. We give you the power to disperse the additional inheritance as you see fit. If, in fact, you do not feel that my grandson and his wife are truly in love, then the remaining five million will be split between the already mentioned charities.'" Mr. Mullins places the papers back in the folder and slides the folder into his briefcase.

There's a buzzing in my ears as I try to process what I just heard. Ten. Million. Dollars. He didn't lose the money. Instead, he got more.

Holy shit!

"Mr. Raines. Legend. I've been doing this job for over thirty years. I've never seen someone so adamant about giving up five million dollars. The love you have for your wife, and your wife for you, is apparent and beyond question. All I need from you is your signature and bank account numbers. Then the ten million dollars will be in your account within forty-eight hours."

"What?" Legend asks, stunned.

Mr. Mullins grins. "I was instructed not to tell you about this clause in the will. However, you've proven to me that your wife is, in fact, the love of your life."

"She is," Legend croaks.

"I can see that."

"Mrs. Raines, I'm glad to see you are home and feeling better."

"T-Thank you." I turn to Legend, and he's obviously in shock. "Babe?"

He shakes out of his stupor. "What do you need? Thirsty? Finally hungry?" he asks. He's ready to push aside whatever it is he's feeling right now to tend to me.

"I need you to go get this man a check with our banking information on it." He stares at me for several long heartbeats before he bursts out laughing.

"I love you."

"I love you too. Now go." I shoo him away, and Mr. Mullins laughs.

Legend does as I ask and comes back with a check with *Void* written on it in black marker. He hands it over and takes his seat next to me. "That's it? That's all you need?"

"There's some paperwork involved, but you and your wife can come to my office to take care of that when she's feeling up to the trip. I have a feeling I can trust you to come and sign."

"You can." Legend nods. "I don't know what to do with ten million dollars."

"I'd be happy to advise you. We have a financial planning team at the firm that could assist you as well."

"Thank you. We'll talk it over and let you know when we come in to sign. Give us a few days?" Legend asks.

"Certainly. Again, Mrs. Raines, I'm glad to see you doing better. I'll see you soon." He stands and smiles at us. "I'll see myself out."

Neither one of us speaks until we hear the front door open and close.

"Did that just happen?" I ask Legend.

"Yeah, baby, it did."

I reach over and wrap my arms around him. "I'm so glad you didn't lose out on your inheritance because of me. That's how this all started."

"It might have been what got us to spend more time together, but that money has nothing to do with the way I feel about you. We could give it all away, and I wouldn't have a single fuck to give as long as you're healthy and happy."

"So happy." I kiss him softly. My heart is so full, I feel as though it could burst.

"You know what this means, right?" I ask him.

"That you can quit your job and raise our babies?"

"I—that's not what I was going to say."

"It's something to think about. Of course, if you want to continue to work, I understand. It's your choice to make."

I nod. "No, I was thinking you need to call the realtor. That land, it's still for sale. That's the dream, right? To build a new state-of-the-art facility. To have guest artists come in, and maybe even add a few new full-time artists to give you all a break."

"The plan is loving you forever."

"Come on." I laugh. "Call them."

He nods and reaches for his phone that's sitting on the coffee table. Ten minutes later, he's made an offer that the agent is emailing over for a signature.

"The guys are going to flip."

"Everything worked out like it was supposed to."

"Yeah, it did." He pecks my lips with a kiss. "I can't believe I was actually asking myself: is this love?" He shakes his head. "I knew better. I knew as soon as you offered to marry me, my life was about to change."

"Regrets?"

"None. You?"

"Nope. I know this is love."

MONROE
EPILOGUE

IT'S BEEN TWO MONTHS SINCE I was released from the hospital. My husband still hovers, but I know he means well, so I don't fuss about it too much. I can't hide my smile as I park outside of the shop and make my way inside Everlasting Ink. I have a surprise for my husband that I know he's going to love.

"Hey, Drake," I greet as I walk toward the reception desk.

"Monroe, you look great. How are you feeling?"

"Never better." My smile is wide, and I'm sure it looks suspicious, but I can't help it. I'm so excited.

He nods. "Want me to get Legend for you? He's got a one o'clock, but I know he's going to want to see you."

"I am his one o'clock. He just doesn't know it yet."

Drake looks down at the books. "'Lilly Morrison,'" he reads.

"I used my maiden name and Lilly's name. I'm glad no one picked up on it," I tell him as Legend walks up behind him.

"Hey, I thought I heard your voice. What are you doing here?" Legend asks.

"I have an appointment with the incredible Legend Raines."

His eyes darken. "You do?" He looks at Drake, and he nods.

"She gave us a fake name."

Legend smirks. "You gonna let me put my mark on you?"

My pulse races as I nod. "I have something." Reaching into my purse, I pull out two pictures. One is of a fancy R, and the other is a fancy M. I hand them to him. "Can you mesh these two together?"

He stares down at the two images in his hands for what feels like a lifetime. When he finally looks up, his eyes are dark and filled with what can only be described as love. "Yes."

"Good. We better get started." I saunter past him and settle into the chair in his office.

"Where do you want it?"

"My left shoulder. That's closer to my heart, right?"

"You're killing me, beautiful."

"I want a piece of us. What we are together."

"You sure about this?"

"Absolutely. Then, when we have babies, I'll need one for each of them too." He moves to the door and shuts it, turning the lock. "You plan on having your way with me, Mr. Raines?" I tease.

"Not even going to chance someone seeing you. Shirt off, gorgeous."

I do as I'm told and strip out of my shirt. He draws up my design, and it brings tears to my eyes. I love it almost as much as I love the man who drew it.

"It's perfect."

"You're perfect." He kisses me softly before he gets to work, giving me my first tattoo.

LEGEND

EPILOGUE

TODAY'S THE DAY. WE'RE HAVING a ribbon-cutting ceremony for the new location for Everlasting Ink. It took some convincing for the guys to concede that they didn't have to pay me back for the land purchase. I didn't want the money to begin with. Putting it into all of our futures, and that of my parents and my in-laws, is a win in my book.

I gave my parents and Monroe's a million dollars each. I told them to retire and enjoy life. They fussed, but eventually, just like I did with the guys, I convinced them to take it. It might have been me telling them they'll have more time to spend with their grandkids. They, of course, assumed Monroe was pregnant. Not yet, but hopefully, it won't be long.

I never wanted the money, but I'm grateful because it brought me my wife. How I didn't see her, see us for what we could have been all these years, is beyond me. That's okay because my eyes are wide open. The ink on the marriage license has long since dried, and her last name has already been changed. Hell, she has my ink representing our last name on her left shoulder.

There is no turning back for us.

So, I had to break out the big guns and get personal. The five of us sat in the break room, and I told them how scared I was when I almost lost Monroe. I told them how I didn't want the money, but as soon as she offered to be my wife, there was a part of me who wanted her, even if I wasn't willing to admit it at the time.

They eventually agreed, not that it mattered. I'd already purchased the land. We still have a lot of work today. We hired an architect to help us plan the new shop. I have a ton of ideas to run past the guys as our families grow. I can't wait to get started.

"This is going to be epic," Monroe says, smiling up at me. I rented a tent and heaters to keep us all warm. I wanted Lilly to be there, and Monroe is just a few months out of being released from the hospital. I can't risk her getting sick again.

"It is. I'm pretty stoked about it."

"Legend?"

I turn to see the guys standing behind us. Emerson is off to the side with Lilly in her arms. Our parents are all here, well, except for Forrest and Emerson's, but they don't deserve the right to see their children's success and happiness.

"Yeah?" I ask as Monroe steps away from me to stand by her best friend.

"This—" Forrest waves his hand around the tent. "—we'll never be able to tell you what this means to all of us."

"Stop. We're in this together."

"We are," Lachlan agrees. "But we needed to do something."

"What did you do?" I ask, eyebrows raised. I told them I don't want their money.

"We might have petitioned the city to change the name of the street," Maddox tells me.

"Yeah? They agreed to Everlasting Ink Ave?" I ask. It's something we've joked about, but I didn't think they'd do it.

"Not exactly." Forrest hands me a business card.

"Everlasting Ink. Legends Way, Ashby, Tennessee."

"Holy fuck. You named the street after me?"

They all nod. "You made this possible. You and Monroe, and while we don't have a million lying around to pay you back, we did want to honor you and what you've done for us."

"Besides," Lachlan speaks up, "Legends Way sounds badass."

We all laugh, and I feel myself get choked up. These assholes are preying on my softer side. The side I found when I married my wife.

Speaking of my wife, she mouths, "I love you."

I would have never guessed this is where my life would end up, but I have zero regrets. I have great friends, a beautiful wife, and a nice, warm home. The only thing we need is a cousin for Lilly, and if I have my way about it, that will be our next move.

THANK YOU

for taking the time to read ***Is This Love?***.
I hope you loved Legend and Monroe's story.

Want more from the Everlasting Ink Family?
Look for Forrest's story, ***Are You Ready?*** releasing November 2024.

Never miss a new release:
Newsletter Sign-up
Be the first to hear about free content, new releases, cover reveals, sales, and more. kayleeryan.com/subscribe/

Discover more about Kaylee's books here
kayleeryan.com

Did you know that Orrin Kincaid has his own story?
Grab ***Stay Always*** for free here
kayleeryan.com/books/stay-always/

Start the Riggins Brothers Series for FREE.
Download ***Play by Play*** now
kayleeryan.com/books/play-by-play/

CONTACT KAYLEE RYAN

Facebook:
bit.ly/2C5DgdF

Reader Group:
bit.ly/2ooyWDx

Goodreads:
bit.ly/2HodJvx

BookBub:
bit.ly/2KulVvH

Website:
kayleeryan.com/

Instagram:
instagram.com/kaylee_ryan_author/

TikTok:
tiktok.com/@kayleeryanauthor

MORE FROM KAYLEE RYAN

With You Series:

Anywhere with You | More with You | Everything with You

Soul Serenade Series:

Emphatic | Assured | Definite | Insistent

Southern Heart Series:

Southern Pleasure | Southern Desire
Southern Attraction | Southern Devotion

Unexpected Arrivals Series

Unexpected Reality |Unexpected Fight | Unexpected Fall
Unexpected Bond | Unexpected Odds

Riggins Brothers Series:

Play by Play | Layer by Layer | Piece by Piece
Kiss by Kiss | Touch by Touch | Beat by Beat

Entangled Hearts Duet:

Agony | Bliss

Cocky Hero Club:

Lucky Bastard

MORE FROM KAYLEE RYAN

Mason Creek Series:
Perfect Embrace

Standalone Titles:
Tempting Tatum | Unwrapping Tatum
Levitate | Just Say When
I Just Want You | Reminding Avery

Hey, Whiskey | Pull You Through | Remedy
The Difference | Trust the Push | Forever After All
Misconception | Never with Me

Out of Reach Series:
Beyond the Bases | Beyond the Game
Beyond the Play | Beyond the Team

Kincaid Brothers Series:
Stay Always | Stay Over | Stay Forever | Stay Tonight
Stay Together | Stay Wild

Everlasting Ink Series:
Does He Know? | Is This Love? | Are You Ready?

MORE FROM KAYLEE RYAN

Co-written with Lacey Black:

Fair Lakes Series:
It's Not Over | Just Getting Started | Can't Fight It

Standalone Titles:
Boy Trouble | Home to You
Beneath the Fallen Stars | Tell Me A Story

Co-writing as Rebel Shaw with Lacey Black:
Royal | Crying Shame | Watch and Learn

There are so many people who are involved in the publishing process. I write the words, but I rely on my team of editors, proofreaders, and beta readers to help me make each book the best that it can be.

Those mentioned above are not the only members of my team. I have photographers, models, cover designers, formatters, bloggers, graphic designers, author friends, my PA, and so many more. I could not do this without these people.

And then there are my readers. If you're reading this, thank you. Your support means everything. Thank you for spending your hard-earned money on my words, and taking the time to read them. I appreciate you more than you know.

Special Thanks:

Becky Johnson, Hot Tree Editing.
Julie Deaton, Jo Thompson, and Jess Hodge, Proofreading
Lori Jackson Design – Cover Design (Guy Cover)
Emily Wittig Designs – Special Edition Cover
RafaGCatala – Photographer (Main Guy Cover)
Chasidy Renee – Personal Assistant
Jamie, Stacy, Lauren, Franci, and Erica
Bloggers, Bookstagrammers, and TikTokers
Andrea, and Stacy - Graphics
The entire Give Me Books Team
The entire Grey's Promotion Team
My fellow authors
And my amazing Readers

Made in United States
North Haven, CT
19 June 2024

53846697R00150